Stories by M.T. Bass

ARTICLE 15

Griffith Crowe Stories #1

BY

M.T. BASS

AN ELECTRON ALLEY PUBLICATION

MUDCAT FALLS, U.S.A.

Electron Alley Corporation
The Herald Building
732 Broadway Avenue
Lorain, OH 44052

This book is a work of fiction. Any references to historical events, real people, or real places are used fictitiously. Other names, characters, places and events are products of the author's imagination and any resemblance to actual events or places or persons living or dead is entirely coincidental.

Manufactured in the United States of America

Edited by Elizabeth N. Love (www.bee-edited.com)

ISBN 978-1-946266-11-8 (Trade Paperback)
ISBN 978-1-946266-09-5 (eBook)
ISBN 978-1-946266-13-2 (Audiobook)

www.MTBass.net

For Denny
Sorely missed…

Everything the power does, it does in a circle.
— Lakota Proverb

It is better to have less thunder in the mouth and more
lightning in the hand.
— Apache Proverb

"And so my story begins, like so many stories, with a woman."
— Daniel Defoe

She was one in a million...and the day I met her I should have bought a lottery ticket instead.

Blonde, slim and well-built, of course, her eyes were darkly blue which, when unsheathed from behind her Jackie Ohhs, glinted like gunmetal at twilight.

I noticed when we first met.

I ignored it after the first time we made love.

I caught it again as she testified against me.

I suppose, I'll just never learn.

The War R

The conference room was small—smalle ... , Big Firm" standards, than the huge public conference room up front used to intimidate clients, adversaries, witnesses, and opposing counsel by swallowing them up whole like Jonahs lost in the belly of a legal whale. Tucked away in a back corner among the partner offices, it was extremely well appointed, though darkly so, in oak furniture and paneling. The quiet confines served as a war room of sorts, a place where grand strategies and hair-brained schemes were incubated, hatched and sometimes celebrated, sometimes autopsied. He knew because Griffith Crowe was sometimes part of them.

There were no windows, which was fine with him. He didn't need to be seen, and, besides, he was just there to get paid and be quickly on his way. Even in the dim, indirect lighting, he found a shadow where he sat and sipped coffee from a massive, dark mug with Stein, Baylor & Stein gilded on the side, patiently waiting for Lance Baylor to come back with his check.

Lance was a master of entering and exiting rooms. So, when he burst into the room like a starlight artillery shell, wearing his white phosphorous rain-maker smile, followed by two junior associates and a young, very attractive Asian waitress pushing a serving cart with no doubt a sumptuous lunch, he knew his escape would be neither clean nor quick.

e?" teased Lance, baring his canines. "I couldn't

u back to…to…where was it you were you off to,

if?"

"Home."

"Right, send you *home* hungry after a job well done. Pull up a chair, and we'll feast before you depart."

Lance naturally took the head of the table with Griff to his right. The two junior associates, veritable bookends with their young, already balding pates, red ties, pin-striped suits, expanding waistlines, and leather portfolios, sat on the opposite side of the table.

They all politely smiled at one another as the waitress set their places and served what turned out to be Beef Wellington. After pouring drinks—Cabernet for Lance, iced teas for the empty bookends and black coffee for Griff—she quietly left them and closed the door.

Like an orchestra conductor, with cutlery for a baton, Lance silently cued the quartet to begin eating.

Lance smiled broadly and looked to his right. "Good. No?"

"Excellent. My compliments to Cookie."

"You know, our friend here was busy freeing Iraq before there actually was an Operation Iraqi Freedom," Lance said, turning to the two associate attorneys, who frowned at the apparent contradiction. As if to explain, he continued, "Special Forces, of course. What was it you did there in the desert?"

Griff watched Lance watch himself surgically cut his Wellington.

"Nothing really so special," Griff said, turning his attention to his own lunch plate. "I suspect much the same sort of things as you may have done here to get your name on the marquee. You know, all's fair in love and war."

Lance pointed his knife at Griff's heart and laughed in a friendly but dignified manner.

The two empty bookends quietly absorbed the banter, knowing that Lance, though extremely talented as both a lawyer and a rainmaker, who would have risen to the top with any firm there in Chicago or any other big city, had married into the Stein family business.

"Yes, fathers love their daughters," mused Lance, then with a sideways glance, "and sheiks love their sons."

"Touché," said Griff.

"How did you two meet?" asked the empty bookend seated furthest from Lance.

At the same time, Lance said "College" while Griff said "Frat house."

The two pointed their knives at each other and chuckled.

"You know, I think I may have been somewhat thoughtless in not introducing you properly." But Lance never did anything without thinking things through beforehand. "Griffith Crowe, this here is Roger Wilkinson and Wes Eply. They are two of our rising young stars in corporate. You know, contracts, mergers, acquisitions and the like."

"Yeah, I know, corporate stuff," Griff said to Lance. Then to Wilkinson and Eply, "I think we may have met at the Christmas Party."

Both empty bookends agreed amiably as they stopped eating to shake hands across the conference table while Lance watched, knowing full well that, though personally invited, Griff never came to any of the firm's social functions.

"You're like, really, the last of the last Mohicans, right?" Lance asked.

"Arapaho, actually. On my mother's side."

"Which is why you are such a sneaky shit, able to bushwhack people in the forest so easily."

"Not that many trees out on the Great Plains—*or the Iraqi desert.* Definitely not enough for any forests. My tribe roamed around Colorado hunting buffalo in the good old days."

Lance smiled. "You know what I mean. You are a bad ass."

"We kicked Comanche butt the hell out of our territory…not to mention Custer's ass, too, if that's what you mean."

"Yeah. Sure. Whatever you say *Chief.*"

"I'm not management."

"Sure thing. Whatever you say, *el Jefe.*"

Griff abandoned himself to circumstances and easily joined the luncheon conversation about the Bears, the Cubs, the Bulls, and golf, demonstrating a good knowledge of sports, though, in truth, he was quite apathetic to subject.

Chicago Executive Airport

"Damn that Daley, closing down Meigs. I loved that place," Lance griped as his Cadillac Escalade lurched along in bumper-to-bumper traffic, northbound on the Kennedy Expressway. "Made it so easy to jump out of the city. Takes me longer to drive to the damn airport than it does for the Citation to actually get me where I need to go."

"Yeah, that guy had some set of balls on him, flipping off God and the FAA and all." Griff gazed out the side window, silently agreeing with Lance and thinking how he'd already be in the air westward bound with Chicago at his six o'clock if the mayor hadn't plowed up the runways at the lakefront airport. He could not get out of the city fast enough.

"Ran in the family. Gotta admire those guys—especially the old man."

"You know, you could have had one of your minions take me to the airport."

"Now, Griff, and miss out on our quality time together?"

"Eh…" Griff shrugged a shoulder. "So, you getting any stick time?"

"Not in the Citation—NetJets frowns upon it. But we still have the King Air. Reminds me of the good old days, ferrying Generals around." Lance sighed, recalling his Army Aviation days. "Winning the war on terror one cocktail party at a time.

So, what are you driving these days? Still got the Aeronca?"

"For fun. The Cirrus gets me where I need to go, fast."

"Nice. You must be doing well, huh. Sounds like you've got more than just Stein & Baylor paying your way."

"Now, Lance, you of all people should respect attorney-client privilege."

"Come on, don't yank me. You don't practice anymore."

"Never did. I still have *my* soul."

Lance chuckled. "Yeah. Right. Keep telling yourself that and maybe one day it will be true."

"So…why didn't you have Wilkinson or Eply drive me to the airport?" Griff asked.

"A sensitive matter for your ears only." Lance merged northbound onto to the Eden's Expressway. "We have this client with a…special request."

Griff shook his head. "It always starts this way, doesn't it."

Lance flashed his pearly whites. "Come on, buddy. I'm making rain for you, too. You could be crossing the great plains at ninety knots in that old rag wing. Take a long, long time to get home, instead of, what, a couple of hours in the Cirrus?"

"Am I going to regret this—*again?*"

"Not so much. He's playing hide-and-seek with his ex. Really, really wants back a piece of art that he was supposed to get in the settlement, but…"

"Let me guess: sentimental value."

"You could say that. But, honestly, who are we to judge which of the one point eight million reasons it really is for him to want his precious Pollack hanging over the mantle in his Idaho vacation home, again."

Article 15

"Sun Valley?"

Lance nodded his head.

"Send me the gory details."

"Thanks, Griff. I owe you."

"Again."

Lance pulled up to the security gate by Atlantic Aviation at the approach end of Runway 16. He rolled down his window and punched the security code into the keypad. When the chain link gate opened, he pulled onto the tarmac and parked next to Griff's Cirrus S-22. "I had them pull it out of the hangar. All gassed up and ready to go. *Thank you very much.*"

"Thanks, pal."

They got out of the Escalade. Griff loaded his duffel bag into the plane and started his pre-flight inspection.

Lance checked FlightAware on his iPhone, then scanned the approach to Runway 16. Soon landing lights glared down the glide path. A Learjet 31 quickly crossed the threshold and touched down with tiny puffs of blue-gray smoke off the mains. Lance watched it roll out, then taxi their way. He smiled.

Griff came around the left wing and stood next to Lance. They watched the Learjet turn onto the apron in front of the Atlantic Aviation hangars and get marshaled to a stop by a baton-waving line boy. Another stood by with a rolled up red carpet, which he placed by the cabin door as soon as the engines spooled down.

"I love the smell of kerosene on the tarmac," Lance said.

Griff looked at Lance staring at the Learjet.

"Wait for it…"

The cabin door opened like a clamshell. The co-pilot

scurried down the stairs and stood ready to assist the deplaning passenger.

A slender blonde in Ray-Ban Jackie-Ohh sunglasses, a skin-tight red dress frosted at the shoulders with a sheer white shawl, and stiletto heels took the co-pilot's hand and stepped down onto the tarmac into the hungry stares of the line boys. Griff pulled off his sunglasses to watch her sashay across the apron, chased by the co-pilot who held the door to Atlantic Aviation open, then followed her in.

"Don't tell me. The stubborn possessor of a priceless Jackson Pollack," Griff said, looking at Lance.

"Now, who owes who?"

Griff put on his sunglasses again, then headed towards the fixed base operator's lobby. "Guess I better go pay my fuel tab."

"But I took care of that," Lance called after him. Then said to himself, "Oh, you dog, you."

~~~

Helena

Griff entered the Atlantic Aviation offices on high alert as if it were a Ramadi residence in the middle of the night, scanning and clearing the lobby corners quickly. No Jackie Ohhs.

The Learjet 31 co-pilot leaned casually on the counter, talking up the young receptionist, Tiffani, as if he might be overnighting in Chicago. Her eyes were drawn to Griff like iron filings to a neodymium magnet. The co-pilot noticed. His banter trailed off, and he looked over his shoulder. As if suddenly confronted by the alpha male of the pack, he stood up straight, reflexively took a step back, and lowered his eyes to his shoe tops.

Griff returned Tiffani's smile. He knew her more or less intimately from his own previous layovers. But this current mission involved another target, and he deemed it tactically unsound to confront a woman emerging from the Ladies Room, so he turned down the hall on his right to lay his ambush in the pilot's lounge.

"That didn't take long. I didn't think it would."

The low, almost husky yet honey smooth female voice poured seductively over Griff and blanked his mind as he turned into the pilot's lounge. Though dimly lit, as they all were to facilitate napping, her red dress glowed like a hearth, yet she still wore her sunglasses as she studied her iPhone's screen, slouching and sitting askew in one of the La-Z-Boy recliners with her legs crossed. Griff's eye was drawn to the slow but rhythmic bounce of her stiletto heel. Predator had become prey.

She took off her Jackie Ohhs, looked Griff up and down, then took a deep breath. "Mmmm...tall, dark and dangerous...just the way I like them."

Griff locked onto her blue-gray eyes and surrendered. He leaned against the door jam. His inside voice taunted, *No plan survives contact with the enemy.*

"I couldn't help but notice Lance's Escalade on the ramp. He is a conniving bastard, isn't he? Of course, he *is* a lawyer, but he does excel at it. Not to mention the unseemly delight he takes in it."

"Always has," Griff said. "As long as I've known him."

"Then, you really shouldn't be surprised."

Griff smiled, realizing it wasn't Mayor Daley's fault that he was still on the ground in Chicago. "Name's Griff."

"Yes. I know."

He waited, his face an implacable facade, one molded and hammered into place on the Coronado Beach while enduring BUD/S training. "You got a name? Or will you answer to minx or vixen?"

"Hmmm...you like the 'X' words. I prefer Helena."

"So...how long will we be playing Three Card Monte with modern art...*Helena?*

"Oh, that. The Pollack is already crated up at a friend's gallery in LA waiting to be shipped off."

"Which gallery?"

"Now, Griff. Have we come to an understanding yet?"

As a Navy SEAL, he had been well-trained never to sigh

out loud. "I've found understandings to be vastly overrated and all too often unreliable."

"Hmmm. So, it often is." She sat up straight, arching her back. She ran her fingers through her blonde hair. "Lance speaks highly of your...*work.*"

"I've solved a problem or two for him—or should I say his clients. What is it you need?"

"Trust me, there is precious little that I *need.*" Helena smiled coyly.

"Well, then, what is it that Helena wants?"

"You're kind of a no-nonsense guy. Don't you believe in foreplay?"

Griff laughed. "Why, yes. Yes, I do. But you and I are a bit too vertical right at the moment. So, it's more like teasing."

"Huh. *Men.* Why must you all be so literal?"

"Because literal is where we live and work and play."

"Well, Mr. Griffith Crowe, this has been a fascinating conversation, but I must be going. I have an engagement to get to, and my limo is surely out front by now." Helena stood up and walked up to Griff. She put her index finger on his chin.

"So, did I pass the audition?"

She pushed his head to the left, then back to the right. "Eh, you'll do."

Griff broke protocol and sighed heavily.

"I'll be in touch," Helena said as she slipped by, brushing his arm with her body.

Griff watched her leave, contemplating the possibility of foreplay—predator, again.

~~~

Wyoming

"Rat bastard," Griff said to himself when he stepped back out on the tarmac and saw Lance's Escalade was no longer parked by his plane.

He climbed up into the Cirrus, started the engine, and called for his clearance to Minneapolis. There was only a short delay after the run-up for his release from ATC until he was rolling down Runway 16. Tower handed him off to Departure Control who handed him off to Chicago Center. Thirty minutes later, Griff canceled his IFR flight plan.

"Squawk twelve hundred. Frequency change approved. Good day," said the voice from Chicago Center over the radio.

With the blessing of Air Traffic Control, Griff turned west towards Laramie, Wyoming. He settled at twenty-five hundred feet and let the North American continent rise up slowly until the Cirrus was clipping along at 175 knots, three hundred feet over western Nebraska prairies.

Griff could not shake the image of Helena's passively aggressive visage—practiced, no doubt, but still stunningly effective overlaid on her Cosmo magazine cover beauty—as well as the firmly feminine curves of a body barely contained or concealed by the second skin of that red dress. Or…the brief, deliberate brush of her breasts against his arms and teasing hint of Ralph Lauren Perfume Notorious as she breezed by on her way to the limo.

God damn it.

Just over the Wyoming border, a herd of pronghorn antelope to the south caught Griff's eye. He banked hard left and dove on the herd, sending them loping off in an amorphous brown flock. Chandelling to the north, he circled to watch them pinball across the plains, then turned back to the west…and involuntarily back to thoughts of Helena.

A half-hour later, Griff called Cowboy Aviation at Laramie Regional Airport on UNICOM to have his Aeronca Chief pulled out of the hangar. After landing, he parked next to it, tossed in his duffel bag and instructed the line boy to top off the fuel tanks in the Cirrus before putting it in the hangar. Ten minutes later, he was on his way to the ranch, north of I80 and not quite halfway to Rawlins.

The day was fading, but he made it home while it was still light, touching down on his grass strip just before sunset with enough time to hangar the Chief and get out on his back deck to watch the daylight die behind the Medicine Bow Mountains with a single malt scotch in his hand. He replayed his skirmish with Helena in the pilot lounge at Chicago Exec yet again.

The family ranch and adjacent Bureau of Land Management leases near Rock Creek once grazed several thousand head of cattle. When he inherited the land, Griff sold down the herd to five hundred or so but kept the leases as well as the small crew of Cheyenne and Arapaho ranch hands, basically three families who had worked with the Crowes seemingly since the end of the Great Indian Wars, preferring to cowboy rather than sit idly on the reservation. During downtime, between "missions" for Lance and his ilk, Griff rode and worked with his crew as much as he could, whenever tending to the business demands of running a ranching operation would allow.

It was three days later when Griff got a call from "Bones," the Laramie Airport Manager. "Hey, Griff, you got a package delivered here."

"I didn't order anything. Sure it's for me?"

"That's what the waybill says."

"Can you have FedEx bring it up to the ranch for me? Might be a week before I'm back that way."

"Well…"

Griff waited. When he got no answer, he asked, "Problem?"

"It's kind of big. Too big for UPS or regular FedEx. A freight company delivered it."

"What the hell?"

"I'd kind of like to get it out of the offices, here. It takes up a lot of room."

"Can you put it in the hangar? I'll be down tomorrow in the Chief."

The next day, Griff taxied up to his hangar in the tiny taildragger. Inside, a wooden crate six feet wide by four feet tall by two feet deep stood in the spot where the Chief usually parked. The paperwork said it was shipped from the Pacifica Art Gallery on Rodeo Drive in Beverly Hills. It was now the most expensive item in the hangar.

Just then, Griff's cell phone rang. "Yeah."

"Who is this Bones guy? And why is he signing for my painting?"

"Hello, Helena. How are you?"

"Really? Chit-chat?"

"How did you get my cell phone number—don't tell me. Lance. But my hangar address?"

"Silly man, I just had my fly boys look up the N-number of your cute little plane in the FAA database."

"So…does this mean we have an understanding?"

"No. But maybe we should discuss it some more. I'll text you details."

Griff's phone went dead.

A moment later, it dinged with a text message: "KSKX. For dinner this Saturday."

He wanted to ask, *Why Taos, New Mexico?* But he decided not to tempt fate. He texted back, "Your treat?"

A smirking yellow emoji face appeared on his phone with a ding.

Griff called Lance's direct dial line at the firm.

"Well, hello there, stranger," Hannah, Lance's Administrative Assistant, answered cheerfully with just a hint of southern drawl. "I missed you last week. Why didn't you come calling?"

He often wondered why Lance tempted himself with the gorgeous blonde parked so close at hand, but his friend claimed she was great at her job and melted the hearts and wallets of clients with her Alabama charm. Griff counted himself lucky that he wasn't married to the boss's daughter. "Just a quick visit. Passing through. Next time?"

"You better…" Hannah let out a huff of *faux* indignation. "Lance has a client in his office right now, can he get back to you?"

"Just a message. Could you please tell him that I found that old drop cloth he was looking for?"

"Now, Griff, not a fan of Mr. Pollack's work?"

Article 15

"It would clash with my decor."

"Well, I will certainly let him know."

"And I'll need a shipping address for Sun Valley."

"Of course. I will get that for you."

"Thanks."

"And, Griff, if you let me know the next time y'all will be in town, I'll bake you a pecan pie."

"I'd like that."

"I know you will. You surely seemed to last time."

~~~

Angel Fire

By Saturday, the Jackson Pollack painting had been picked up from Griff's hangar and delivered to an address in Sun Valley, Idaho; an invoice had been sent to Stein, Baylor & Stein for services rendered; and the Cirrus was crossing North La Veta pass into the San Luis Valley of southern Colorado with sixty nautical miles left to go to Taos, New Mexico.

Twenty minutes later, with the wind calm, Griff entered downwind for Runway 22 and landed. He noticed a familiar Learjet 31 parked on the ramp. A set of car keys awaited him at the front desk of Taos Aviation with an address near the Angel Fire ski resort on the other side of the Carson National Forest. He smiled reflexively when the key fob lit up the parking lights on a black Mustang convertible outside. Griff tossed his go-bag into the back seat, fired up the engine, put down the top, and loaded the Angel Fire address into Apple Maps. He pressed "Go" and did.

Exceeding the posted speed limits all along U.S. 64, he made the trip in far less than the predicted one hour and sixteen minutes with Brad Paisley competing against the ridiculous 5.0 L Coyote 435 hp V8 to fill the valley with the most noise the whole way. Once to Angel Fire, Siri's directions led him up into the mountains to a mansion masquerading as a cabin in the woods. A Post-It note on the door instructed Griff to "come in." As he dropped his go-bag in the front entryway, the aroma of sautéed onions and garlic triggered a growl in his stomach.

"Lucy! I'm home," he called out in the best Cuban accent he could muster. Griff expected to see a hired chef in the kitchen but found an apron-clad Helena instead. "Slaving over a hot stove for me?"

"Shut up and make yourself useful. Try opening some wine."

"So…this isn't an eat-and-run situation, then."

"You got some place you need to be? Bad?"

Griff smiled and opened the 2010 Screaming Eagle Cabernet Sauvignon sitting out on the counter. "I've heard about this, but never had it. Any good?" Griff's inside voice finished his thought, *Better be at two grand a bottle.*

"I like it."

"Works for me." Griff set a glass of wine on the counter near Helena, then pulled a stool up to the kitchen island, spinning to survey the great room with its panoramic view of the Sangre de Cristo Mountains as he sipped the cab. "Kind of off the beaten path. I have to admire your courage…or is it recklessness."

"What do you mean?"

"Remember me? Tall, dark and…*dangerous?*"

"Oh, that. Yeah, well…" Helena pulled back her apron to reveal a Smith and Wesson revolver tucked into the waistband of her shorts.

"Is that a Chief's Model 36?"

Helena scowled at Griff over her shoulder. "M&P Bodyguard 38. FBI Plus-P loads."

"That'll put a man in his place."

Article 15

"Mmmm... I'll bet you're still hanging on to your SIG."

"Oh, yeah?"

"Men are so predictable."

"Well, you gotta dance with the one that brung you home."

"So, a sentimental choice."

Griff smiled. He got up and went over to the sliding glass door in the wall of windows. It opened to a deck that ran along the back of the house looking down the mountain.

Helena turned, leaned back against the kitchen counter, and sipped her wine as she contemplated Griff from behind. She smiled. "Don't smudge up my windows like a puppy. Go on out. And light the grill while you're at it. That should keep your tiny man-brain occupied."

Griff looked at Helena's smiling reflection in the glass. He nodded, then went out on the back deck. A Kingsford bag leaned against a well-used Komodo Kamado grill. He loaded the chimney starter and fired up the coals. Griff leaned on the rail, looking down the mountain, sipping his Screaming Eagle, and mentally plotting his next move. *Love is a battlefield...*

Helena brought out a tray with two thick Kobe Delmonico steaks and set it on the Komodo. She parked herself in one of the Adirondack chairs.

Griff turned and looked down at her. With the apron and revolver left inside, he savored her body dressed in short-shorts and a tight tank top. "I didn't notice any empty spaces that need filling on the walls inside."

"The painting was Edward's all along. He bought it to prove his cultural *bona fides,* I suppose. I wanted to get in one last squeeze—just for fun, you know."

"So, why am I here?" Griff asked.

"You know why you are here." Helena smiled coyly, slowly crossing her legs. She leaned seductively towards him. "Don't you."

Griff sighed. He sat down next to her. "You are right. We are *so* predictable."

She reached out and stroked his cheek. "There, there."

"I guess, in my defense, I could invoke Article 15."

"What's Article 15?"

"I did a little work in Africa during my, ahem, military career and learned a bit about the 'Takings' clause of the Zaïre Constitution. When the government is corrupt, there's really nothing a citizen can do to fight it. So, the only reasonable response is *Débrouillez-vous!*"

"Get it while you can. I like that."

"Yup. Article 15."

"Wait a minute—are you calling me corrupt?"

"You *are* trying to corrupt me. And doing a damn fine job of it."

Helena smiled.

They drank and watched the daylight fade against the mountains. When no more smoke rose out of the chimney starter and an orange glow reached the top, Griff dumped the coals into the grill and pre-heated the cast iron grate so the Delmonicos sizzled loudly when he put them on. He assumed Helena preferred her beef on the rare side, and he was right.

When he turned the steaks, Helena retrieved silverware, napkins, and the bottle of wine from inside to set the patio table. She went back for two plates, steaming with servings of *au gratin* potatoes, which Griff loaded up with the Delmonicos.

A quick toast, then they ate.

"So, Griff…do you miss it? You must, or why else would you do what you do for the likes of Lance."

"The pay's good, but the benefits suck. I work my own hours, which is nice. And most days no one is trying to kill me." He winked at Helena. "And, of course, I get to meet interesting people—and I'm always interested in *interesting* people."

Helena sighed. "I suppose."

"That's why I'm here, right? You have some kind of…*interesting situation?*"

"Yes…and no."

"Let's have it."

"I have everything I need. But there are some things that cannot be bought. And why is it those are what you always want the most?"

"Want is a four-letter word."

"So is need."

They finished dinner in silence. Griff took the dishes inside and returned with a second bottle of wine. Helena had moved back to the Adirondacks. He filled their glasses, and they sat, swallowed up by the infinite dark of the mountain night.

"Lance said you were the only one he knew who could help me."

Griff learned patience from the many ambushes laid and sprung. He waited.

Finally, Helena asked, "You know who my father is?"

"I did some homework. Hedge fund manager. Early investor in damn near everything on the Internet that's been a success…and a couple that went sideways. But ended up worth, what, north of a billion dollars or so.”

“Close.”

“And you got half, right?”

Helena nodded.

“Sweet.”

“Yes, it is. But…”

“There’s always a but. Even with five hundred million.”

Helena sighed and swirled her wine. “There are things yet unresolved.”

“With your dad?”

Helena nodded.

Griff leaned forward and put his elbows on his knees. He stared out at the freckles of light scattered about the mountains. “I think Lance may have been wrong. I, ah, I’m not much use in resolving…you know, those kinds of issues.”

“Daddy issues? You think that’s what it’s about?”

“I’m an outside, meatspace kind of guy. That’s where I get things done.”

“You are a jerk.”

“Yeah. So I’ve been told.”

“What is unresolved is that there are things—my father’s things that are missing. Nothing of great value, but family things. Personal items that were important to him…and me. I want them back.”

“Who’s got these *things?*”

“I don’t really know for sure. If I did, I would have them.”

“You got a list?”

Helena nodded.

“Well, then, that I can help with.”

Article 15

"Good."

"I'm suspecting, though, that you suspect your half-brother."

"Good guess, Einstein."

"So, may I presume we have our *understanding?*"

Helena sipped her wine. "Lance will handle the details—and your fees."

Griff sat back. It was hard to tell where the lights on the ground stopped and the stars began.

After the last of the Screaming Eagle had been consumed, Helena showed Griff to a guest suite in the loft above the great room, then retired to the master bedroom downstairs. Sometime during the night, she came back upstairs, climbed naked into bed beside him, and woke him to make love.

~~~

JR

The aroma of fresh brewed coffee greeted Helena when she woke. She padded out barefoot from the master bedroom to the kitchen, poured a mug for herself, then leaned on the island as if to brace herself with caffeine to face the day—to face Griff.

He was already out on the deck in an Adirondack chair. Helena smiled at the sight of him sitting like a man-sphinx, shirtless in only Levi's, staring blankly at the pre-dawn glow growing behind the mountains like a big, dumb Saint Bernard. She went to join him but hesitated at the sliding glass door. Up close, even in profile, the expression on Griff's face gave her pause. She sensed an intensity, a grim tension in his stare at the horizon, more like a dangerously hungry wolf than a furry family pet.

"There you are." Griff turned his ravenous gaze towards Helena as she came out on the deck and the rays of morning sun reaching around the mountains gave him x-ray vision to see her naked body beneath a sheer, gauzy summer dress. "You left me all alone last night."

"Mmmm…well, three times—you know, there's only so much a girl can take." Helena sat down beside Griff.

"Yeah. I know. I feel so…*used.*" Griff smiled at Helena. "But, still, glad to be of service."

Helena hid her smile behind a sip of coffee. "You always up this early?"

"Cattle don't water themselves."

"Yeah. They do, actually."

Griff laughed. "Caught me. I figured you for a city-girl."

"Daddy had a ranch in Montana. We'd spend summers there."

"And a mansion in Bel Aire, a spread in Carmel, and a condo in Aspen, not to mention the apartment in Manhattan…and San Francisco…and Paris…Did Lance get them all?"

"Lance?"

"Already hard at work in the Windy City, sending me intelligence reports." Griff held up his iPhone. "So, when did you text him? Before or after we consummated our *understanding?*"

"After, of course. You don't think I just bought that Mustang in the driveway without test driving it, do you?" Helena poked Griff's bicep with her index finger as if testing the firmness of his muscles. "Daddy didn't raise some bubble-headed Barbie doll."

"Yeah. I get that. What about Junior? He doesn't strike me as the sharpest knife in the kitchen."

"Oh, he pales into an albino in comparison to our dad. But people underestimate him because, well, he definitely doesn't interview well. The camera hates him. Makes him look like a prototypical evil capitalist. I think 'cause he got my step-mother's deep-set eyes. Daddy was so smooth and easy-going, and no matter who it was he was talking to, he made them feel like they were just a couple of old chums from the neighborhood catching up on good times." Helena shook her finger at Griff. "Careful. Don't you underestimate him, too. He's got a grisly kind of determination."

"Just not your smarts…or good looks."

"Well, that goes without saying." Helena flipped her blonde hair off her shoulders. "Oh, just so you know, he hates being called Junior."

"And that would be his problem, not mine."

"For the record, he prefers JR."

"And you think Junior has your father's stuff?"

"You are incorrigible." Helena sighed. "Or he knows who does. He was the executor of Daddy's will."

Griff leaned forward in the Adirondack. "What's the point of all this?"

"I don't know. I just don't know. But I want it back."

"All right, then. I've got my marching orders."

"Good." Helena looked at Griff. "So, what's keeping you?"

Griff stood up, effortlessly lifted Helena out of the Adirondack chair, and carried her inside. He headed towards the master bedroom.

"No. Not there."

He laid her on the rug in front of the fireplace and clawed at the hem of her dress.

Helena pushed back on his chest, then sat up to pull the dress off over her head. Griff stood and stepped out of his jeans. When he went to lay on top of her, she rolled him over and, straddling his hips, ever so slowly lowered herself onto him.

He lay back and closed his eyes, his arms outstretched.

Helena sat up straight and methodically rode him with her hips for a long, long time, savoring the smile on Griff's face, until he arched his back and they both came.

After, Helena rested her head on his chest listening to his heartbeat and breathing return to normal. Then, she found her dress, pulled it back on over her head, and left Griff on the floor to go make them breakfast.

Griff's drive back to the airport was much more leisurely than the night before. He noticed the Mustang's odometer had only four hundred thirty-seven miles on it.

Once over North La Veta Pass, he throttled back the Cirrus and floated along the Front Range heading home to his ranch in Wyoming.

The List

When Griff remodeled the ranch house, he added a windowless hideaway to his upstairs bedroom suite and furnished it sparsely with a roll top desk, a large oak table, and an old comfortable leather wing-backed chair and ottoman. Behind a vault-like door, it also held a FireKing filing cabinet, a Liberty gun safe, and an NSA/CSS 02-01 - Level P-7 approved paper shredder. There, Griff conducted business for Lance and his clients, completely separate from the first-floor office where he handled affairs for the ranch.

Stein, Baylor & Stein arranged to have the more sensitive documents hand-delivered to Griff via messenger service, including the list of items Helena wanted him to find and return. At first glance, it seemed innocuous enough: a footlocker evidently filled with personal mementos, photos, service medals, and private correspondence; her father's private journals; family photo albums; an A-2 leather flight jacket; an old felt fedora; and a long list of *objects d'art,* souvenirs, and knick-knacks collected while globetrotting for business and pleasure.

Ranch work done and the sun long set, Griff pulled his desk chair over to the oak table where four stacks of papers were neatly lined up, one each for mister, missus, JR, and Helena. Lance was anything if not thorough in his background preparation. He stared a long time at the pile for Helena—the shortest one—sipping at the Balvenie 40-Year-Old Single Malt Scotch Whisky she FedExed him with a promise to hand-deliver a bottle of fifty-year-old Balvenie—a $50,000 bonus—*when* he got her father's items back. A distinctly wolf-looking Siberian Husky wandered into the hideaway and pressed its muzzle against his thigh. Griff scratched behind its ear, then pulled his SIG Sauer P226 pistol out of his waistband, placed it within easy reach to his right, and sat down at the table. Rodya sniffed Griff's shoes, then curled up to lay at his feet.

After a bracing gulp of scotch, Griff pulled the pile of papers for Helena's father towards him and began to read the story of Cliff Nickolson's life—and a particularly charmed and lucrative life it was.

Mr. Nickolson was a proud fifth-generation Californian whose ancestor successfully chased the gold in them thar hills around Sutter's Mill in 1849. The son of a Lockheed Aerospace Program manager, Cliff grew up in the San Fernando Valley, lettering in baseball and swimming while taking flying lessons at Van Nuys airport. He won an appointment to the Naval Academy at Annapolis, which Griff might have held against him, but rather than become a Fobbit—a "Rear Echelon Mother Fucker"—Nickolson opted to become a Marine Corps fighter pilot, all of whom are required to go through The Basic School, because they are considered Marines first, then pilots. Towards the end of his second tour of duty, by then a Major, he flew an F/A-18 Hornet in relentless ground attacks against bridges, roads, and Iraqi military assets in Desert Storm.

Figuring those 42 days of combat for Commander-in-Chief George Bush were likely the pinnacle of his career as a warrior, Nickolson mustered out into the reserves, which allowed him to

Article 15

fulfill both his "need for Mach 2 speed" as well as the freedom to pursue the accumulation of an obscene pile of wealth, an obsession that started with the acquisition of a Harvard MBA and a meticulously cultivated and maintained network of Ivy League contacts which led to stint as a researcher, then portfolio manager at Bridgwater Associates, the largest hedge fund in the world. Not content to play with OPM—Other People's Money—Helena's dad went out on his own and rode an incredible wave of early investment successes with X.com, Google, and Facebook, among others.

Griff became bored with the details entombed in the accolades of business journal articles of how Cliff continued to pile up ludicrously tall stacks of cash, so he skipped to the bottom of the pile, looking for the NTSB accident report for the helicopter crash that took the lives of Helena's dad, step-mother, and a corporate pilot near Pebble Beach.

Griff's cell phone rang, and he dug it out of his pocket. Lance's name appeared on the screen. "Yup?"

"Cramming for finals, again?" Lance asked.

"Yup."

"So, you got everything, then."

"Yup."

"I wish you'd let me get a word in edgewise."

Griff pulled out the NTSB report. He read the Probable Cause and Findings: The National Transportation Safety Board determines the probable cause(s) of this accident to be: IMPROPER PLANNING/DECISION BY THE PILOT, AND HIS FAILURE TO ATTAIN ADEQUATE ALTITUDE BEFORE FLYING OVER RISING TERRAIN AT NIGHT. FACTORS RELATED TO THE ACCIDENT WERE:

DARKNESS, FOG, HAZE, RISING TERRAIN, AND THE LACK OF VISUAL CUES THAT WERE AVAILABLE TO THE PILOT. Griff mumbled to himself, "Hmm, wonder who was flying…"

"What?"

"You still at the office?"

"Yeah, long day." Lance sighed.

"The price you pay."

"Not all of us get to live the life of Reilly—speaking of which, how are you treating our very important client?"

Griff slurped his scotch loud enough to be heard over the phone.

"You two playing nice together?"

Griff said nothing, thinking of Taos.

"You dog, you."

"It was before anybody inked any contracts, so there's no conflict of interest…yet."

"Careful, my friend. You're punching above your weight class."

"I made it to the bell."

"Yeah…of round one."

"Cut me, Mick. *Cut me.*"

"I'm telling you, these folks, they are way above my weight class, even."

Griff thought for a moment. "Yeah. Duly noted."

"Don't get complacent. Condition Yellow, man."

"Always."

"Yeah, I know."

"You know something that ain't buried in all this paper," Griff asked.

"Not specifically. I just know their kind—and I clean up a lot of their kind's messes. Sometimes lists aren't just lists."

"Duly noted."

"Anyway, sleep tight and don't let the bed bugs bite."

Griff grunted.

Lance hung up.

Griff pushed Mr. Nickolson's briefing papers back into line, skipped ahead, and pulled Helena's pile towards him.

~~~

The North Forty

Griff got up early, saddled his favorite quarter horse, Winston, and rode north, followed by Rodya. A severe clear morning, the horizon stretched out to infinity and beyond, and the mixed-breed spirit inherited from his Arapaho mother and cowboy father reverberated from centuries back across the eternal great plains.

Griff smiled at Rodya's attempts to run down jack rabbits, which zigged and zagged upslope to wear out their larger, heavier predator. The Husky roamed and returned, panting from his hunt, then took off again on the next futile footrace. It gave Griff pause to consider the power of such instinctual urges. Eventually, he led Rodya down a draw to a clump of cottonwood trees by a shallow creek where he and Winston could drink. After, they headed west up a trail that followed rising terrain into the foothills.

Griff did his most productive thinking when he wasn't trying to think, something early morning rides or flights were best for. He got to a familiar rock outcropping, tied off Winston to a lodgepole pine, and went to sit at the edge with his feet dangling. Ninety-mile visibility allowed him to look far beyond his ranch land below. Clear to the north. Nearly to Nebraska, east—or so it seemed. A brownish smudge of smog to the south along the Colorado front range. Rodya came and sat beside him. He tried to imagine the ground blackened with a great herd of buffalo as it once was.

"Temptations abound, my friend," Griff said out loud. He scratched the scruff of Rodya's neck.

After reading Helena's bio, the urge to make a quick trip to Sun Valley to debrief her ex welled up inside him. *A fool's errand,* he decided, but didn't entirely rule it out…yet. Griff thought a while about Taos and its luring siren's song preying on his own instinctual urges—not to mention the Ford pony Helena evidently bought special just for the occasion of his visit. He wondered where in the world Helena's Learjet might have taken her that day. And if Chicago wasn't so far, he might be tempted to confront Lance face-to-face about what he obviously knew but left out of the wood pulp dump his minions prepared and delivered to his doorstep.

"Hey, Boss," Ben, the elder ranch hand, called out from behind. "Figured you'd be here."

Griff turned and looked up at Ben on his horse. Just down the trail, Johnny Eagle and Shep waited, their rides pawing at the ground. "Men…"

"We're moving some herd over from the BLM," Ben said. "You want in?"

"Yup. Thanks."

Griff mounted Winston and followed Ben, Johnny Eagle, and Shep down the trail onto the government's land.

The men worked the scrub oak in the foothills rounding up cattle without banter or chit-chat, communicating in whistles and shouts directed more at the cows than each other. Though the "Boss," Griff fell in as part of the crew following Ben's natural lead just as he had when, as a boy of twelve, his father sent him out with Ben's father to start learning to be a man, though he let Shep ride drag once they had the small herd gathered and moving.

Back home after a long, hard day of riding and driving cattle, Griff relaxed on his deck with a glass of Helena's ridiculously expensive but exquisite scotch and realized that sometime during the day, the decision was made unconsciously to start his quest on her behalf in Los Angeles.

So, the next day he flew himself into Van Nuys Airport and picked up a Chrysler 200 rental from Hertz—a distinct let down compared to Helena's Mustang—then drove to Bel Air.

~~~

Sun Tzu

Griff parked the Chrysler rental car down the street from Cliff Nickolson's contemporary-style mansion near the Stone Canyon Reservoir in Bel Air. Watching and waiting until the regular cleaning crew left, he noted the company name, website, phone number, and license plate number on the Dodge Caravan parked in the driveway. Through the telephoto lens on his Cannon Rebel T6, he took close-up shots of each of the four women who got in the Maid-In-LA minivan. He wanted to put eyes on the people who were regularly inside Cliff Nickolson's home. He planned to come back the next day to similarly scout the landscaping crew. Both companies were holdovers retained by the realtor to maintain the thirty-nine-million-dollar listing in pristine condition for prospective buyers.

He waited a half hour, then did a perimeter walk of the property before approaching the house. Once at the front door, he discreetly donned latex gloves from a small tool bag. Using the code Lance got from the listing agent for the lock box, he quietly let himself into the mansion and stepped into the posh setting for Helena's formative years.

Griff punched the security code into the keypad to disable the alarm system and stood still in the foyer for a full three minutes, listening closely for any human sound. He then quickly walked the memorized floor plan, clearing each room and closet of the three-story house. A half-hour later, he was back at the front door ready to go to work.

The interior was pristinely kept but also very much unalive, having been unoccupied since the helicopter crash in Pebble Beach eighteen months prior while JR and the family lawyers sorted out the final affairs of the elder Nickolsons. Fresh flowers did little to cut the pervasive odor of cleaning solvents. Of course, there were no lingering aromas of cooking or any human hints of cologne, perfumes, bath soaps, or even body odors. Only Glade air fresheners in the closets, which were empty of any apparel. The home had a sad sterility to it. Marble mantles, walls and staircases, along with the granite countertops in the bathrooms, wet bars and kitchen chilled the luxurious ambiance, like a morgue. The effect was aided and abetted by predominantly arctic white furniture. Griff highly doubted the residence would yield up any items on Helena's list, as the home had been meticulously scrubbed of any personally identifying effects—no doubt in part to mask the family tragedy that put the house on the market, which made a big splash in the national media at the time.

Nevertheless, he worked the rooms methodically, checking every closet, drawer, and shelf for drill. What he really hoped to gain was at least a faint sense of the family dynamic when the Nickolson family was alive, intact and filling the house with life, so once his search for physical items was done, Griff took the time to sit in each room, surveying them from every different angle and perspective the furnishings allowed. He worked his way from the first floor up, spending the most time in Cliff Nickolson's office. All evidence of his personal collection of memorabilia had been polished out of the bookshelves lining the walls, which were now filled with fake books.

Article 15

Upstairs, JR's and Helena's rooms betrayed their former occupants: Dark wood furniture, browns, and an LA Dodgers poster for JR; a white enamel canopy bed, matching dresser, and warmer blue colors—not lavender or purple—with a Van Gogh print of *Starry Night* for Helena. He went to her bedroom window and, as the sun set, absorbed the panoramic view of Los Angeles that surely filled Helena's childhood dreams and wondered what those dreams might have been.

Griff's phone rang. He knew who it was before even looking at the screen. "Hello...*Helena*..."

"You must be stalking me through the past, no? You certainly aren't going to find anything there. The realtor made sure of that."

"If you know the enemy, you need not fear the result of a hundred battles," Griff said, quoting Sun Tzu.

"Forgetting something, aren't you?"

"What's that?"

"If you know the enemy *and know yourself...*"

Griff smiled at her correction. "You never fail to surprise me."

"I know. That's my job."

"Thank you. It keeps life interesting."

"Yeah, and I know how interested you are in *interesting* things."

"Nice place." The lights of LA began to glitter in the gathering darkness like spilt diamonds below.

"I had a happy childhood."

"I'll bet. So, you going to get the thirty-nine million asking price?"

"Doesn't really matter. Daddy bought it with petty cash for nine hundred thousand out of foreclosure in the Nineties."

Lance is right, Griff thought, *way above my weight class.*

"Some movie producer bet the farm on an Oscar and flopped hard."

Don't do it—do not ask—don't, don't don't, Griff told himself inside his head, but he could not resist is own instincts. "And where are you now?"

"Just doing a little shopping."

"Fifth Avenue or the Miracle Mile?"

Helena laughed. "Why, you are a sly devil, aren't you?"

"Say hi to Lance for me."

"Maybe I'll buy you a little something."

"Like a five-thousand-dollar bottle of scotch?"

"You no like?"

"It is awesome."

"Well, there you go. Don't forget to stop by Daddy's office."

"Next on the list."

"Off you go then. We'll talk again soon."

Before Griff could put the iPhone back in his pocket, it dinged with a text message: "Let your plans be dark and impenetrable as night, and when you move, fall like a thunderbolt."

Griff could only smile.

~~~

The Art of War

Griff took a last look out Helena's bedroom window at downtown Los Angeles, then went back downstairs. Automatic timers had cycled on lamps throughout the house. At the kitchen, he paused to look out back at the pool which glowed blue from the underwater lights. The quick sweep of an errant shadow caught his eye.

Griff moved into an interior hallway without windows, pulled out his iPhone and logged into the house's security system with the ID and password provided by Lance. He swiped through the CCTV camera views. A van was parked out front just around the corner. It had not been there when he went in. The cameras around the pool showed nothing, but the far reaches of the backyard near the fence line were veiled in darkness. He brought up the front door camera and studied it intently. At the fringes, the shape-shifting of shadows led him to conclude that two, possibly three assailants lay in wait. Griff checked, then re-holstered his P226 pistol.

He went to the kitchen, grabbed the bottle of Dawn dishwashing soap from beneath the sink, then went to the foyer and poured it out on the Italian marble tile just inside the door. He got what he needed from his tool bag, biting down on zip ties and quietly pulling his baton to full length. In his left hand, he turned on the TASER Strikelight, pointing the beam of the flashlight down and away. Griff stepped to the side of the front door. He turned the deadbolt.

At the faint click of the latch opening, the front door was violently pushed in, and two men came lunging into the foyer skating uncontrollably on the soap-slicked marble, cursing as they crashed into a tangled heap. After a couple of quick shots from the stun gun, Griff had the two men hogtied with zip ties faster than a rodeo calf roper. Duct tape from the tool bag sealed their mouths. He stood and stepped back to the side of the front door and waited. A minute later, he heard a quiet shuffling on the walk outside. He drew his SIG Sauer.

"Alan? Steve?" came whispered from just outside the door.

The muffled replies of the two bound men were indecipherable.

A head and a Glock came into view through the doorway.

Griff pressed the muzzle of his P226 against the intruder's temple and grabbed the barrel of the Glock. "I'll have that if you don't mind."

He led the third man to a Queen Anne chair in the foyer and zip tied his wrists and ankles to the arms and legs. Griff closed the front door again, pulled out his iPhone, and studied the CCTV camera views again.

"You can't—"

"Shut up. I just did," Griff cut off the man in the chair. He swiped through the camera views again. "Just the three of you then?"

The ungagged man smirked.

Griff smiled. He surveyed his quarry. The two larger, hogtied men were obviously the muscle; the slight man in the chair the "brains" of the operation. He retrieved wallets from the back pockets of the men on the floor and took out their driver's licenses. "Not really good tradecraft, fellas. Oh, look, you really are Steve and Allen. So, who hired you guys? Cliff Junior?"

The man in the chair glared at Griff.

"And who might you be?"

"Bite me."

Griff shrugged and pocketed the driver's licenses. He held up and fired the Strikelight, so the unnamed man could see the blue arc clearly. Griff smiled at the grimace of despair on the man's face when he heard the electrode crackle loudly. "Don't feel like conversating a little?"

"I—I—I…"

Griff leaned over, pulled the shirttail out of Alan's trousers, and pressed the stun gun against the small of his back.

Fear etched itself deeply into the "brains" of the operation, but he remained silent.

"Okay, then." Griff fired the stun gun. Alan had a brief spaz attack against the zip ties. "Looky there. Soap bubbles. I think he pissed himself."

The man in chair swallowed hard.

Griff came over to the chair and leaned down into the man's face. "Now…let's say we talk."

"I don't know. I don't know. I don't know. We're getting paid by some law firm."

"This law firm have a name?" Griff touched the stun gun to the man's cheek.

"Perkins, Holmes and something. I don't know. I just cashed the check."

"Here in LA?"

"No. The Bay Area."

Griff smiled. "Now, was that so hard?"

"Is he—is he okay?"

"He'll be fine." Griff retrieved the man's license and pocketed it with the others. He packed up his tool kit and paused at the front door. "You fellas have a nice night."

Griff punched the panic button on the alarm system control panel, then left.

Bungalow 7

Griff parked on Oxford, then cut through Glen Way on foot to the Beverly Hills Hotel, slipping discretely into Bungalow 7. Despite the late hour in Chicago, he called Lance.

"You never call. You never write," Lance answered. "Trouble? Or do you just want money...*again*. You are worse than my kids."

"Perkins, Holmes and whatever. What's the scoop?"

"Why should I know?"

"Seem to have an annoying interest in the Nickolsons. Client or a cutout?"

"Doesn't ring a bell." Lance thought for a moment. "I do not recall seeing the name in any of the background I read. Likely a cutout."

"Supposedly from the Bay area."

"Ahh...probably JR. He haunts Silicon Valley. Fancies himself the next Zuckerberg-in-waiting and, from all accounts, has burned through an unhealthy chunk of cash trying to make it happen. Kind of an entrepreneur without a clue." Lance snickered. "You know he and Helena...well, let's just say there's more warmth between the Israelis and the PLO."

"Ah, family. I do miss the holiday rock throwing."

"Well, she never did embrace Mrs. Nickolson number two. That's why she went all Ivy League on her education. Maybe three thousand miles away wasn't far enough."

"Maybe."

"So, where are you bunking out there?"

"Beverly Hills Hotel."

"Ouch. A room or…"

"Bungalow. Number seven. Bill Shatner highly recommended it."

"The Norma Jean."

"Yeah. I guess. Off the beaten path."

"That's your style. Am I going to see a bill for this?"

"Maybe. We'll see. Can you check out those Bay area clowns for me?"

"Will do."

"West LA PD blotter might be a good place to start. You know the address in Bel Air. There were three of them. Ask for Allen, Steve or Dominic."

"Sure. I'll let you know."

Griff changed clothes and went to the fitness center to work out for an hour. After a quick shower, he roamed the neighborhood streets, a walking meditation. He window-shopped a bit while passing by the closed Pacifica Gallery on Rodeo Drive. After a leisurely patrol through the jungle of wealth and fame, he went back to Bungalow 7 and went to bed.

~~~

The next morning, Griff got up early and swam laps in the pool for an hour. He ate breakfast poolside while he read Lance's email, then dressed in a lawyerly pinstriped suit. He drove by the Stone Canyon mansion to discreetly photo the landscaping crew on his way downtown to Century Plaza which held the offices of the Hornet Investment Group on the 32nd floor of Tower 1. A gorgeous dime-a-dozen former starlet wannabe with a slightly disqualifying crooked smile the camera likely did not love at the reception desk showed him into the conference room—a huge one up front with a panoramic view to the west which failed to either impress or intimidate Griff—for his mid-morning appointment with Managing Director Donald Wallace.

Wallace stood up from the conference table and motioned to a chair pulled out across from him, too far away to shake hands. Behind him another man, dressed like a golf pro, scowled and scanned the Pacific coastline with his arms crossed over his chest. Griff correctly surmised: *JR.*

Griff plopped a leather messenger bag heavy with aviation magazines for effect down hard on the highly polished conference table with a dull thud, eliciting an ever so slight grimace from Wallace. He smiled as he sat down. "Thank you, Mr. Wallace, for taking time to meet with me."

Wallace glanced over his shoulder at JR, then back, and said, "I'm not sure what exactly the purpose of this meeting is, Mr. Crowe."

"Call me Griff."

"Okay…"

JR sighed heavily and marched over to the table. He was a solid six foot three, in excellent shape, and, just as Helena said, had the stereotypical visage of an evil capitalist: thick, protruding eyebrows, dark deep-set eyes, and a five o'clock shadow at ten in the morning—though with blonde hair like Helena's. He looked like a weird combination of a surfer dude and Richard Nixon. JR leaned on the table with both hands. His biceps bulged and his throat muscles clenched tight as he directed an angry, greedy smirk down at Griff. "Enough. *Enough.* Just what is my sister up to this time?"

Wallace leaned back in his chair and clasped his hands on top of a leather FranklinCovey planner like a poker player who just folded his hand.

Griff smiled. His inside voice reminded him, *Be polite, be professional, but have a plan to kill everybody you meet.* "You mean half-sister, right?"

Wallace's poker face cracked with a hairline grin, obviously no stranger to the Nickolson sibling rivalry.

"Where does she keep finding you guys? Huh?"

"I'm in the book," Griff said in a soft and casual manner.

"She is always stirring up trouble for me."

"You mean like making bail for Steve, Allen and Dominic?" Griff shook his head. "Where do you find your guys?"

"Fuck you."

"Yeah…I don't think so. Not you, anyway." Griff smiled broadly. "Not my type, if you catch my drift."

"Jesus Christ."

"Him either."

JR turned to Wallace and growled, "Get this guy out of here."

"Your office, then?" Griff asked Wallace.

Wallace stood up and headed towards the door.

"I said get this guy out of here!" JR barked.

Wallace sighed. His shoulders slumped. He did not look back. "Helena owns the same number of shares as you do."

Griff got up and followed Wallace out of the conference room. "Nice to meet you, *Junior.*"

"Son-of-a-bitch."

~~~

Article 15

"Can I get you a cup of coffee?" Wallace asked as they made their way through a maze of hallways.

"Sure." Griff never declined an offer of java, as it usually allowed for a bit of recon and loose lips chit-chat. Wallace led him to the breakroom and handed him a corporate mug with a silhouette of an F/A-18. Griff poured. "JR is wound a bit tight."

"Mmm. Yes." Wallace answered. "Always has been."

"The shadow of a legend is usually a stressful place to live."

Wallace gave Griff a knowing smile and led him deep into the executive suite, passing by his own nameplate on the wall to go into Cliff Nickolson's office. Though it was lit, the computer screen on the desk was dark. He led Griff inside, and they sat at a round glass table. "My office is a bit of a mess. End of the quarter, don't you know."

"Sure." He surveyed Cliff Nickolson's office, pausing at the "I Love Me" wall with its framed citations and pictures of airplanes and fellow warriors. "Marines, too?"

Wallace nodded. "You?"

"Navy. Special Warfare."

Wallace relaxed visibly.

"I got no dog in this hunt. In fact, I am the dog in this hunt. That's all."

"What is it that Helena wants?" Wallace asked wearily. "And how can I help?"

"Some items seem to have gone M.I.A. She'd like them back. Personal stuff. Probably just some tit-for-tat shell game with JR. That's all. You been through this drill before?"

"No. Not this particular one."

Griff laughed. "Yeah. I get it. Anyway, you knew Mr. Nickolson well?"

Wallace nodded. "We served together. Desert Storm. His wingman. And worked closely after."

"She said he kept a journal—personal stuff, not business. Travels, I guess. Interesting people, places and events…"

"He did."

"What, was he going to write a memoir or something?"

"No. Just a lifelong habit. A mental exercise, he said. Always had a notebook with him—except on missions, of course. So, I imagine the last one…"

"Lost."

"Yes. Lost." Wallace sighed. He looked around the office as if searching for a ghost, his eyes ending up on the "I Love Me" wall. "The Major was a quite remarkable man. Would have earned a star easily, if he had stayed in the Corps."

"I've met guys like that—not many. Could count them on one hand and give away a couple-three fingers. You'd follow those guys anywhere."

Wallace nodded.

"I read the NTSB report…"

Wallace locked on Griff's eyes.

"Did that read right to you?"

Wallace started to shake his head but shrugged a shoulder instead and looked away.

"Was he on the stick?"

"I doubt it. He was in the left seat."

"But…"

Wallace gave Griff the thousand-yard stare. "You read the report: Pilot Error."

Article 15

"It's always pilot error, isn't it."

"No. Not always."

"Gut feel?"

Wallace shrugged. "The Safety Board has spoken."

Griff waited then said, "He must have filled a lot of those Moleskins. A hundred, maybe."

"Leuchtturms."

"What?"

"The brand he used, Leuchtturms. Not Moleskins. They're German."

"Oh. Well, is there another place he might have kept them? Somewhere, maybe someone...*off the books?*"

Wallace looked back at Griff with a stern expression.

"Be better if I could get in, get out. No one gets hurt." Griff took a sip of coffee. "You know, rather than stumble into a shit storm. No one wants a fire fight here."

Wallace stared.

"I'm going to find them. That's what I do. And I'm good at it."

Wallace began, nearly imperceptibly, to nod his head. He opened his planner and wrote something down. He tore out the page, folded it in half, then slid it across the glass table top. "Need-to-know basis only."

"Helena?"

Wallace shook his head. "And I have no idea how you found out about it."

"Understood."

"Now, if you will excuse me, I have an angry share holder waiting to see me." Wallace stood up.

Griff pocketed the paper without reading. He stood.

"Does Hornet use Perkins, Holmes and Bond for legal services?"

"From Frisco?"

Griff nodded.

"No. We have local representation."

"Sure. Thanks."

Downstairs on level D of the subterranean parking beneath the Towers, Griff opened and read the paper Wallace gave him: Blue Wing, LLC.

He lit the paper on fire with his father's Marine Corps Zippo lighter, then left.

~~~

Bungalow 7 was empty when Griff returned, but a faint tease of Perfume Notorious hung in the air. Griff smiled. He changed into cargo shorts, a T-shirt and Ray-Ban Wayfarers, then went out poolside. He stood across the water from Helena, savoring the sight of her sunning in only a tight red one-piece bathing suit and her Jackie Ohhs.

"It is impolite to stare, *mister,*" Helena called out across the pool.

Griff felt all the eyes around the pool drawn his way.

"Darling, there you are. Done shopping so soon?" He walked around the pool and laid back in the lounge chair next to her. "You are resurrecting lurid *Baywatch* fantasies from my childhood."

"So to speak…" She reached over and quickly grabbed his crotch, then let go. "So, how was your day, honey?"

"I met Junior—"

"I told you, he hates that—"

"Yeah, I know, but I had to find out first hand."

"Did you boys play nice together?"

"I didn't feel any love in the room, so we left."

"We?"

"Mr. Wallace and I."

"Oh, Donnie? How is he? I always liked him." Helena raised herself up on an elbow and turned to face Griff.

He looked over at her. "He says hi."

"Was he helpful?"

"Eh…" Griff shrugged a shoulder. "We'll see."

"He was always my father's guard dog."

"So…did you want me to bill Lance for the room?"

"No, silly. He'll just mark it up with his outrageous overhead, so I took care of it already."

"It is good to see you, Helena."

"You just wait." She stood up, took Griff's hand, and led him back to Bungalow 7.

~~~

Spyglass

Griff woke the next morning rested and contented but alone in an empty bed. He lay on his back with eyes closed and listened. The bungalow was quiet. He contemplated whether to check for Helena poolside or in the restaurant.

He got up to find the receipt for Bungalow 7 on the breakfast bar with a hand-written note from Helena scrawled on it: "Darling—I've gone out shopping. I'll see you at home later. Feel free to send this to Lance for a little bonus. ~H"

Suddenly, Griff was not so contented any more, so he put on his suit and went to the pool to swim laps. After, he showered, dressed and drove the non-descript rental car back to Van Nuys Airport. He checked the weather and saw it was clear up and down the California coast, so he paid his tie down fee and fuel bill, then departed to the northwest, skirting Santa Barbara to the north, then turning west out over the water far enough to stay out of Vandenberg Air Force Base's airspace. He flew up the coast in the smooth air over the water taking in the sights.

An hour and a half later, Griff landed at Monterey Peninsula Airport. He drove the Avis rental out to the Pebble Beach resort. The Nickolson's condo had sold quickly, so it was no longer accessible, but that wasn't why Griff was there. It was still early, so he paid his toll and drove the 17-Mile Drive. After, Griff headed back to the resort and found the Tap Room where he ordered a Kobe burger and draft ale. He ordered a second beer so he could linger 'til dusk.

Griff walked the grounds until he found the site of the temporary helipad and scanned the surrounding area. On his iPhone, he pulled up the pdf copy of the NTSB accident report and read it again. He walked the short flight path that led to Cliff Nickolson's doom at the site where the Bell 407 slammed against rising terrain to the northeast. It made little sense if the weather was as marginal as the METARs indicated, no doubt from low stratus blowing in off the bay. A west departure out over the water to gain altitude would have been prudent—and seemed to be the path chosen by the other pilots that evening.

Griff wondered what their intentions were—something the government report did not delve into. The NTSB noted that the Hornet Group Gulfstream was parked at the Monterey airport, which they presumed to be the destination of the doomed flight based on an FAA flight plan filed for the G-5 to fly to Burbank that evening. But Lance's information showed that Nickolson held a first-class ticket on United Airlines Flight 869 out of San Francisco International to Hong Kong later that night.

No doubt, then, the G-5 was taking Mrs. Nickolson home to Bel Air after a long weekend at the Pebble Beach corporate golf outing for select Silicon Valley investors at Spyglass. Griff made a note to check with Donald Wallace about the ticket to Hong Kong. He would ask Lance more about the meeting of Silicon Valley investors, something Wallace would likely be tight-lipped about since the way Lance's reports described the outing made it sound like a high-tech Bilderberger-type event.

As Griff scanned about the crash site, he tried to imagine the grief brought down on Helena with the death of her

Article 15

father and the irony of surviving war only to die on a battlefield of high finance.

~ ~ ~

Griff drove back to the Red Roof Inn at the airport, checked in and went to bed, scanning the room and involuntarily comparing it—unfavorably—with Bungalow 7 at the Beverly Hills Hotel.

In the morning, he called Lance. "So, tell me about Spyglass."

"Yeah. Tough course. I hate it—well, not really, but it sure hates me. Evidently it was Cliff Nickolson's favorite, though."

"I wouldn't know."

"Sure, 'cause there's no gun powder or gasoline or oats involved, right?"

"Eh…chasing a little white ball just doesn't seem to be a worthy quarry."

"Yeah, you're right, since it can't shoot back. But it can hurt you bad, inside—you know, like women. Speaking of which, how's Helena?"

"We weren't. But she's good. Very good."

"I'll bet."

"So, this golfing group, they do this every year?"

"Since the late nineties. Nickolson was one of the founding fathers. Pretty exclusive club. All the huge technology investors no one has ever heard about conspiring, no doubt, to rule the world while they humped the links."

"Was Cliff any good at it?"

"What, golf or investing?"

"I know he was good at making money."

"Scratch golfer. Most all of them were. Rumor has it that the NASDAQ dropped ten points for every stroke he shot over par."

"Figures."

"Don't you just hate guys like that?"

"Aren't you a *Guy Like That?*"

"In my dreams." Lance sighed. "How is this going to help you find any of that stuff?"

"Don't know yet. Tell me about the Bell 407."

"Nice. State of the art with Garmin glass and FADEC. Been in a few, but not much stick time."

"Hmmm."

"Why do you ask?"

"I don't know. Something just ain't sitting right with the crash."

"Well, I know one thing for sure. If it hadn't been for Daddy Nickolson's misfortune, you'd have never met Helena."

"What was in Hong Kong?"

"Man, you are all business, aren't you? You need to take a lesson or two in maximizing billable hours."

"Hong Kong?"

"Come on. You know, the gateway to all the tech and finance locked up in China. Just 'cause they're Commies doesn't mean they're immune from the greed virus, you know." Lance chuckled at his own observation of human nature. "Those Bilderberger guys play on the world stage. Some of them could buy and sell small countries for fun like they're just squares on a Monopoly board."

"Cliff?"

"He's on the list."

"Was."

"Yeah. Was." Lance cleared his throat. "Anyway, just make sure you don't land on Boardwalk."

Griff silently shook his head.

~~~

Sun Valley

Griff should have asked to meet at the McDonald's in Hailey instead of letting him pick the pretentious Ketchum coffee shop, just to set him on edge.

Edward, Helena's ex-husband, gave the barista such detailed instructions for his latte that the speech could have filled a section of a phone book-thick aircraft maintenance manual or, perhaps, half a chapter of a Tolstoy novel. Griff had plenty of time to think of several other comparatives while he waited to order a cup of the "free trade" Sumatran Sunrise roast with no cream, no sugar, much to the disbelief of the young girl behind the counter. Of course, when they sat down outside at a cafe table on the sidewalk patio, Edward grimaced at his first dainty sip.

"Problem, Eddie?"

"It is Edward. Please." He sipped again, shook his head and complained in a nasally New England accent, "Too much cinnamon. It is Arial's annoying habit."

Yeah, life is tough. Griff nodded, idly trying to come up with a plan to kill the pasty-faced, patrician Ivy League-legacy bastard. *Not so much the killing itself as the disposal of the body...*

"Bonita knows the proper balance. She's a natural. A barista artista," Edward chuffed under his breath at his own rhyme. "So, what can I do for you Mr. Crowe."

"Just a courtesy follow-up visit to make sure your Jackson

~ 67 ~

Pollack painting arrived intact."

"You work for the shipping company?"

"No. As I said, Stein, Baylor and Stein. You know, the firm your father retained to resolve the matter."

"Oh, sure. Sorry I didn't recognize the name at first. Not our usual. So, you're an attorney there?"

"Something like that." Griff smiled. "And Ms. Nickolson?"

"What about her?"

Griff could have sworn Edward literally shrank ten percent in size right before his eyes at the mere mention of Helena. "Well, I have to ask…I mean, she seems somewhat…spirited?"

"Oh, she's a scamp alright."

"Scamp?" Griff was having a hard time imagining Helena and Edward as a couple, which, of course, lasted less than three years and thankfully did not lay down a challenge to evolutionary theory with any offspring. "Stealing a two-million-dollar work of art hardly seems the work of a scamp."

"It was appraised at four point six million, actually."

"Still, a scamp?"

"It was all covered in the pre-nup that Father insisted upon. She just, well, she gets emotional at times and often acts out as a rather spoiled child when she does not get her way."

"So, you do not wish to press charges?"

"Oh, Lord, no. I am quite content to be finally done with the Nickolson clan."

"Yeah, I know. *Nouveau riche.*" Griff knew from Lance's report Cliff Nickolson could have bought and sold Edward's father's rum running inheritance at least ten times over.

"She was quite the ride, though," Edward said wistfully.

"You gotta stay on for the full eight seconds, though."

Article 15

"Huh?"

"Nothing." Griff sipped at his Sumatran Sunrise. "College sweethearts, then?"

"Yes. Something like that. She was a drama queen—literally. Theater Studies, don't you know. Crashed one of our Deke frat parties with some of her sisters. That's how we first met."

"I don't see her as the sorority type."

"No, no—her thespian sisters. Or lesbros? If you catch my drift. Or so we all thought."

"Really…" Griff wasn't buying it.

"Or maybe she swung both ways. Funny thing…."

"What's that?"

"I almost felt *selected.* Sometimes, I wonder if I might have been her beard."

"Hmmm…" Griff could not square Edward's observation with his own hands-on experiences—*then again, Yale drama school?*

"Anyway, we tried New York City. The girl is indefatigable. Didn't work much on the theater boards but was a smash hit with the backstage crowd at the after parties. Of course, my father had other ideas for my future: politics. And that lifestyle certainly didn't fit the plan. Besides, he never did like her from our first visit to Nantucket. So…"

Griff studied the faraway look on Edward's face and saw the oil and water of regret and relief swirling about his eyes.

"Where is she now?"

"I honestly don't know," Griff said.

"When I learned about her father's death, we were, you know, already separated and in the middle of our meltdown, so I figured she needed some space." Edward sighed. "But no. It was Helena being Helena."

"Were there any other…contested items she might have stashed away somewhere?"

"Do not know. Do not care. She might have some things still in our old Tribeca apartment. Rent controlled, so she held on to it. Obviously, the painting was acquired through *my* family resources, so it was rightfully mine. Quite a stunning work, don't you think?"

"It is…" Griff finished his own sentence inside his head…*for a drop cloth.*

"My campaign begins in earnest this summer for next fall's elections. Fund raising and such."

"Congress?"

"No. My father has charted out an executive branch career path, so mayor, then the governor's mansion."

"Being VP in his company must fit the bill."

"It didn't for Helena. It was the beginning of the end, I suppose. I went home, and she stayed in Manhattan."

"You running here? Or back East?"

"Back home. Connecticut."

Good.

"Um, she's not going to make waves for me, is she?"

One last squeeze, Griff recalled Helena saying. "You never know. She's a—what did you call her?"

"A scamp."

"Yes…*a scamp.*" Griff could only smile. *Maybe it did fit.*

Edward, on the other hand, seemed to shrink yet another ten percent in size.

~~~

Rock Creek

After the flight back from Hailey, Idaho, and the quick commute from Laramie to the ranch's sod strip, Griff taxied up to find Ben at the hangar when he shut down the Aeronca Chief.

"You got a visitor," Ben said, as he grabbed the horizontal stabilizer on the passenger side of the plane and helped Griff pull it into the hangar. "Pretty one, too. Blonde. Blue eyes."

Griff shook his head. "Her name's Helena."

Ben nodded sagely. "Dropped out of the sky in a helo, just like a Greek goddess. The woman has style."

"And a boatload of money."

"But that's not why she's here…Or why you got that smile on your face."

"Shows that bad, huh?"

Ben chuckled as they set the empennage down. "She's out on the back deck. I'll close up here."

"Thanks."

Griff walked around to the backside of the ranch house and stepped up on the deck. He savored Helena's profile in the sunset as she leaned on the rail gazing towards the Medicine Bow Mountains. Barefoot, she wore only a gauzy dress like the morning at Angel Fire. He went and stood next to her, with his elbows on the railing.

Helena leaned her head against Griff's shoulder.

"Made yourself at home, I see," he said.

She nodded against his arm.

Griff looked at her, then off to the west, wondering at the absence of a snarky comeback.

"Donnie's dead," she said softly.

"Huh?"

"Donald Wallace. You met with him at my father's company."

"Yeah, I know. What—When? How?"

"He was assaulted in the parking garage. Working late. They found his body yesterday morning, so a couple of days ago. The police think it was probably a carjacking, 'cause his BMW is missing." She stifled a sniffle and cleared her throat. "I liked him. And he was Daddy's best friend."

"I know." Griff put his arm around Helena. "He seemed like a stand-up guy."

"I didn't really have anywhere else to go…or anyone else I wanted to be with right now." Helena sighed. "I hope you don't mind."

"Absolutely not."

"Thank you."

"Sure. You want me to get you set up in a bedroom?"

"Why? You got other company?"

Griff smiled. "No. Of course not."

"Good," she said wearily. "Do you still have any of that scotch I bought you?"

"I do. On the rocks?"

"Neat, please."

Griff went inside to get glasses and the Balvenie. Before he came back out, he texted Lance, "Donald Wallace Dead. WTF?"

He left his phone on the kitchen counter.

Article 15

Griff and Helena sat and drank scotch on the deck in the cold moon shadows of the Medicine Bow Mountains. Rodya came wandering up out of the darkness, sniffed around their chairs, then lay at Helena's feet.

Around midnight, a reply from Lance dinged on Griff's phone: "I guess JR is in charge now."

But by then, Helena and Griff were upstairs in bed.

~~~

In the morning, Griff saddled up Winston for Helena and his second favorite quarter horse, Hannibal, for himself.

They rode north, walking and trotting casually across the high plains, moving deep into the Crowe ranch land with Rodya alongside. The calm, crisp morning air faintly seized their breaths for an instant, then set them free again until the sun rose high enough to warm the thin atmosphere.

Griff noted Helena's ease in the saddle, then recalled she spent her summers at the family ranch in Montana. He tried to hold on to pleasant thoughts of Helena, the morning and riding, but his mind was roped back to Lance's message about JR and gnawing questions about the coincidence of Donald Wallace's death just days after their meeting.

Griff turned Hannibal to climb the path up to a ridgeline looking down on Rock Creek. Helena and Winston followed. A small clump of cattle grazed and drank in and along the water. Griff reflexively counted and mentally logged the location.

Suddenly, Helena galloped past Griff, charging ahead along the ridge with Rodya chasing to catch up.

Griff spurred Hannibal after her.

Once past the herd, Helena turned down off the ridge towards Rock Creek, where the stream spread out. She guided Winston into the shallow water and galloped up the rocky bed, splashing up water that glittered in the sun.

Griff followed at a pace to keep a hundred feet behind her.

Rodya ran along the shoreline.

Helena reined Winston to a stop beneath a stand of cottonwood trees. She turned to watch Griff, who slowed Hannibal to a walk as he approached. She patted Winston's neck and let him drink.

"You must be the new school marm, ma'am," Griff drawled out as he came towards her. "Might not be safe to be out here all on your lonesome and such. Injuns, you know."

Rodya ran through the creek between them to the other side to chase a jack rabbit.

"Why, Marshall, so kind of you to notice…and care," Helena breathlessly teased back. "But I hear tell you're part Injun yerself."

Griff grinned and motioned upstream with a nod. "Come on."

Helena turned Winston to fall in beside him and walk on in the middle of the rocky creek bed. "Do you believe in coincidences?"

Griff squinted at the horizon. "Not particularly."

"What about divine intervention?"

Griff shrugged.

"Karma?"

"Maybe."

"And Donnie?"

"JR's in charge now, right? At least that's what Lance thinks."

"We each own forty-two and a half percent of the voting

stock. Donnie held the other fifteen."

"And now the tie breaker is dead."

"He wasn't married. Never was. I honestly don't know about any family he might have had."

"So, where does that fifteen percent go?"

Helena shook her head. She watched Rodya race ahead of them along the shoreline. "What's going on, Griff?"

"I don't know."

Up ahead, Ben, Johnny Eagle and Shep were working strays their way to join up with the small herd upstream. Griff waved then turned west up out of the creek bed towards the foothills. Helena waved at Ben and followed.

Griff and Helena spent the balance of the morning exploring the trails that led in and out of stands of aspen trees and lodge pole pines and along the lacework of unnamed rivulets, which formed the runoff capillary system that fed Rock Creek. As they rose higher into the foothills, the western wind brushed the tops of the trees in an arid imitation of ocean waves. Their ride ended at the familiar rock outcropping which overlooked the ranch and beyond.

"Oh my God, it's been years—too, too many years," Helena said as she dismounted Winston. She bent over, stretching her back and legs. "I'll be sore. But it'll be worth every Advil. Thank you."

"Montana summers?" Griff took Winston's reins and tied him and Hannibal off.

"I'll be damned. You *do* pay attention when I speak."

Griff dug in his saddle bags for sandwiches and his canteen. He waved her on to the lip of the overlook. "Hungry?"

"Famished."

"They're not aged Kobe Delmonicos, but your sandwich has a name."

Helena grinned and followed him out to the edge. "As in: Mayer-comma-Oscar?"

"All beef. Only the best for you, ma'am." He handed her a sandwich.

"I love it." She sat down shoulder-to-shoulder beside Griff near the edge with a huge boulder of granite for their backrest. "You know bologna was officially frowned upon in 9-0-2-1-0."

"Well…not here." After a few bites, he offered her the canteen. "We bottle our own water and swap spit, too."

"How positively barbaric of you." She took the canteen and drank. "I get the feeling you come here often."

Griff shrugged, took a bite of bologna sandwich and peered out over the plains.

"So…*do you?*"

"Yup. Ever since Ben's dad taught me to ride and I could head out on my own."

"And what do you call this place?"

"What do you mean?"

"Well, your sandwich has a name. Seems like your favorite place should have one, too."

"Huh. Never gave it much thought."

"Thoreau had Walden Pond. Superman had his Fortress of Solitude—and he's a stupid cartoon character for crying out loud."

"I guess I've always been busy thinking of other things."

"Typical…*Men.*" Helena ate another bite of sandwich. "Do you at least get good reception up here?"

"Don't know. Never tried."

"But I should let my flyboys know what's going on.

They're parked down in Denver."

"Oh, I think they'll find something to keep themselves occupied. Us pilots tend to be somewhat resourceful types. Besides, we got dinner plans tonight at Ben's."

"You don't even have your phone, do you."

Griff shook his head. "Nope."

"Wow. So, not even any Facebook posts from the top of the world? It really is like living two centuries back around here."

"Yeah. I kind of like it."

They finished their sandwiches in silence.

"Well, I must admit, it does have its charms." Helena yawned, stretched, laid down, and rested her head on Griff's lap. Moments later she nodded off.

Griff softly stroked her hair and wondered if he should name this place.

~~

The third Thursday of every month, Ben invited Griff, the hands, and a few friends from the reservation who were occasional day laborers on the ranch over to his house for dinner. He lived with his wife, Swan, on a plot in the southeast corner of the ranch which had been willed to him by Griff's father, along with their house and the couple of nearby cabins where Johnny Eagle and Shep lived. Their three children had grown and moved away—the daughter to Denver, one son to Cheyenne and the other to Washington DC—so the third Thursday filled the homestead with family again.

Griff drove Helena the three miles to Ben's place in his father's antique Willys MB he continued to keep in pristine condition as if it had just rolled onto Normandy Beach on D-Day. With the top off and the windshield down, he couldn't help noticing Helena's blonde hair blowing back like a palomino's mane as the Jeep bucked down the unpaved road. She held on tight, but smiled at Griff, as if careening across the plains was a thrill ride at Elitch Gardens. When they got there, Ben was stoking the fire pit out back and tending to the dozen T-bones sizzling on the grate over the open fire under Johnny Eagle's and Shep's watchful eyes. Allison, one of Johnny Eagle's many girlfriends, sat at a row of three picnic tables pushed together talking with Swan, while the men from the res milled about drinking beer out of long-neck bottles.

Helena bounded out of the Jeep when it skid to a stop and headed for the fire pit.

Griff went to grab a beer out of the washtub filled with ice then waded into the huddle of men from the res. Their talk wandered aimlessly about the Broncos, the Rockies, and the National Stock Show and which of the men might try to ride or work the rodeo. Griff watched Helena talk with the boys, showing the usually bashful Shep some flattering female attention. He could tell even from across the way it made the young ranch hand blush.

When Ben turned the steaks and called out to Swan, who got up to set the table with Johnny Eagle's girlfriend, Helena went to help bring out the side dishes served family style, chatting with Swan as they went in and out of the house carrying bowls and plates full of food. It was as if she had been coming to Ben's third Thursdays for years, which made Griff smile.

The chow line started with the men from the reservation, cycling past the fire pit to have their plates filled with a huge T-bone. They settled together at the far end of the picnic tables. Then came Johnny Eagle next to Allison with Shep across from them in the middle. Helena sat down beside Shep. Griff slid in by Swan opposite Helena. Ben parked next to Helena at the end.

After the chaotic choreography of passing dishes had filled everyone's plate with baked beans, corn, coleslaw and potatoes, the feasting began in quiet earnest. Halfway through her steak, Helena smirked at Griff, then nudged Ben with her shoulder and asked, "What was it you called Griff when he was a kid?"

Ben looked over at Griff, who shook his head. He answered anyway, "Geronimo Crowe."

"Yeah. That's it." Helena winked at Griff. "And that was because, what, he was some kind of wild half-breed?"

"He was a handful and a half, for sure," Swan said. "I'm just glad he wasn't one of mine to raise. Maggie was a saint."

"I've met kinder and gentler drill sergeants," Griff said.

"Shame on you talking about your mother that way," Swan scolded. "What did you expect? You boys were the worst."

"You boys?" Helena asked. "You mean there's more than one of you?"

"Used to be," Griff said.

"Car accident," Ben said. "Wil's senior year in Boulder."

"Sorry." Helena looked across at Griff.

"Yeah. Me, too."

"But this one here was more than enough trouble for three," Swan said. "The stories I could tell."

"Oh, I love stories."

Griff cut hard into his steak and scowled at Helena.

She grinned back. "Do tell."

"Oh, just boys being boys," Swan said, looking back and forth between Helena and Griff.

"I like boys, too." Helena's comment drew stares from the

other end of the table. She got up and walked around the table. Leaning over between Swan and Griff so he could hear, she half-whispered in Swan's ear, "We'll talk later."

Griff watched Helena work the table like a good hostess at a high society *soirée,* pausing to talk with Johnny Eagle and Allison, then each of the men from the reservation until she got back around to Shep, who she cajoled into joining her by the fire pit.

"You are in some serious trouble, my friend," Ben said to Griff as he followed Helena around the table and over to the fire with his eyes.

"I know it." Griff pushed away his empty plate.

Ben stood up. "I think I need to stoke the fire."

"I'd say she's got an ornery Maggie streak running through her that'll keep you in your place right proper," Swan said. "You are in trouble."

"I know. I know."

All the boys from the reservation—and even Johnny Eagle, too, with his girlfriend beside him—watched Helena walk arm-in-arm with Shep to the fire pit, then turned their envy towards Griff before getting up to head over to the washtub for a beer, then to gather around Shep and Helena.

"There, there. It was bound to happen sooner or later." Swan patted Griff on the arm.

The erratic glow and shadows of the stoked-up flames danced on Helena, and Griff could not take his eyes off her either.

~~~

In the morning, Griff sat in the overstuffed chair angled to look both out his bedroom window and, with a slight sideways glance, at Helena still sleeping naked tangled in the bedsheets.

She snored softly.

Griff smiled as he sipped his second cup of coffee, trying to decide if his little experiment of taking Helena to Ben's had been a surprising success or a dangerous failure by not giving him an easy out exposing her as an elitist snob. Either way it was quite a performance.

I am in trouble.

He checked email with his iPad and read the police report on Donald Wallace's murder attached to Lance's email. He followed the link to the *Los Angeles Times* story from the day before, but it was equally cryptic in terms of assigning a motive for the crime beyond Wallace's missing BMW.

Junior may be a jerk, Griff thought, *but I bet he's more bark than bite.*

Griff petted Rodya laying on the floor beside him.

Helena stirred. The Husky raised his head to stare at her.

Besides, a voting deadlock between the two of them while Wallace's estate is settled will probably be even more frustrating for him.

Helena rolled towards Griff and gave him a sleepy-eyed smile. "Morning…"

"Sleep well?"

"I did."

Griff smiled. "You're leaving today, aren't you?"

She nodded.

"Where to?"

"New York, I think."

Tribeca, Griff thought.

"I need to get away—not from you. I mean, you know, Donnie."

"I know what you mean. Besides, I've got work to do."

Helena threw back the sheet to reveal her naked body. "But first…"

Griff smiled. He rose and moved back towards the bed.

Rodya growled lowly, which made Helena roll on her back and laugh.

And made Griff want her more. He put Rodya out and closed the door.

They made love.

After, Griff fixed breakfast of pepperoni and eggs, then took Helena to the Laramie airport in the Aeronca Chief. He stood on the tarmac and watched the Learjet 31 fly her away.

"Who was that?" Bones asked as he meandered up next to Griff.

Griff sighed. "A client."

"Huh." Bones took a sip of coffee from his Cowboy Aviation coffee mug. "Where do I get a job like yours?"

~~~

Blue Wing, LLC

With Helena eight miles high or so over the Midwestern United States in her Learjet 31 heading to White Plains, New York, Griff pulled his Norton Commando out of the hangar and rode downtown to the Albany County Public Library. He parked himself at an unoccupied computer and began searching in an incognito session of Chrome.

Google returned fifty-one million, three hundred thousand items for "Blue Wing LLC." Griff ignored the home inspection company in Idaho and the pet supply company in Kansas. He checked the websites of a consulting firm in Boulder, a freight company in Oklahoma and a property management firm in South Carolina, but his gut feel told him those were dry holes.

Only fifty-three million, two hundred ninety-nine thousand, nine hundred and ninety-five to go.

On a hunch, Griff went to the Kentucky Secretary of State web site and searched there. A Blue Wing, LLC, was listed in Pine Hollow. The company had no web site, but it moved immediately to the top of Griff's list. According to Lance's briefing papers, the first Mrs. Nickolson—Helena's mother—was born and raised northwest of there in Maysville, Kentucky. Given his strong disinclination towards coincidences, Griff figured a flight plan to the Bluegrass State would be in order, with a stopover in Chicago.

~~~

Lance's Escalade was parked on the tarmac when Griff taxied the Cirrus up to Atlantic Aviation and shut down where the line boy marshaled him to park.

"Did you call Hannah?" Lance asked when Griff got in the Cadillac. "She's been asking after you."

"I did."

"Hungry for pecan pie, are we?"

"Just dinner. No dessert," Griff said.

"Yeah. Sure." Lance gave Griff a skeptical sideways glance as he waited for the security gate to open. "You gonna want to eat something or save your appetite for later?"

"A dog sounds good for now."

"I know just the place." Lance pulled out of Atlantic Aviation, drove around the airport, then down Milwaukee Avenue. He pulled into the strip mall behind an old Denny's building and parked in front of the Dog Walk. He winked at Griff. "A diamond in the rough."

"As long as they don't serve MREs."

"You won't be disappointed." Lance punched Griff's arm hard but didn't get a reaction. As they went in, he called out, *"Hola, Kim."*

"Señor Lance, me alegro de verle de nuevo," the Korean man behind the blue counter replied fluently.

"Este gringo es mi amigo, Griff."

"Encantado de conocerlo, señor Griff." Kim bowed towards Griff.

"Gracias. Y tú también." Griff waved. He drifted over to the only table in the place and sat down as Lance ordered their lunch.

"Actually, his Spanish is better than his English," Lance said as he set down their hot dogs. "Chicago style, right?"

Article 15

"When in Rome…"

'So, what's going on?" Lance asked around a mouthful of hot dog dragged through the garden. "You're not two-timing our very important client, now are you?"

Griff shook him off like a pitcher to a catcher. "I told you, no dessert…*This time, anyway.*" Griff knew well how his casual on-again off-again relationship with Hannah gnawed at Lance's unrequited lust for his assistant. He grinned broadly.

Lance closed his eyes and sighed heavily.

"Besides, I want to get to Cincy tonight."

"Got a date there, too?"

"No, an early morning appointment across the river."

"Is this on my nickel?" Lance asked.

"You mean Helena's, right?"

"Just looking out for my client—*as usual.*"

Griff dug out his wallet. He pulled out a dollar bill and slid it across the table to Lance.

"What's that?"

"A retainer. Now I'm your client, too."

"I don't know if it will hold up in court."

"No worries. That's not where we're headed."

"Okay." Lance pocketed the dollar. "But my hourly rate is a bit higher than this. Like five hundred times higher."

"But it's full service, right? Privilege and all?"

"Usually I charge extra, but in your case…"

"Not even for another client, right?"

"Helena?"

Griff nodded.

"So, what privileged information are you going to share with your attorney?"

"Blue Wing, LLC. It wasn't in any of your reports."

"Should it have been?"

Griff nodded slowly. "Donald Wallace gave it up to me on the promise of total confidentiality. A few days later, he's dead."

"And you don't believe in coincidences."

Griff shook his head. "And I'm not buying the carjacking angle."

"Me, too, neither. Mmm." Lance frowned. "I don't know how we missed it."

"Well, here's how you can make it up to me. Get me an appointment tomorrow with The Leonard Group. Lawyers in Newport, Kentucky. They're listed as the registered agent of record."

"Can do. Then what?"

"Then a little side trip to Pine Hollow."

Lance nodded. "But first, a little pecan pie?"

"All work and no play…."

"You know, Hannah and Helena get along famously. They have ever since my first sit down with Helena."

"She knows, doesn't she?" Griff asked.

"They always do, my friend. Always do."

Griff's shoulders slumped. He shook his head. *"Damnit."*

"As your attorney, I advise you to begin drinking heavily."

~~~

E. Leonard, Esq.

All through dinner, Griff could not help but dwell on Lance telling him how well Hannah and Helena got along. They shared a pleasant meal, as always, surprisingly free of the dangers of intimate entanglement, which he was prepared to fend off, if only that one time. Griff half suspected the two women were conspiring against him to tease, torment, and test his mortal being.

Hannah dropped Griff off at Chicago Executive Airport. He departed due east into the pure darkness over Lake Michigan to get out of the Chicago terminal area as quickly as possible. He turned southeast as soon as the air traffic controller called him clear of the Class B airspace and landed at Lunken Airfield in Cincinnati a little over an hour later.

The next morning, Griff sat in the reception area of the dingy law offices of The Leonard Group across the Ohio River in Newport, Kentucky. The decor, which seemingly had not been updated since the Seventies, was a stark contrast to Stein, Baylor & Stein's legal palace in their Chicago Loop skyscraper. Griff felt thrown back into the frosted-window gumshoe digs of an old black-and-white Humphrey Bogart movie.

Though not audibly snapping gum, the secretary, who might once have been as alluring as Hannah—forty or fifty years ago—silently worked her jaw as she plodded methodically through unkempt stacks of paperwork on her desk, oblivious to Griff's presence until the ancient intercom on her desk scratched out either a drive-through order of French fries and a chocolate milkshake or his invitation in to see the managing partner and only other employee of The Leonard Group.

"Mr. Leonard, I'm Griffith Crowe." He could barely see the short, skinny octogenarian in thick-rimmed glasses slouching behind a massive desk drifted high with a blizzard of legal briefs and documents. "From—"

"Call me Johnny. Everybody does," E.J. Leonard called out in a drawling hillbilly twang as he waved Griff in without standing up. "Come on in and take a load off those tired old dogs of yours."

"Thank you, Johnny."

"Yup, yup, yup. I talked to your boss man—what, Baylor, is it? Yesterday. Or the day before? I forget. Anyways, you're here."

Griff nodded as he surveyed the office and its dusty collection of no doubt personally priceless, yet publicly worthless, memorabilia. The wall behind Johnny's desk was tiled with framed eight-by-ten photos of the attorney posing beside dignitaries through the ages, his hair graying and thinning as the photos transitioned from black-and-white to color. Most of the dignitaries were unknowable to out-of-towners, though Griff recognized Pete Rose, Jimmy Carter, and Bill Clinton—who was ironically hung next to Lonnie Anderson from *WKRP in Cincinnati*. "How long have you been here, Johnny?"

"Criminy, it's been since the wife and I graduated from U of K. Sixty-seven. We once had half the floor filled with young fellas such as yourself. But, you know, those days have faded away. Just me now. And Patty Ann in the front office."

Article 15

"And Mrs. Leonard?"

"She passed. A few years back." Johnny took off his glasses to wipe a moist eye. "So, it's just me now."

"I'm sorry to hear that."

"Yeah…me, too—least ways around supper time." Johnny grinned mischievously. "She was a hell of a cook. Best apple pie in the tri-state region. Kind of a tyrant here in the office, so it's quieter at work nowadays—You like baseball, Griff?"

"I don't follow it religiously, but—"

"Here, let me give you a ticket to this afternoon's game." Johnny put his glasses back on and started digging in his desk drawer.

"You know, that's okay, I've got—"

"Nonsense. I insist. We still have season tickets for the Reds. Don't know why, but we do." Johnny reached out across his desk to hand Griff a ticket. "Just don't get across the river as much as I used to. But can't let them go to waste. Here, take it."

"Really, Johnny—"

"See that there Louisville Slugger there on the shelf?"

Griff looked and nodded.

"Johnny Bench himself signed it. Don't make me tattoo you with it. Now, take the ticket, dang it. Enjoy yourself."

"Sure thing." Griff took the ticket and stuck it in his shirt pocket.

"I do believe you'll find it rather…enjoyable, if not enlightening."

"Thank you, Johnny. I owe you."

"You say that now. Anyways, what does your bossman, Baylor, want with this crusty old country lawyer?" Johnny leaned his elbows on his desk and stared at Griff, unsmiling now, his face set hard in cross-examination mode.

Griff met and held his glare. He made a decision, even though he wasn't under oath. "It's not Lance. It's me. I'm the one who needs your help."

Johnny just nodded slightly.

"You know a Cliff Nickolson?"

"Heard of the fella. Heard he died hard a while back. A whirlybird wreck or something."

"Donald Wallace?"

Johnny's right eye twitched ever so slightly behind the thick lens of his glasses.

"He was killed a few days ago."

"You appear to know a lot of fellas taking dirt naps, don't you?"

"Not my doing, Johnny. Not my doing."

"But you're involved."

"That I am."

"And what brings wanton death to my door and yours, Mr. Crowe?"

"You know Helena Nickolson?"

"Can't say as I do."

"Cliff's daughter."

"And what's she to you?"

Griff smiled. He was losing the cross examination. "That, Mr. Leonard, is a very good question."

"Not my business, I reckon. But I'm suspecting it brung you here to brighten my morning."

"Not directly. Rather, it's Blue Wing, LLC. You are listed as their registered agent."

"Could be." Johnny slapped the intercom button. "Patty Ann. Blue Wing, LLC. Where's the file?"

Article 15

A moment later, Patty Ann trundled in and over to the desk. She stuck her palsied hand in and pulled a file folder out of a stack. She handed it to Johnny, then trundled out.

Johnny opened the folder and read. "Evidently, you are correct. Says here, they're situated over in Pine Hollow. So?"

Griff smiled. "Man, I would not want to play poker with you, sir."

Johnny cracked a sly smile. "Just a country lawyer, son. I used to split rail, too, in my younger days."

"Just like honest Abe."

"Whall, I ain't making that comparison, 'cepting maybe to the honest part."

"And your arrangement with Blue Wing?"

"I am indeed the registered agent for the company. I drew up the original articles of incorporation nearly a decade ago at the behest of the reportedly late Donald Wallace. I was retained as legal counsel to handle contracts, patents, copyrights, and other such legal matters."

"Are there any patents or copyrights?"

Johnny smiled. "A matter of public record. No."

"And these other legal matters?"

"We'd be finding ourselves straying into privileged territory there, Mr. Crowe."

"Shareholders?"

"Not at liberty, unless you're a pesky revenuer with a subpoena." Johnny shook his head. "Privately held."

"And if one had business with Blue Wing?"

"Pray tell, just what business would that be?"

Griff smiled. *"Touché."*

"Your interest gives me pause, young man. You say Donald

Wallace, personally his own self, told you of this company?"

Griff nodded his head. "Face-to-face."

"And he's since expired?"

"Yes, sir. He has." Griff looked out the window at downtown Cincinnati across the river. "What if...what if one would wish to acquire Blue Wing, LLC?"

"I reckon, as their registered agent and legal counsel, I'd be obliged to pass on any such tendered offer to the Board of Directors."

"Hmmm." Griff pulled a pad of yellow paper out of his brief case. He thought for a moment, then wrote. When he finished, he tore the paper off the pad, folded it, then leaned over to hand it to Johnny.

Johnny's lips moved as he read. He looked up at Griff. "One million, two hundred thirty-four thousand, five hundred sixty-seven dollars and eighty-nine cents? One might feel compelled to inquire as to how you came upon such a figure...that is if one hadn't learnt to count in grade school."

"You will convey my client's offer to the Board?"

Johnny's right eyebrow arched above his glasses. "Client? Would this be one said Helena Nickolson?"

Griff sat back and smiled. "I believe we had a prior discussion on issues of privilege."

"Indeed, we did."

"The offer will find its way to the Board?"

"Rest assured, I will do my duty, Mr. Crowe. 'Course, no guarantees of acceptance nor negotiation."

"Understood. There never are."

"Very well, then, Griff, if there is nothing else." Johnny stood up from his desk.

Article 15

Griff stood up, noting that Johnny was taller than he first imagined, though still four inches shorter than his own six-foot two-inch height. They shook hands across the desk. "Thank you for your time, Mr. Leonard."

"It was a pleasure to meet you, Mr. Crowe. I hope you enjoy the ball game this afternoon."

"Right, right. The Reds and..."

"Why the Atlanta...*Braves.*" The old man winked knowingly. "And whom might you be rooting for?"

A blank look of incomprehension hung on Griff's face as he turned to leave.

"And Griff...I'm not going to end up room temperature like them other fellas you were acquainted with, will I?"

It gave Griff pause. He looked back over his shoulder. "I look forward to seeing you again. That's my plan."

"Good, then."

"Thanks for the ticket, Johnny."

~~~

Great American Ball Park

Griff found his seat in Section 117 of Great American Ball Park. He had no intention of using the ticket Johnny gave him when he left the Newport office building, but the little voice in his head nagged him relentlessly to go to the game. Since that little voice often showed great wisdom and foresight in the past—and having saved his life on at least two occasions—he abandoned his original plan to drive to Pine Hollow to check out Blue Wing, LLC.

Johnny's seats were good ones, in the lower deck behind the third base line. Being a 1:05 game on a Tuesday afternoon, the stands were sparsely filled, so Griff took the end seat on the aisle, opened his Cracker Jack and watched the Reds and Braves battle to a 2-2 tie by the bottom of the fourth inning.

"You're in my seat," a woman called out coming down the steps behind him.

Griff pulled his leg off the empty seat in front of him and sat up from his slouch. He made a show of pulling out his ticket to check the seat number. "Oh, so I am. Sorry." He slid over two seats to his left.

The skinny woman in her late twenties with jet-black hair and dressed like a glammed-up biker—breast-hugging tank top, black leather jacket scarred with big silver zippers, skin tight jeans, and stiletto heeled boots—stepped in and sat down in the seat next to Griff. She pulled off her aviator sunglasses and, without taking her eyes off the field, asked as if the huge outfield scoreboard was invisible, "Who's winning?"

He eyeballed her with a sideways glance. Something in her facial features struck him as familiar. "Tie game."

One row back, a huge muscular biker, his hair pulled back tight in a ponytail, sat down behind the woman and stared at Griff.

Griff immediately regretted disarming himself to attend the ball game.

The three watched an inning of play in silence. The Braves scored an unanswered run, and the home team went three up-and-out.

"Well, that should make you happy, eh, *Tonto?*" The woman looked at Griff and smirked.

"So…you know Mr. Leonard, too." Griff glanced over his shoulder at the biker behind him, then directly at the woman. "Didn't really figure you two for baseball *aficionados,* on first impression."

"Grandpa used to drag us to the games all the time. Broke his heart a little when I declared myself a Dodgers fan."

Griff squinted to look through the dark, blood-red lipstick and heavy eyeshadow. "I see the family resemblance now."

"How observant of you."

"Who's our friend back there?"

"Oh, he works for me."

"And what business would you be in?"

"Why? You want to talk shop?"

"Nah, I was enjoying the game." Griff looked back towards the field. "Tonto?"

"The name Griffith Crowe seems to pop up on a lot of legal filings for folks on an Indian reservation in Wyoming.

Mostly *pro bono.* Figure there's got to be a blood connection."

"I didn't catch your name."

"I ain't throwed it out yet."

"Well, I can call you Ms. Leonard, but that seems a bit formal for the occasion."

"Maura."

"Pleased to meet you, Maura."

"Hmmm. You want a beer? My treat this round."

"Sure."

Maura turned to the man behind them. "Dewey, get us a couple of beers, would ya?"

"Be a good boy now." Dewey patted Griff on the shoulder hard, then got up and headed for the concession stand.

Maura smiled at Griff. "He looks out for me."

"Like you look out for Johnny?" Griff asked.

"Nothing's going to happen to him, right?"

"Is that a question or a command?"

"You got a problem taking orders from a woman?"

Griff laughed. "I got someone you need to meet."

"Oh, yeah? Who's that, Helena Nickolson?"

"You know what they say, the customer's always right…"

"Is that so? My clients are usually ill-informed, ill-advised, and often down right ornery." Maura scoffed.

"Yeah. Mine, too. But they're still right—as long as they pay their bill."

"And who are you working for now? Helena?"

Griff shook his head. "I'm always working for myself."

Maura smiled and nodded her head. "Good answer, Mr. Crowe."

Dewey came back and handed Maura and Griff their beers.

"Thanks, Dewey." Then to Maura he said, "And call me Griff. After all, you just bought me a beer."

Maura took a swig of her beer. "So, *Griff,* you up for taking a ride tomorrow?"

"The three of us?"

"Nah, just you and me. A little road trip to Pine Hollow, maybe."

"Is this your idea or Johnny's?"

"You're lucky. He seems to have taken a shine to you for some reason." Maura looked Griff up, then down again with her dark green eyes.

"I'm honored."

"Oh, he doesn't trust you. But he says you seem like the kind of guy who gets things done. You found him after all."

"And he wants you to help me get things done?"

"Don't flatter yourself. He don't like you that much. He's got questions, too."

"About Donald Wallace?"

Maura nodded. "A fellow Marine, evidently."

"And you?"

"Two tours in Afghanistan."

"I was there once."

"So, we've all seen the ass end of the world, then."

Griff smiled. "Dewey, too?"

"We became acquainted through our work."

"Which is?"

Maura smiled. "Bail recovery and such. We mostly work the north side of the river here where it's still legal."

Griff sized up Maura and nodded. "What time do you want to leave in the morning?"

Article 15

"I'll pick you up at eight."

"Good, then."

Griff bought the next round.

Maura, Griff, and Dewey watched the Braves beat the home team 6-3.

~~~

Maura

Maura picked Griff up the next morning at Christopher's Bed and Breakfast in a granite-colored, four-door Jeep Rubicon Recon with the top open.

"Nice place," Maura said when Griff got in. "I presume you slept alone."

"Why's that?"

"You want to burn in hell for having sex in a church?"

"Former church."

"The site of countless weddings, baptisms, funerals, readings from the good book, yearning prayers, mournful hymns and sermons on reaching the pearly gates? And you're going to tempt the Almighty by doing the horizontal mambo in *His* house? You SEALs are crazy insane."

Griff laughed. "And that coming from a Devil Dog."

Maura grinned and pulled away. She crossed the Ohio River, then followed Route 52 along the north shore heading southeast.

Wind noise made conversation difficult, so Griff sat back and enjoyed the scenery—inside and outside the Jeep. An easy, blissful smile rested naturally on Maura's lips as she passed the world by, her fingers tapping on the steering wheel to the beat of some song in her head, since the radio was off. He didn't mind that she seemed unconcerned with obeying Ohio speed limits. Her black ponytail, pulled through the back of a black Los Angeles Dodgers baseball cap, danced crazily in the slipstream like the tail of a racing thoroughbred. An occasional tugboat churned the water, pushing barges laden with coal upstream. Four lanes became two, but Maura held her speed, and the centrifugal pull in the curves leaned Griff towards Maura, then her to him.

An hour later the Rubicon crossed the river back into Kentucky at Maysville. She turned right down West 2nd, then onto Rosemary Clooney Street on the west side of town.

"Rosemary Clooney is from Kentucky?" Griff asked.

"George, too." Maura said. "Hillbilly blood runs deep in them thar Hollywood hills. Probably why they call it Tinsel Town."

She pulled into the parking lot of the Blue Wing Diner overlooking the river.

"Is this what I think it is?"

"Let's grab a bite." Maura hopped out of the Jeep.

Griff followed her into the diner. They took a booth next to the windows facing the Ohio River. Maura opened a menu and studied. Griff warily surveyed the restaurant's nondescript Denny's-like interior, fighting back a haunting *Twilight Zone* sense of foreboding. The tables and booths were a third full of late breakfast eaters and coffee klatches of senior citizens, who arrested their conversations to seriously eyeball Maura and Griff.

"Coffee?" asked a young waitress coming up to their table, holding up a pot.

Griff nodded as he turned over his mug, staring down a quintet of nosy old men in overalls across the room. He looked up at the waitress to say "thank you" but couldn't get the words out as he recognized the twenty-something blonde.

Maura lifted her eyes from the menu to savor Griff's expression. She turned over her mug, then patted Griff's hand gently. "Now, honey…it's not polite to stare."

Griff glared at Maura, then looked back up at the waitress, who mustered a weak smile.

"Thanks." Maura smiled back at the waitress. "I think my friend and I will need a minute or two."

"No hurry. I'll check back." The waitress gave Griff a wary once over, then headed back to the counter.

"Is that…" Griff tracked the waitress to the Bunn coffee machine, then into the kitchen.

"Helena's cousin." Maura looked down into her menu to hide her growing grin. "Too bad we're here so early. They have a chicken fried steak to die for—and world class derby pie."

"Cousin?" Griff looked back to Maura.

"Quaint, huh. I mean, a family-run diner in the middle of a heartland Mayberry? Mom and dad and the kids all slaving away over a hot grill for their piece of the American dream. It's what this country is all about, isn't it. Of course, they don't have a Learjet. Just an old F150 pickup truck."

"Her aunt?"

Maura pointed to a stern looking woman behind the register.

"But this is Pine Hollow?"

"Patience, Griff. Patience. We'll get there after breakfast. I'm hungry."

~~

After suddenly coming face-to-face with Helena's doppelgänger, Griff wasn't in the mood to talk, so breakfast was a conversational vacuum. Maura ate her French toast, humming a cheerful melody purposely chosen to annoy Griff, who, between agitated glares her way, intently studied each and every employee of the Blue Wing Diner like a hungry wolf while he choked down his bacon and eggs.

When Helena's cousin, Angie by the name tag on her uniform, set down the check, Maura cleared her throat loudly to get Griff's attention and slid it across the table to him. "I paid for gas."

"How was everything?" asked Helena's aunt at the cash register with a sudden warming smile that transformed her countenance.

Griff grunted, dug out his money clip, and handed her two twenty-dollar bills. He read her name tag, which said "Willa," then studied her face.

"Everything was delicious…*again*," Maura said, poking Griff in the ribs with her elbow.

"Yes, ma'am. Very good," he said in a mild-mannered voice.

"You know, hon, I thought I recognized you from before," Willa said to Maura.

"I just had to bring him by to see for himself."

Griff glanced sideways at Maura with his eyes as he collected his change. He started to say something but just turned for the door instead.

"*Griff…*" Maura scolded. "Don't you forget about Angie."

"Oh, yeah." He went back to the table to leave a tip.

"Is your friend all right?" Willa asked.

Article 15

"There's been a death in the family," Maura said. "But we're working through it."

"My condolences."

Maura nodded as she watched Griff. "Appreciate it."

"Thank you for stopping in and come back again."

Maura smiled then scurried to catch up with Griff, who was halfway out the door.

They sat in the Jeep with the engine off. Griff searched the river out his side window. Maura stared at Griff and smiled.

"Remarkable resemblances, eh? Say what you will about us hillbillies, we got some strong and deep and dominant gene pools," Maura said.

"That was kind of a dirty trick." Griff watched Angie work her station through the window into the diner.

"Yeah. I know."

He turned in his seat to look Maura in the eye. "You're something of a...*scamp.*"

Maura laughed. "That's a new one. Been called worse, so I guess I'll take it."

Griff smiled at Maura. "What now?"

Maura started the Rubicon. "Just wait 'til you see Pine Hollow."

"Great. More surprises."

Maura playfully patted Griff on the thigh, then backed out of the parking spot and headed south out of town.

~~~

Pine Hollow

Maura picked up AA Highway east and followed it up into the Ohio River watershed for forty-five minutes. An unnumbered, unnamed road led south deep into a narrow valley. At the intersection with another unnumbered, unnamed road, she pulled into the parking lot of the Pine Hollow General Store.

The dandruff of old peeling paint clung to the siding of the hundred-year-old wood building. A broad porch fronted the store with a line of empty rocking chairs separated with whiskey barrels for tables on each side of the entrance. The clouded display windows revealed little of the contents of the store.

Mac's Garage sat catty-cornered from the store. Two-story houses flanked each business, one of which had been converted into the Uptown Beauty Salon, complete with a flashing neon "Open" sign in the window.

"A teeming metropolis," Griff said as they got out of the Jeep.

"Don't be snobby." Maura climbed the steps to the front door.

"No. It's a lot like home. Only greener. And more…deciduous." Griff followed her up and in.

"Hey, Cap!" Maura hollered out.

"That you, Maura?" An elderly gentleman came out of the office behind the counter. He smiled at her, then noticed Griff.

He moved quickly beside the twelve-gauge shotgun leaning next the cash register.

"It's okay, Cap. He's with me." She waved Griff forward. "He looks ornery—and acts it, too—but he's pretty much harmless. Besides I just fed him, so he should be pretty docile."

"I'm Griff." He extended his hand, but it hung unanswered over the counter.

Cap sized Griff up, then grunted. "Is he going to buy something or just be another looky-loo?"

"Need some ammo, Griff?" Maura asked.

"Nah. I'm good. Load my own." Griff looked around the cluttered five-pound-sized store stuffed with eight pounds of hardware, groceries, and sundries. "Been looking for a brass spittoon. Happen to have one?"

"I might. Don't take credit."

"Well, let's have a look, Cap."

Cap shuffled out from around the counter and dove directly into his inventory, knowing exactly where the item was located. He brought it back and set it on the counter. "A little spit polish should bring her back to life just right—"

"So to speak."

Cap growled out loud. "Two hundred dollars."

Griff smiled at Maura, then scowled at Cap. He inspected the spittoon from all sides. "Can't help but suspect you might be taking liberties with the tourist trade, sir."

"That thing's older than me by a long shot. Genuine antique. Early American. Two hundred's fair for a piece of history."

"No doubt George Washington himself spat there. Well, I make it a policy never to pay full retail. I'll give you one ninety-five, that is if you can make change for a couple of Franklins."

Article 15

Maura looked at Griff in disbelief.

He winked back at her. "It's a write-off."

Before Griff could look back at Cap for an answer, the old man was holding out a five-dollar bill.

Griff peeled off two hundreds, handed them over, and pulled the five dollar bill out of Cap's fingers with some difficulty. He picked up the spittoon. "Hope you have room for this in the Jeep."

"Pleasure doing business with you. Come back anytime, Griff."

"Any mail in the box?" Maura asked.

"Yupper. And that package, too. I'll fetch it." Cap disappeared into the back office.

Maura went over to a wall of antique post office boxes. She spun the combination to one of them, retrieved a handful of mail, and slammed it shut.

"A tad heavy," Cap said, hauling out a small moving box. "Good thing you got this feller here to help. Where's Dewey?"

"Sitting on a runner's mom's place over in Hillsboro. Where's the box from?"

"California. Los Angeles."

"Now, isn't that interesting," Griff said, taking the box from Cap. It was heavy. "From the Hornet Investment Group. We know them, don't we? And—whadda ya know—addressed to me in care of Blue Wing, LLC."

"Small world, huh?" said Maura, sorting through the mail.

"Been the same size for a real long time," Griff answered.

"Got any root beer, Cap?" Maura asked. She turned to Griff. "You want a sarsaparilla?"

"Sure."

"Make it two, please."

Cap scowled at Maura.

"Now, Cap. He just paid you two hundred dollars for a worthless old hunk of brass."

"One ninety-five."

"Cap…"

"Oh, bother." Cap pulled two bottles of Stewart's Root Beer from a noisy, old, red Coca-Cola cooler behind the counter. He popped the tops and handed them over to Maura.

Griff followed her outside, carrying his box and his new old spittoon. They sat in the rocking chairs on the porch to watch the Pine Hollow afternoon traffic.

"So, what's in the box?" Maura set Griff's soda on the whiskey barrel between them.

Griff shrugged his shoulders. He put the box down beside his chair with the spittoon on top, then grabbed his root beer. He sipped and rocked. "Is this why you invited me along today?"

"Well, Cap's curiosity was roused up good over who this Griffith Crowe feller was and why he was getting packages sent here."

"Yeah. So, what's the deal with Mr. Cap and all?"

"Papa Johnny has me come down here every two weeks to collect the mail. That's all. Been doing it for years."

"Why?"

"You don't know my grandfather very well. You can ask him anything you want, and he won't take offense. Just don't expect him to necessarily answer." Maura sipped her soda. "Just for the record, I never bothered to ask. It was for Papa Johnny. Good enough for me."

Article 15

"Curiouser and curiouser."

"Well, who's it from anyways?"

"You're kind of nosy."

"Hey, I chauffeured you down here and all."

Griff looked up and down the road that brought him into the fringes of the Cumberland plateau. "Kind of peaceful here. I like it."

"Yeah? How might you be planning to get yourself back to civilization?"

"Donald Wallace sent me this box."

"Who's he, exactly—besides a fellow Marine?"

"Never asked your grandfather about him?"

"Never had the occasion."

"Donald Wallace is dead. Recently passed."

"What? Was he old or something?"

"Murdered." Griff took a long drink of root beer.

"Oh…"

"What's the connection between Cap's place here and the diner?"

"He's just the post office in town. That's all. Johnny figured you knew Helena's roots were here abouts."

"I did."

"And you wanted to see for yourself, didn't you?"

Griff nodded. "I did."

"You're welcome."

"Thank you."

"So…What's in the box? Aren't you gonna open it?"

"Are we working together?"

Maura shrugged her shoulders. "Another thing I ain't asked Johnny. Just naturally curious, I reckon."

"I've found uncompensated curiosity to be something of a liability."

"Come on, Griff, you're killing me here. What's in the box? Open it already now."

Griff set the spittoon aside, sliding the box in front of him with his foot. He pulled a knife out of his pocket and, with a quick flick of his wrist, snapped out the blade. "If this is what I'm thinking it is…"

"What?"

Griff cut through the packing tape on the top flaps and opened the box. "Yup. Journals."

"Journals? Like diaries? What the hell. That sounds boring."

"He knew."

"Who knew? What?"

"Wallace. He knew."

"Now you're just being annoying about all this mysteriosity." Maura slouched down in her chair and pouted.

"Looks like me and Papa Johnny should have a conversation."

"Well, not for a few days. He's in Louisville on business."

"What kind of business?"

"Now who's the nosy one?"

"*Professional* curiosity."

"Well, ain't that special."

"Drive me back?" Griff savored Maura's mask of Shirley Temple-like consternation. "Please?"

"You're buying me dinner—and not no greasy spoon fare neither."

"Sure thing."

Article 15

Maura launched herself out of the rocking chair and pulled open the door to the store. "See ya next time, Cap."

"Tell Johnny, *Oorah!*"

"Should have known—another jarhead," Griff said to himself, as he picked up his box and spittoon to follow Maura down the steps to her Rubicon.

~~~

Ghostrider

"Anyways, I wouldn't entertain any...*notions,*" Maura said when she stopped at the front of Christopher's Bed and Breakfast after dinner at Ruth's Chris Steak House, where Maura bested a T-bone almost as thick as her. She kept her hands at ten and two on the steering wheel and studied the speedometer.

But Griff looked over at her and realized just such a notion—involuntarily—was already rattling around in his head. "The church thing, right?"

She gave him a sideways glance and smiled. "Mmmm...whatever works for you."

Griff's iPhone vibrated and glowed faintly through his front pants pocket. He took a deep breath.

Maura teased Griff by tapping on the phone. "Besides, someone really, really, really wants to have a conversation with you—*Helena?*"

"Likely."

"Too bad." She grabbed his thigh and squeezed.

"Yeah...too bad." His phone went dark and quiet. "Well, tell Johnny I'll be in touch."

"Soon, I hope."

Griff smiled and got out of the Rubicon. He retrieved his box and his spittoon from the back seat. He leaned over to look through the front door window. "Thank you."

"We'll catch another Reds game the next time you're in town."

Griff watched Maura drive off, then went up to his suite in the converted Christian church. He checked his phone. Helena had called four times and sent three text messages. He looked at the box full of her father's journals, then decided to go for a stroll—without his iPhone.

Griff walked three blocks north on Ward Avenue to the river. The reflected lights of the "Queen City" on the water didn't much distract Griff from competing thoughts of Helena and Maura. He walked the trail around Bellevue Beach Park. Even though it was pushing midnight, his Spidey sense nagged him with the tingle of not being alone; so, he left at the east end of the park, headed down O'Fallon Street to Poplar, then back to the B & B.

If it wasn't for the wine and scotch at dinner with Maura, he would have checked out and headed home in the Cirrus right then. Instead, he opened the box of Cliff Nickolson's journals. There were at least fifty or sixty medium-sized hardcover notebooks in the box, each one around two-hundred fifty pages. Griff picked up and flipped through the pages of a few at random, grateful the hybrid cursive-block print handwriting was neat and readable. He then realized Donald Wallace had packed them carefully in chronological order with the oldest on top.

He went back to the very first journal. The entry on page one, dated June 12, 1979, described Cliff Nickolson's first flight as a student pilot at Van Nuys Airport when he was sixteen. The boy's jumble of excitement, trepidation, wonder, and—once his feet were back on the ground walking to his car in the parking lot—elation, brought a smile to Griff's face as

Article 15

he recalled his own first flight with an instructor. Such were the innocent beginnings for the Marine Corps Aviator, call sign "Ghostrider," who rained death and destruction down from his F/A-18 over Iraq. But Griff was most interested in what Helena's father wrote in his very last journal, so he carefully emptied the box, keeping the notebooks in order. At the bottom he found it along with a box within the box. The final entry in the notebook—dated forty-two years after Cliff Nickolson's first flight—was written in Singapore seven months before his death. His last, unfinished journal no doubt perished with him in the helicopter crash.

Griff opened the second box. Inside were hinged jeweler's boxes containing Cliff Nickolson's lieutenant, captain, and major uniform pins; his golden Naval Aviator wings; Desert Storm campaign ribbons; a Silver Star; and a Navy Cross.

Griff stared at the Navy Cross, then snapped the box shut and set it aside. He knew what it took to get one as his was tucked away in the Liberty safe in his hideaway. The medal brought back ugly memories of a "bad day at work" as a Navy SEAL in Afghanistan. It gave Griff pause, then he shook it off.

Beneath all the medals was a small notepad-sized piece of paper with "From the Desk of Donald Wallace" preprinted at the top. A hand-written message said only, "HF = Highlands Forum."

Griff Googled "Highlands Forum" on his iPad and read—ironically enough in an article via a link in a WikiLeaks tweet titled, "How the CIA Made Google"—about the secret network of Military-Industrial Complex elites; its connections to Booze Allen Hamilton, SAIC, DARPA, and In-Q-Tel; the Forum's role in examining "the strategic and tactical offensive and defensive aspects of information operations by state and non-state actors to achieve political, military and economic goals"; and its meetings in the Carmel Highlands in California…

Griff set aside his iPad and flipped slowly through the pages of Cliff Nickolson's most recent journals, scanning for "HF." The code Donald Wallace provided was peppered liberally throughout the pages. He carefully repacked all the notebooks in order, except for the very last one. He set it and the box of medals on top.

Griff studied the representation of Jesus praying in Gethsemane rendered in his room's stained-glass window, wondering if information about "HF" was really what Helena hired him to find.

Even though it was two o'clock in the morning, he returned Helena's calls.

"Finally…" She answered on the first ring. Her voice betrayed no sign of being asleep.

"You weren't worried about me, were you?"

"Um…Not particularly. Just sitting out back on my deck, looking at the stars. Remembering…"

Griff heard her sip, wine he presumed.

"So, where have you been spending my money this evening?"

"Kentucky."

"Do tell."

"Well, I met some of your family this morning."

"Aunt Willa? How is she? It's been a month of Sundays since I've seen her."

Griff looked up at the stained-glass window. "And cousin Angie."

"Did you get the derby pie? An old family recipe. It's to die for."

"So I've heard." Griff thought of Maura. "Sadly, no. It was too early."

"It is never too early for pie."

"Maybe you could bake me one someday."

"Well, you're just lucky all us girls had to memorize the recipe—family tradition. So, I just might do that the next time you come calling…" Another sip, then Helena asked softly, "And when might that be?"

"When might you be up for company?"

"Now…might be nice."

"If I weren't so far away…"

Helena sighed. "And if my Aunt Willa had balls, she'd be my uncle."

"Helena…"

"What?"

"I've never asked. The accident—"

"Crushed my world. It's as simple as that."

Griff wished he had some of Helena's scotch right then. "What do you know about it?"

"What is there to know? It wasn't right. It doesn't matter what some government report says. My father should not be dead."

"And Junior?"

"JR…is, well, *Junior*. He's all about *him*."

Griff felt himself nodding in agreement.

"Sometimes you can hear them."

"Hear who?" Griff asked.

"Sometimes far away. Sometimes close, like now. Wolves."

"Wolves?"

"So, Mr. Crowe. Do I have any hope of finding my father's things?"

"I believe so."

"And when will you be returning from Kentucky?"

"Tomorrow."

"Tomorrow I have to go to a funeral."

"In Los Angeles?"

"Donnie."

Silence filled the gap between Kentucky and New Mexico.

"Can I come calling...after?" Griff asked.

"It's damn good pie."

"I'll be there."

"You better." Helena hung up.

Griff stared for a long time at the box which held forty years of her father's life and, likely, the reasons for its abrupt end.

He sent a text to Lance: "Got time for a dog tomorrow?"

Less than two minutes later, Griff got a reply: "Absolutely."

He grabbed Cliff Nickolson's last journal and began to read.

~~

Hot Dogs and Lemon Bars

"No cell phone, right?" Griff asked when Lance sat down across from him at the only table in the Dog Walk.

"Man, you do not wear paranoia well," Lance said shaking his head. "In the car. Power off. *Sheesh.*"

"So, do I have to give you another dollar, or is my retainer still good?"

Lance adjusted the knot in his bright red tie. "Who's buying lunch? You? Me? Or…"

"Helena?"

"I don't want any conflicts of interest."

"I'll buy."

"Fair enough. Besides, I'd just have to expense it back to your ledger if I paid." Lance waved to catch Kim's attention behind the counter. He held up two fingers. "Two usuals, *por favor.*"

"Besides, it's not paranoid if they're really after you."

"For Christ's sake, don't tell me you've been reading *Infowars.*"

"What's that?"

"Never mind. Be blissful in your ignorance."

"Well, what do you know about the Highlands Forum?"

Lance pointed at his own face with both index fingers. "Me? Happy guy. Don't spoil it for me."

"Seems to be an alphabet soup of Pentagon and Langley minions swapping spit with the corporate world."

"Ah, the vaunted Military-Industrial Complex. People complain, but the bottom line is they get shit done."

Griff and Lance sat back as Kim came over and served two chili cheese dogs.

"And if people get in the way?" Griff asked, after Kim left.

"What people?"

"Cliff Nickolson, for one."

Lance scowled and took a bite of hot dog. "What?"

"Sometimes accidents aren't accidents, when the spooks are involved."

"Langley?"

Griff shrugged a shoulder.

"Please don't go all Alex Jones on me. The world doesn't need more conspiracy theories. We're still not even done with the Kennedy assassination, for crying out loud."

"When you've lived in the shadows, you get used to seeing things in the dark."

"You're serious?"

Griff nodded.

Lance took another bite and stared Griff down. He swallowed and asked, "Okay. What do you need?"

"Your rising stars—Eply and…"

"Wilkinson."

"Yeah, Wilkinson. The corporate dudes. Can they get me some insider info?" Griff pulled a piece of paper out and slid it over to Lance. "I made a list."

"*In-Q-Tel…Hornet Investment Group…SAIC…Booze Hamilton…Blue Wing LLC…*" Lance read. "Is this for you or for Helena?"

"Not sure, yet."

"Bottom line it for me—And not the full King James

Article 15

Version. Sunday school it and cut to the chase."

"In the beginning was darkness and light. Then Al Gore invented the internet. Then government decided that maybe working with all the fallen angels would make creating a New World Order easier. Then 9/11 happened and they bulked up by putting their plans on steroids with the Patriot Act. Then Snowden Skywalker takes on the evil empire. Then a helicopter crash kills Helena's father."

Lance stared at Griff with a half-chewed mouthful of chili dog. He swallowed. "You make a compelling argument—*for Oliver Stone's next movie.*"

"Call me crazy—"

"You're crazy."

"Yeah? Ask Donald Wallace."

Lance chewed on that thought as well as his hot dog.

"What do these so-called Masters of the Universe do?"

"Write software," Lance answered.

"And what's behind all the glass in a cockpit panel and rattling around in the FADEC?"

Lance swallowed. "Computer code…"

"Bingo."

"You sure this isn't just the tiny G.I. Joe in your pocket sounding off?"

Griff shrugged. "Her dad's journals make for some *interesting* reading."

"You found them?"

"I did—all except the last one, which no doubt vanished in the smoking hole where he augered in." Griff crashed his index finger into the table top.

Lance winced.

"Courtesy of the late Donald Wallace…now, why would he give them to me? Then he gets killed? *And,* why didn't the family have them in the first place?"

"But you've got them back now. That's what Helena wanted, right?"

Griff nodded.

"And you're going to give them to her, right? That's what she hired you for."

"In due time."

"Why do I sense a messy conflict of interest heading my way?"

Griff finished his chili cheese dog and sat back. "That's why you call me, isn't it? To deal with messy situations?"

"Right. I don't call you to create them."

"Would you rather not know?"

Lance scowled. "I was having such a good day. Hannah brought in a batch of her momma's lemon bars. And I settled the Mitchell suit for eight figures."

"Well, I guess the lesson is, when life tosses you lemons…give them to Hannah."

"You are a riot. But seriously, Griff, where is this headed? What's the point? She doesn't need the money. Or is this for truth, justice, and the American way?"

"Like your buddy Henry Lee said at the O.J. trial, *Something not right here…*" Griff stared at Lance.

"So? Just another day in the paradise we call America. Enjoy it. Don't fight it. That's what I do."

Griff nodded slowly.

"You're not going to take my advice, are you?" Lanced asked.

"I'm not going to go to war with city hall. Look how that

turned out for the guys at the Hornet Investment Group—"

"Exactly my point."

"But…"

"Griff…take the money and run. Run hard. Run fast."

"But…"

Lance shook his head.

Griff smiled.

"I'll get Eply and Wilkinson on it for you."

"Thanks."

Lance sighed. "I just hope there are some lemon bars left back at the office."

~~~

Dead Doggies

The sun had yet an hour before setting when Griff crossed the southern boundary of the ranch coming home in the Aeronca Chief. A column of smoke rose to the northeast. He banked in its direction.

Below him, buzzards swirled around the column. Griff spiraled down, taking care to avoid them and the smoke. On the ground, Ben tended to a large bonfire built from old pallets, scrap lumber, and logs loaded haphazardly in the back of his Silverado pickup truck. Johnny Eagle dragged a cow carcass to the fire with a Bobcat UTV. Shep disconnected the chain, then Johnny Eagle pirouetted and placed the carcass on the fire with a pallet fork. A uniformed officer leaned against an Albany County Sheriff's Department SUV and watched.

The men all looked up at the plane. Griff circled lower until he was less than a hundred feet off the ground.

Hatless, the deputy shaded his eyes with his hand.

Shep waved.

Griff rocked his wings.

Ben's right arm swept up with an open hand from his side in an exaggerated gesture. He spread his arms out wide, then brought his hands together, touching his index fingers in front of his face. He dropped his hands to his side, then put his index fingers together at an angle in front of him.

Griff understood the Plains Indian sign language: "Go. Meet. Teepee."

Since there was no level ground in the area to land on, Griff leveled his wings, rocked them in response to Ben, and climbed away. Ten minutes later he landed. He hangared the Chief, then waited for Ben on the back deck, sipping a Bass Ale with Rodya at his feet.

A second ale bottle had long been empty and darkness blanketed the mountains when Rodya lifted his head and turned his ears to the driveway.

Griff reached behind and gripped the SIG Sauer pistol tucked in the waistband of his jeans. A moment later he heard footsteps approaching, then boots on the wooden steps of the deck.

Rodya leapt up and trotted over to greet Ben with his tail wagging.

"You look tired," Griff said, noticing the soot smeared on Ben's face in the light through the kitchen window. "Sit down. I'll get you a beer."

"Thanks. I need it." Ben fell into the chair beside Griff.

Griff got up and squeezed Ben's shoulder as he passed by on his way through the sliding glass door. He returned with a can of Olympia—Ben's favorite—and another Bass for himself.

Ben just nodded as he grabbed the beer and lifted it for a three gulp pull.

Griff sat back down and sipped his ale.

"We got trouble?" Ben asked.

"We might. What's going on?"

"Three dead cows. I called Deputy Walt 'cause they were all shot with a thirty-aught-six or three-oh-eight—at least."

"Three?"

"This was no hunting accident." Ben shook his head.

"What did Walt say?"

"He said, *'This was no hunting accident.'* Also, there ain't been any other such reports in the county."

"Sounds like we got trouble, then."

"The woman? Helena?"

Griff shook his head. "I think it might be her problem, too."

"Too bad. Nice lady. 'Course every one of them is trouble of some sort."

"Even Swan?"

"Yup. Even Swan." Ben sighed. "But I love her just the same."

They sat and drank in silence.

"You and the boys haven't noticed any strangers passing through or hanging out, have you?" Griff asked.

Ben shook his head. "Anyway, now that we've got the mess cleaned up from the scavengers and such, I'll go back tomorrow and look to find where those shots came from."

"You want company?"

Ben nodded. "I think I would, indeed."

~~~

The next morning, Ben leaned against the corral outside the barn looking east at the sunrise with his gray mare, Shadow, tied off beside him as Griff led Winston out of the barn.

Griff noticed the .44 caliber Smith and Wesson Model 29 holstered at Ben's side and his Henry .308 Winchester in the scabbard on Shadow. Winston carried his MK11 sniper rifle. His saddle bags held a half-dozen loaded Magpul PMAG 20s. Griff's SIG Sauer P226 was holstered on his belt along with two extra magazines.

With a quick nod, Ben climbed up into the saddle.

Griff mounted Winston and they headed northeast.

Their shadows were still long in the dawn when they got to the site of the bonfire. Magpies hopped around the cold, black scar in the plains, picking at the bones and tufts of hide that had not burned up completely.

"All three were within fifty yards of this spot," Ben said, getting down off Shadow. He walked off to the north, following the tire tracks and drag marks made by Johnny Eagle in the Bobcat. "This way."

Griff dismounted and followed, leading Winston.

"Here." Ben gestured to show how one of the slain cows laid. "This one was a head shot. Put down instantly."

"All of them?"

"Just this one. The other two were center mass. Likely did not have the angle. The last one took two shots. Trailed blood off that way."

"Spooked by then, probably."

Ben nodded. He turned and squinted towards the rising terrain to the east.

Griff looked east as well. "Which one?"

Ben pointed and sighted down his arm. He aimed back and forth along the horizon. He settled on a rise at his two o-clock. "That one."

They mounted up and rode towards the ridge line, circling around behind the hill Ben pointed out. They got down, tied off their horses to sagebrush, grabbed their rifles from the scabbards, then spread out to climb the backside of the hill looking for signs of the sniper.

"No easy shot," Griff said looking down from the crest at the spot where the cattle had been slaughtered and burned. "At least five hundred yards."

"I make it half a mile." Ben began surveying the ground around where they stood.

Griff lifted his rifle and looked down range through the scope.

"There." Ben pointed to the grass to their right. "Lodging."

Griff looked over at the grass stalks bent over from the weight of a body lying in the prone firing position. "Four shots?"

"At least."

"I'm thinking this guy didn't waste any rounds."

Griff and Ben carefully combed the area to the right of the sniper's nest looking for shell casings.

"He probably got them all," Ben muttered.

Griff circled around to put the sun in his face. He methodically scanned the grass until a spark caught his eye like a distant, silent muzzle flash. He reached into the stalks and pulled out a brass shell casing. He read the engraving around the firing pin. "Three-hundred-win mag."

Ben stood upright and grunted. He scanned the horizon. "Sniper round. I guess Walt was right."

Griff nodded as he twirled the shell casing in his fingers. "Yup. *This was no hunting accident.*"

~~~

Derby Pie, Interrupted

It was dark when he landed. Griff drove the Mustang from the Taos airport at the posted speed limits nearly the entire way without music. Outside, his headlights pierced the night. Inside, he continued the debate which consumed him the entire flight down from Wyoming, trying to decide what to do with the box of journals in the trunk and what to tell Helena about his suspicions.

As he pulled into the long, uphill drive, he noticed Helena's house was completely dark. He turned off the headlights and slowly crept the Mustang up towards the house, stopping fifty yards from where the drive circled around by the front door so he would not trigger the motion detectors on the lights. He killed the engine. Every window was dark. He watched.

After a full five minutes, he drew his pistol and quickly got out of the car, closing the door quietly with his hip pressing against it, grateful the convertible had no dome light. Griff stepped off the stone drive and into the woods. He moved closer and circled counterclockwise around the house, his eye scouring every corner and shadow for movement or an errant reflection. Around back, the wall of windows offered only a blurry mirrored image of stars and the crescent moon at the top. On the north side, Griff moved further out to avoid the motion detectors by the garage doors, which were closed.

Griff circled back around the house the way he came and silently climbed the wooden steps up to the back deck. He paused at the back corner by the Kamado grill and peered into the great room. The only light came from the clock on the microwave and the keypad for the security system. He waited two minutes then moved to the sliding glass door. It was unlocked. He pulled it open and slipped in, backing into the nearest inside corner. The smell of fresh-baked chocolate chip cookies hung in the air. On the kitchen island, he could make out the vague shape of a pie in the blue glow from the LED display on the microwave. He methodically scanned from left to right through the sights of his SIG Sauer. Across the room, the door to the master bedroom was an open black hole.

"Marco," Griff said softly.

He heard Helena's husky voice answer from inside the master bedroom, "Polo."

Griff instinctively moved away from the windows to avoid presenting an easy target and crossed to Helena's bedroom. He stepped inside. In the dim moonlight, he could make out the curves of her naked body lying on the king-sized bed.

"Are you all right?"

"I made you a derby pie."

"What? What's going on?"

Helena propped herself up on her elbow and patted the bed.

Griff stepped over and sat down beside her.

She took the pistol from his hand, set it on the nightstand next to her revolver, then pulled Griff towards her and began to kiss him madly on the mouth, holding his head in her hands at first, then moving down to undo the buttons on his shirt. She pulled it down off his shoulders.

Article 15

Griff kicked off his shoes. He stood up and slipped off his shirt, then his pants.

When he was naked, Helena grabbed his wrist and pulled him down on top of her to make love immediately, without foreplay. When finished, they slid beneath the blankets. Griff sat against the headboard. Helena rested her head on his shoulder and held herself tight to him with her arms around his neck. She clamped her legs to Griff and pressed hard against him.

The animal in him slowly receded. As badly as he wanted to ask what just happened, Griff kept quiet and looked around the room. On the wall opposite the bed was a framed print of Van Gogh's *Starry Night*—just like in her childhood bedroom in Bel Aire.

He looked out the wall of windows that continued across the back of the house from the great room with its view of the mountains across the valley and the night sky above. High on the window two stars were especially bright, like the ornament on top of a Christmas tree. He was trying to figure out which constellation they were part of when he noticed the dark hole in the center of each and the spider web-like like sparkles surrounding the darkness. He realized what they were. He turned and looked up over their heads and saw two black dots in the wall above the bed.

Griff put his arms around Helena and held her tight.

She pressed herself harder against him. "I'm glad you're here."

Griff stared at the bullet holes in the window, figuring Helena would understand his suspicions and trying to decide what to do about them.

~~~

Griff woke with a start. Helena, still tight against his body, stirred then nuzzled her head into his chest. He was still naked, except for his watch. It was 1:47 in the morning.

He listened, gently tucking Helena's blonde hair behind her ear and stroking her cheek. He leaned over, his lips close to her ear, and whispered, "Come on. Let's go."

Helena moaned, pressing her face into Griff's chest. "Go? Go where?"

"We should leave. Now."

Helena's eyes opened wide. She clutched at Griff tighter. Now fully awake, she asked, "What is it? What's wrong."

"Spidey sense. We should get out of here. Right now. Can you pack without turning on the lights?"

"You're scaring me."

"I'm not the one to be afraid of." Griff slid to the side of the bed and dressed. He tied his shoes, then grabbed his pistol from the nightstand and stared at the bedroom door. "Get some things together. I'll be back in a minute."

Helena grabbed his shoulder.

He patted her hand. "We'll be okay."

Helena started to get out of bed.

Griff got up and, without a sound, followed the wall around to the bedroom door. He peered out, the SIG held down at his thigh. He heard Helena at the dresser, gently pulling out drawers. He slipped out into the great room.

Griff stalked the perimeter of the room opposite the wall of windows. He stopped at the front door to check outside, then moved through the kitchen and upstairs to clear the loft bedrooms and bath. He sat down on the top stair, studying the window panes on the back wall, looking for more bullet holes.

Finding none, he holstered his gun and came down into the kitchen. He cut a wedge of derby pie and ate it with his fingers out of the pan.

Helena's silhouette appeared in the master bedroom doorway, holding a carry-on suitcase.

Griff walked over, took her hand, and led her to the sliding glass door. They went out the way Griff came in and circled through the woods to the Mustang. He depressed the clutch and let the convertible roll backwards, using the emergency brake to control his speed to avoid the red glare of the brake lights. Once out on the road, he fired up the V-8 and sped down the switchbacks out of the mountain, throwing their bodies violently back and forth in their seats. With ten miles of U.S. 64 put behind them, Griff slowed to eighty, heading west to Taos.

"You've got someone to check on your place, right?" Griff asked Helena as he slowed coming down out of the Carson National Forest and into Taos.

"Uh-huh. But…"

"Good. We'll call them later."

Helena just nodded as Griff passed through town, obeying every speed limit and traffic light.

"Where's the Lear?" He asked pulling into the airport.

"Wichita for maintenance," Helena answered.

Griff parked. He got his go bag and the box of journals out of the trunk.

"What's that?" Helena asked wheeling her suitcase in trail behind Griff.

"One, twenty-two, eight." Griff answered.

"Huh?"

"Key code for the gate. One, two, two, eight."

Helena punched the four numbers into the keypad and pushed the gate open.

Griff passed through and headed to the Cirrus across the dark, deserted tarmac. He loaded their luggage and the box in the plane, then did a quick walk around, undoing the tie downs. Seven minutes later they were rolling down Runway 22. He banked hard to the east and the glow of Taos disappeared under the nose of the plane as Griff clawed for altitude at the best angle of climb. He circled back around the city to gain more altitude to clear the wall of mountain peaks in their flight path. At 13,500 feet, Griff rolled out on a heading of 080 degrees and leveled off.

"Where are we going?" Helena asked

"I don't know."

"What do you mean, you don't know. You're the pilot."

Griff looked over at Helena and saw her smiling in the glow of the G1000 displays in the instrument panel.

"I expected more." Helena sighed.

"Where do you want to go?"

"Your place?"

"Maybe not a good idea."

"Why's that?"

"Same reason we had to get outta Dodge."

Helena's smile melted.

Griff swiped around the EFB sectional charts on his iPad. "Hmmm…how about Oakley, Kansas? Home of the world's largest prairie dog and a five-legged goat."

"What? No giant ball of string?"

"Come on, Honey. It'll be good to get away."

Helena rubbed the top of Griff's thigh. "From what?"

Article 15

"I don't know."

"Boy, you sure are full of answers, aren't you?"

~~~

Oakley

They landed just before dawn at Oakley Muni Airport in western Kansas. Griff tied the Cirrus down on the dimly lit ramp. They walked the half-mile to the Sleep Inn motel across the street and checked in with their bags and the box of journals.

Griff set the box down on the table by the window and drew the curtains closed. He threw himself down on the bed, covering his eyes with his arm. "I'm beat."

"Oh, no you don't," Helena said sitting down beside him and poking his ribs. "Where's this world's largest prairie dog?"

"I lied. It's not what you think. Just a huge, eight-foot-tall concrete lawn ornament."

"And the five-legged goat?"

"Now, that's real. Preserved for the ages through the miracle of taxidermy."

"So far, I'm underwhelmed." Helena looked around the sterile room. "So, who's shooting at us—and, hey, what's in the box?"

Griff moaned, thinking of Maura's relentless curiosity in Pine Hollow and pondering on the cat-like nature of women. He rolled off the bed and went over to the table. He took out the smaller box of her dad's medals. He handed it to Helena.

She pulled out a jeweler's box and opened it. "You found them?"

"His Navy Cross." Griff sat down next to her on the bed. "They found me is more like it."

Helena gently stroked the blue and white ribbon. She traced the cross of gold. "Thank you."

"What did he do to get it?"

"I don't know. He never said. He didn't talk about it much."

Griff nodded. "I got his journals, too."

Helena looked up at Griff.

"All of them. Starting from when he was sixteen."

She looked at the box.

"Yup. They're all there."

"And this is why someone is shooting at me?"

"At us—well, my cattle. What could your dad have been involved in?"

"Money. That's what he was involved in."

"Well, money makes people crazy, but I think there's something else. Something with the government." Griff rubbed the small of her back. "Come on, let's get some shuteye."

Helena got up off the bed and went to the box. She picked up a journal off the top. "Have you read them?"

"Not all of them. Just the last couple."

"And?"

"Sometimes accidents are just accidents..." Griff laid back down on the bed and covered his eyes. "And sometimes not..."

Helena looked over at Griff. "My dad?"

"There's a seven-month gap leading up to the crash."

"Was the last one lost in the crash?"

"Maybe...maybe not. I thought so at first, but, then again, it was the NTSB that investigated the accident—you know, the *National* Transportation Safety Board."

Article 15

"You think the government is trying to kill us?" Helena came back over to the bed and sat down facing Griff. She pulled his arm off his face. "Seriously?"

"Seriously? We'd be dead by now, if that's what they wanted." Griff met and held her eyes. "The guy who shot up my herd didn't miss. Three cows from half a mile away with four trigger pulls ain't luck. Whoever shot at you didn't miss either. It was a warning. A brush back. I don't know who the bad actors are, but there's definitely a bad DC stink on it."

"And the reason is my dad's journals?"

"Evidently. Lead didn't start flying until they were in my hands."

Helena rubbed the leather cover of the journal in her hand. "What are we going to do?"

"Right now? Sleep. We don't need to give them a helping hand by making stupid mistakes from fatigue."

Helena leaned over and gave Griff a kiss.

He held her hand and squeezed gently, then rolled over. A minute later he was asleep.

Helena sat next to Griff on the bed and began reading her father's journals.

11-25x, 11-56, 11-6

Griff slept for five hours. When he woke, Helena was asleep with a half-dozen or so of her father's journals scattered about her on the king-size bed. He rolled out of bed and went to the window. He squinted when he pulled back the curtain. A shaft of hard light cut into the room.

"What are you looking at?" Helena asked in a voice dry and gravelly from sleep.

"They don't call it the Sunshine State for nothing."

"Florida is the Sunshine State," Helena said. "Kansas is the *Sunflower* State."

Griff looked over his shoulder. "Why are you always correcting me?"

"Because you obviously need adult supervision."

Griff looked back out the window. "You sleep at all?"

"Not much."

"Get some. Then we'll make this pop stand a memory."

Helena rolled over and buried her head beneath the covers.

Griff got his cell phone and sat down at the table by the window. He thought for a long while, then texted Lance a series of California Highway Patrol radio codes: "11-25x, 11-56, 11-6."

Female motorist needs assistance.

Officer being followed by auto with dangerous persons.

Illegal discharge of firearms.

M.T. Bass

Lance answered, "Hot dog."

Griff went over to carefully gather the notebooks from around Helena without waking her. He put them all in the box, except for the last two going back two years before the helicopter accident. He scanned through them again, making a written list in a small spiral notepad of the dates and places of Cliff Nickolson's travels. He starred those meetings with the initials "HF" beside the destination.

When he finished, Griff planned a flight from Colonel James Jabara airport in Wichita to Chesapeake Regional in Norfolk, Virginia. After, he watched Helena sleep until sunset, then went down to the front desk and settled up their bill. He paid the hotel clerk a hundred dollars to order a pepperoni pizza, a six pack of Budweiser, a bottle of Cabernet and a two-liter Pepsi.

When the desk clerk delivered dinner, Griff took the six pack and wine into the bathroom and began pouring the beer down the bathtub drain.

"And what, pray tell, are you doing?" Helena asked appearing at the door, rubbing the sleep from her eyes.

"Eight hours from bottle to throttle."

"What?" Her question morphed into a yawn.

"If we're being watched—or the desk clerk gets loose lips, they'll have to figure we won't be flying outta here til morning. Give us a head start."

"The wine, too?"

"Be my guest."

Helena picked up the bottle of Cab and read the label. After a heavy sigh, she handed it to Griff. "I'll drink the Pepsi. It's a better vintage."

Article 15

They ate, showered, dressed, and packed. Leaving the key cards by the TV, they walked back to the plane.

Helena watched Griff refuel the Cirrus. "You know, if the government is really after us, they can no doubt track us by following our credit card purchases."

"Not this card," Griff said, waving the card for Helena to see before putting it back in his wallet. "You'll get one from Lance. Maybe two."

"Lance?"

"They're Stein, Baylor corporate cards. They've got hundreds." Griff pulled the receipt from the pump. "Come on. Let's go."

"Where? Chicago?"

"Wichita. Oh, and make sure your phone is powered off."

She did.

Helena let Griff go through the ritual of his checklists and depart to the southeast, rising into the night. Civilization seemed to disappear, as the stars and the few farm lights in western Kansas melted together at the horizon. It was an hour-long flight from Oakley to Wichita.

"Here's what's going to happen," Griff began, once he leveled off at the Minimum Safe Altitude of four thousand four hundred feet and set power for best economy. "When we get to Wichita, call your fly boys from the airport landline and have them send a courtesy car to get you. Tell them to file for Chicago Exec. When you get there, ask Tiffani at the desk to drive you to the Dog Walk."

"Tiffani?"

"Have her or one of the line boys do it. Don't use a cab. Tip them good, of course."

"Of course."

"You still have the apartment in Tribeca, right?"

"How do you know about…*Edward*. Stupid Edward. You talked to him, didn't you."

"Just due diligence."

"And how is my ex-husband?"

"Prepping to be his father's political puppet on a string."

"I never could stand his parents. Nor they, me. A real mutual disadmiration society we had going there."

"Anyway, Lance will have their Citation take you to New York—probably Republic out on Long Island. Maybe MacArthur. He might even fly you there himself in the King Air to get out of the office and get some stick time."

"He's a pilot, too?"

"You'll be safe. He flew generals around in the Army. No medals in it for him, though."

"What about my plane?"

"He'll send the Lear west—probably to San Francisco. He'll hire some local McCormick booth babe he's got on speed dial to be your double and send her off for a weekend at your apartment there, then bring her back commercial."

Helena sighed loud enough to be heard over the headsets. She looked out into the night. Wichita glowed on the horizon.

"He'll set you up with burner phones and credit cards. Cash, too. That'd be best to use."

"All this cloak and dagger stuff…" Helena shook her head. "And where are you going?"

"I'm gonna look up an old Navy buddy."

"Great. So, what do I do in New York while you're swapping war stories?"

Article 15

"I believe you've got some reading materials."

"Oh, yeah…but I don't know if I'm ready to know everything—you know, Mom and the Wicked Witch of the East and all."

"Take the last five or so. Maybe ten. We need to figure out what got him killed. You can leave the rest with Lance for safe keeping. Or park them in a vault or safety deposit box."

Helena nodded.

"I have to ask…" Griff looked at Helena.

"What?"

"Do you think Junior could be involved in something deeper than probate games?"

Helena thought for a long full minute. "I don't know."

"We'll find out."

Griff began his descent. He skirted the Class Charlie airspace to the north, avoiding the need to contact Wichita Approach Control. He landed at Colonel James Jabara Airport where there was no control tower to log his N-number.

After her Learjet co-pilot picked Helena up, Griff departed to the east towards Norfolk.

~~

T-Rex

Griff came in the back way of the Trident Lounge in downtown Norfolk just after seven the next evening. The tables were still half-full of diners; not bad for a Wednesday. The place was meticulously neat and clean, just as he remembered and expected.

Donna, the forty-something barmaid who still dressed twenty-something—yet had the figure to pull it off—and held the gray in her brunette hair at bay with a standing monthly appointment with her hairdresser, talked it up with a couple of burley military types in civilian clothes at the end of the bar near the front door. A few singles nursed their beers and feigned interest in ESPN on the nearest flat screen.

Griff sat down at the abandoned back corner of the bar facing the entrance. He exchanged nods with a pair of younger men in their late twenties catty-corner from his stool, who quickly returned to their animated conversation. Their strong family resemblance and easy manner screamed "brothers." Griff sat patiently surveying the familiar surroundings with its hidden "Where's Waldo" clues about the proprietor mixed in with the muted nautical theme of the decor.

One of the military types at the opposite end of the bar pointed his way, and Donna looked back at him over her shoulder. She smiled, patted the man on his forearm and headed Griff's way.

"Well, well, well...look what washed up from the briny depths," Donna said, setting a cocktail napkin in front of Griff. "Long time, no see, *Big Chief Runs-With-Scissors*. Got a tribe of your own yet?"

The brothers broke off their conversation to listen.

Griff smiled. "Ain't found a squaw who could measure up—since you won't have me."

"I got enough wild Indian problems as it is, pal. So, the usual?"

"Club soda and lime."

"Ouch. You on duty or something?"

"Or something. Is 'T' around?"

"He's in back." Donna filled a glass with ice, shot seltzer into it from the soda nozzle, squeezed a lime over it and dropped it into the glass. She set it down in front of Griff. "I'll tell him you're here."

Donna disappeared into the kitchen through the swinging doors behind the middle of the bar.

The two military types at the end of the bar stared at Griff. No doubt they were SEALs from nearby Joint Expeditionary Base Little Creek. He met and held their gaze as he sipped his soda water.

"Who the hell is asking to see T-Rex?" bellowed out from the kitchen. The doors swung open and a cigar chomping ex-Chief Petty Officer stormed out and looked up and down the bar. At five-ten, he wasn't as tall as his voice advertised, but he was still trim and powerfully built, even though he was on the downhill side of fifty.

"Are you *the* T-Rex?" Asked one of the brothers at the bar.

"You want me to bite your fucking head off to prove it? Who's asking?"

Article 15

Griff smiled, knowing the Jurassic moniker came not from the man's ferocity but from his oversized head and the fact that he was never once known to reach out to pay a bar tab.

"Uh-uh-uh…" The brothers exchanged confused and frightened glances like little kids.

"Our father was in your unit," said the other brother.

If T-Rex's eyes had been lasers, he would have burned the skin off the brothers' faces. "Yeah…the polack, Sitkowskowicz."

The brothers nodded.

"He passed away this summer. Cancer."

"Yeah. I heard." T-Rex took a deep draw off his cigar and blew it out slow. "Donna, give the polack's boys a round."

"Thank you, sir."

T-Rex growled.

"Chief," Griff mouthed silently when the perplexed brothers looked his way.

"Thank you, Chief," the brothers said in unison.

"Damn good man, your dad—of course, they all were. Except for *that* motherfucker." T-Rex pointed at Griff. "Can't seem to rid myself of the son-of-a-bitch—just like the dose of pogey clap I got me in Manila."

"Good to see you, too, Chief."

"Makes my dick burn like a roadside flare." T-Rex chomped down hard on his cigar and grinned. "Don't suppose you liked us on Facebook, you twat."

Griff shook his head and laughed. "Facebook is a feedlot. I'm free range."

"Yeah, well, my grandson says I got to have it. Claims it's good for business."

"Seems to be working." Griff looked around the dining room.

"Fucking computers. Good thing for me you can't eat and drink online." T-Rex puffed on his cigar three times. "So, what do you want?"

"A word."

"Step into my office, then."

Griff got up and went behind the bar. He followed T-Rex through the doors into the kitchen.

"Want some grub?"

"What's the special?"

"For the public? Some healthy chicken crap," T-Rex said. "Made myself carbonara."

"I'll have what the cook's having."

"Smart choice." T-Rex served up a plate of pasta. They sat down on stools pulled up to a stainless-steel prep table in the back of the kitchen. "What's up, Griff?"

"I seem to find myself taking fire." Griff took a bite of carbonara. "Mmmm, good stuff."

"Of course it is, you twat. I made it. So, you got muzzies raining jihad down on you?"

"Don't really think so. I'm not the one bragging about shooting Bin Laden. So, nobody knows who I am."

"Who then?"

Griff looked T-Rex dead in the eye. "Blue-on-blue…I think."

The Chief stared back, chomping his cigar a little more vigorously.

"Not the Community, of course. But I think it's coming out of some dark corner of the Beltway."

T-Rex nodded. "And what did you do to get sideways with the suits?"

"Not exactly sure. Nothing I did personally. But this case I'm working—"

"There better not be a dame involved. Is there? There is—Goddamn it. I ought to pound you over the head down to my size and kick the crap right out of you. Won't you ever learn?"

'I…" Griff gave up. There was no point. "Anyway, somebody somewhere has got to know something."

"Usually is the case. You talk to Kevin?"

"I don't need a biography written about it. I just want to know what spider hole it's coming from."

"He's pretty plugged in. I'll chum it out, and we'll see what floats to the surface outta the teams."

"Anonymously."

"Yeah, yeah, yeah—all anonymous-like." T-Rex drew and blew a stream of blue smoke. "Nobody's gonna like the idea of it—suits taking pot shots at one of our own."

Griff nodded as he finished his pasta.

"And if I find the weasel fucks, I'll shoot 'em 'til they catch on fire and change shape."

"Thanks, Chief."

~~~

Saigon Sam's

T-Rex offered to let Griff crash on the couch of his apartment above the Trident Lounge, but he opted instead for the recliner in the pilot lounge at Chesapeake Regional where he could keep an eye on the Cirrus.

Griff settled in and sent Maura a text: "You checking the mail anytime soon? Like tomorrow maybe? ~G"

He just felt himself start to doze off when his phone dinged with an answer: "You expecting another package?"

"I could use one from Saigon Sam's to fill my TAP." Griff figured Maura would recognize the military surplus store outside Marine Corps Base Camp Lejeune and understand.

"What do you need?"

Griff got up and, at the flight planning desk, he started writing out a list: Body Armor-Large; M-4 Carbine with 3 extra mags & 500 rounds; Federal 9mm hollow points - 500...

When finished, he took a picture of the list with his phone and sent it to Maura.

"Catch a game?" was Maura's reply.

"Rain check. A picnic with the Clooney's? KFGX?"

"On it."

"Thanks." Then Griff let himself sleep.

~~

On the flight from Norfolk to Maysville the next day, Griff caught in himself a rising tide of warm anticipation at the prospect of seeing Maura again. So, he was surprised and chagrined to see Johnny standing next to her on the tarmac outside the terminal building when he taxied up. The pair were definitely a modern American Gothic: her in studded black leather accented with chains; he in a nappy suit and a wide, loud tie leftover from the Seventies which should have been reeking of mothballs by now.

"Papa really wanted to see you again," Maura said with a shrug of helplessness as Griff walked over. She held up a carryout bag from the Blue Wing Diner. "But I brought enough for three."

They went over and sat at a picnic table outside the terminal building. Maura began emptying the bag, laying out sandwiches, chips, slaw, and Pepsi-Colas.

"Good to see you, Johnny."

"Is it?" Johnny smiled mischievously. "I got a notion there might be trouble afoot."

"Nothing I can't handle."

"Ain't worried about you. You ain't family."

"Just here to collect a few supplies and be on my way." Griff nodded towards Maura sitting beside Johnny on the opposite side of the picnic table. "She's not involved."

"I seen what's in the back of my granddaughter's Jeep. I'd say she's involved."

"Papa—"

"What's going on, son?"

Griff could feel Johnny's stare bore into his skull. He reached into his pocket for his money clip, peeled off a twenty-dollar bill and slid it across the table to Johnny.

Article 15

"What's this?"

"A retainer."

"You need a lawyer?"

"Everybody needs a lawyer. Most folks just don't know it—until it's too late."

"I reckon you hit upon a truism there…I'll give you that, but—"

"What I mostly need is to be on my way with…you know, no loose ends to snag me."

Johnny snatched up the twenty. "Tell me. *Straight.*"

"She works for you, right?" Griff nodded towards Maura. "No third-party exceptions?"

"Maura, darling, there is something I'm going to need you to do—professional like."

"What's that, Papa?"

"Not rightly sure yet." Johnny slid the twenty across to Maura without taking his eyes off Griff. "But I have me this client…"

She picked up the twenty, stared lovingly into Andrew Jackson's eyes, then folded it neatly and slid the bill into the front pocket of her tight black jeans." This will do…" Maura smiled at Griff. *"For now."*

"Consider yourself hired, then." Johnny's lips parted in a huge, toothy grin aimed at Griff. "And, of course, I'll brook no hanky-panky with the clientele."

Griff shook his head, feeling outfoxed again. "Of course. That would be *unprofessional.*"

"Yes. *Quite.*" Johnny unwrapped his sandwich. He scowled at Maura when, looking inside, he found turkey.

She swapped her roast beef sandwich for his turkey.

"Now, then, Mr. Crowe, thank you so much for choosing The Leonard Group for your legal needs. How may we help you?"

Griff watched Johnny take a carnivorous bite. He checked inside his own sandwich and found roast beef. He offered it to Maura, but she shook him off.

Johnny chewed and chewed and chewed, then swallowed. "Go on now, son. Don't be bashful. We're here to help."

"Well...I'm getting a little taste of what came Donald Wallace's way." Griff explained the sniper incidents at his ranch and Helena's place in Taos as they ate, sticking to just the facts of the shootings.

"Hmmm..." Johnny wiped horseradish sauce from the corner of his mouth with a napkin. "I feel compelled to ask, whether you, your own self, might be acting in a completely professional and ethical manner with *your* client? Don't worry, now, what you say is completely and absolutely protected by this thing we call attorney-client privilege."

Griff hung his head in defeat but caught Maura's wry smile.

"Yes, Mr. Crowe, you can trust us to keep your affairs completely confidential," Maura said. *"We're professionals."*

"Oh, let's not embarrass the poor fellow now, darling. It sounds like he's got a world of worry already," Johnny said. "One last thing, though. I'd be remiss if I failed to inquire as to your intentions for these...*supplies,* what that we were discussing earlier. Should you have any notions to use them to commit an act or acts of an illicit nature, well then, I'd be obliged by my oath as an officer of the court to make the authorities aware of such ill intent."

"Strictly self-defense," Griff said.

Article 15

Johnny crumpled up his sandwich wrapper. "Very well, then, I shall have Patty Ann set up an account for you."

"I'm paying for this lunch, aren't I."

"We do pride ourselves on being a full-service legal firm, Mr. Crowe. Or might I address you as Griff?"

"Of course."

Maura and Griff went to load his supplies in the plane. At the back of her Jeep, she nudged him with her hip.

"Glad to have you as a client," Maura said in a breathy voice.

Griff could only sigh.

When the Cirrus was packed up, Griff departed westbound, while Maura and Johnny stood on the tarmac and waved good-bye.

~~~

Sand Hill

After two days of hard flying, riding the bucking bronco of mechanical turbulence down low through uncontrolled airspace to literally "stay off the radar" as much as possible, Griff arrived on the far fringes of the Bay Area civilization in Hollister, California. He caught up on sleep in the "Jungle" room at the Cinderella Motel. Early the next morning he drove his nondescript Hertz Ford Fusion north to Silicon Valley.

JR's company was located in the nation's highest high rent district on Sand Hill Road in Menlo Park. Griff staked out the entrance to his building in the office complex from a park bench conveniently provided by the developer. He fit right in with the herd of venture capitalists and their techie petitioners by staring at his iPhone screen reviewing Lance's briefing paper on Helena's half-brother again as he waited for him to show up for work.

As far as anyone could tell, JR's company, PulseTech, was still in the vaporware stage after three years of bouncing back and forth between the Menlo Park moneybags and Mumbai code jockeys. The fact that he was still getting private equity sit downs and still getting face time from cable TV talking heads was due primarily to his father's reputation and an impressive burn rate on his inheritance, most of which was being spent on public relations rather than programming. With the ossification of cyberspace into FAANG—Facebook, Amazon, Apple, Netflix and Google—JR's business plan for yet another social media network had been so far greeted with respectful disinterest.

Just after nine-thirty, JR cut across the plaza from the parking lot flanked by two burly men Griff recognized from the Nickolson mansion in Bel Aire: Allen and Steve. After they entered the building, Griff placed a GPS tracking device on JR's Maybach, then went to hang out at the Stanford Shopping Center, where he could hop from one Wi-Fi hotspot to another to track JR's movements without drawing attention to himself for loitering.

Griff got a one-day snapshot of JR's routine: office hours 9:30 to 12:30 with a quick lunch break at the Sushi Shack on Ramona Avenue by Stanford University; eighteen holes and dinner at the Half Moon Bay Golf Links; a night cap at the British Banker's Club; then home to his Silicon Valley condo for the night.

Griff got a burger at The Melt, then went back to the tropical figurines, colorful macaw paintings, and rattan furniture in his motel room in Hollister to plan for the next day. He thought of Helena—and Maura—but resisted the temptation to contact either.

According to the GPS tracker the next morning, JR arrived at PulseTech at nine-thirty again. Griff dressed, checked out, and drove north to stake out the office building, planning to follow JR to lunch. A creature of habit, JR returned to the Sushi Shack, shadowed by Allen and Steve.

Griff parked in Lot N on Emerson, then gave JR time to order.

"Hi, guys. Good to see you again." Griff patted Steve on the shoulder as he walked through the Sushi Shack. He made a pistol with his fist and pointed it at Allen. "No hard feelings, right? Zzzzt. Zzzzt."

Article 15

Before Allen and Steve could react, Griff moved on and sat down at JR's table, just as Helena's brother stuffed a hunk of sushi in his mouth.

"So, we meet again, eh?" Griff put his hands flat on the table and shrugged his shoulders. "Got a minute?"

JR swallowed his yellow fin tuna. He shook his head at his body guards to have them sit back down, then asked, "What happened? My sister toss you out on your ass?"

"Not yet."

"Yeah? Just wait. She'll kick you to the curb like all the rest."

"Well, you know, you can visit the Magic Kingdom, but nobody actually lives at the fun park."

"You got some balls fucking my sister then coming here to talk trash at my face."

"I'm trying to look out for your sister. She doesn't have a pair of gorillas to protect her like you. Just me." Griff looked over his shoulder at Allen and Steve. He waved. "They aren't holding a grudge about the taser thing, are they?"

"Evidently, it left a mark." JR chuffed. He waved his chopsticks at his plate. "You want some?"

"No, thanks. I prefer to eat what I catch with my bait—not the bait."

"Suit yourself."

"So, what's with the muscle? Getting death threats? Or maybe someone took a shot at you?"

JR stopped in mid-bite. He pointed at Griff. "That better not've been you."

"You'd be dead by now if it was." Griff shook his head. "Like my cows."

"Huh?"

"And Donald Wallace…" Griff let that sink in. "Besides half your DNA, do you and your sister share anything else…like enemies, maybe?"

"You think this has something to do with Donnie?"

Griff shrugged his shoulders.

"Nah. That was a carjacking. That's what the cops are saying."

"So…no one out to get *you?*"

"I got enemies. Who doesn't? But most of them wouldn't know which end of the gun to aim my way." JR pointed around the sushi bar with his chopsticks.

Griff surveyed the clientele of pasty-faced millennials. "Fair enough."

"What is this about?"

Griff debated whether to ask JR about the Highlands Forum. "You tell me. I'm just hired help."

"Some loon, no doubt. Occupational hazard, I guess. I'm on TV a lot—and I'm rich, you know. Some people take offense. That's their problem."

"Well, evidently, this loon is a pretty good shot." Griff watched JR casually dip his sushi into wasabi sauce and pop it into his mouth. "So, be careful."

"Yeah, well, you, too," JR said with a mouthful of octopus. "You know, next time I might not be able to keep them on a leash." JR pointed at Allen and Steve. "Not that I really want to."

Griff looked at them, smiled and gave a thumbs up. "Fair enough."

"She okay?"

"Who? Helena?"

JR nodded.

Article 15

"So far."

"Okay."

Griff smiled at the underwhelming outpouring of brotherly love. He decided his inside voice should stay inside, then went to stand up, but suddenly felt two hands on his shoulders holding him down in his chair.

"Hi, boys. What are you talking about? Little old me?" Helena's voice came from behind Griff.

"Hi, Sis. As a matter of fact, yes. I was just asking how you're doing." JR skated a piece of sushi around on his plate like a hockey puck. "What brings you to town?"

"I thought you were in New York," Griff said, looking back over his shoulder at her, mad at himself for letting her get the drop on him—*again*.

"Yeah. No. I decided to visit family." Helena came around and sat between Griff and JR. "Aunt Willa says hi."

JR sneered at Helena. "My maternal bloodline runs through Beacon Hill, not hillbilly country."

Helena pouted at Griff. "Why is he always so mean to me?"

"Now, kids..." Griff shook his head.

"Make him stop."

JR smiled his evil, capitalist grin. "No offense."

Helena let out a huff. "That's okay. Dad liked me best anyway."

"In your dreams, Sis. In your dreams."

Griff suddenly wished he was sitting with Allen and Steve. "Seriously, why didn't you go to New York?"

Helena simply smiled like a sphinx.

"See what I put up with growing up? She was always misbehaving."

"I'm not the one with a police record."

"Expunged."

"You're welcome, Daddy." Helena hummed a little ditty as she looked around the restaurant, then at Griff. "Want to get some real food?"

"Yes, please."

"I saw your posse when I came in," Helena said to JR. "How are the boys?"

"Fine."

"Pathetic how they're still following the varsity quarterback around hoping for cheerleader sloppy seconds."

"They work for me," JR said. He tapped his index finger on the table impatiently.

"So, now you have to pay them to hang out? That's even more pathetic." Helena stood up. "Come on, Griff. Let's go downtown. I like my seafood cooked."

Griff smiled and stood up. "Good to see you again…Junior."

"Next time…" JR pointed at Allen and Steve.

Griff leaned over to look JR directly in the eye and held out his hand. "Deal?"

JR shook Griff's hand. "Deal."

"Come on, Helena. Let's make this bait shop a memory."

As they left, Helena brushed Steve's cheek with the back of her hand. "Hi, boys. Bye, boys."

Griff noticed both men strained their necks turning to follow her figure as she left the restaurant.

~~~

The Golden Gate

Griff really, really wanted to ask why Helena didn't go to New York; why Lance agreed to take her to Kentucky instead; why she was now there in California; and how in the hell she knew where he and JR would be. But he figured he wouldn't like the answers he got—if he even got any answers from her at all—so, he just drove instead.

Helena let Griff stew, savoring the musky aroma of simmering male angst and enjoying the quiet ride into downtown San Francisco along the Bayshore Freeway. When Griff parked, she hopped out and sauntered off towards the west end of Fisherman's Wharf.

Griff got out, stood by the car, and watched. Fifty feet off, she stopped and waved him on, so he slowly shuffled her way.

"Stop acting like a tired old hunting dog ready to be put down," Helena scolded when he got to her.

Griff stared her down.

Suddenly, she took him in her arms and forced a passionate kiss on him. She felt the tension in Griff slowly melt until he returned her kiss and embrace. "There now. Better?"

Griff gave Helena a half-smile.

"*Come on.* I actually missed you." Helena discreetly grabbed the inside of his thigh and smiled.

"It *is* good to see you."

"So, come on, now. Let's have some fun. I know it's kitschy, but I like doing the touristy thing." She took Griff's hand and led him to Alioto's where they joined the blue-hair crowd for an early dinner at a table overlooking the marina. "And I got us a room at the St. Francis."

"Not your apartment?"

"We're on vacashe. And I want to ride the cable cars, too."

"Whatever Helena wants…"

"That's the spirit."

Helena ordered Noma Rose's Cioppino with Chianti. Griff got fried calamari with an Anchor Steam.

Griff clinked Helena's wine glass, then took a pull off his beer. "So…"

"So?" Helena smiled seductively.

"I can't believe Lance let you go to Kentucky."

"He works for me. Remember?"

"So do I."

"Oh, Griff, don't think of it as work. Not now anyway." Helena looked out the window. "Why do you suppose they call them sea lions?"

"Don't know."

"Hmmm…"

Griff gave in, sat back and enjoyed the view.

"Who's Wes Eply?" Helena asked gazing out the window.

"Why?"

"Oh, Lance kept fretting about him, 'cause he hadn't checked in or something."

Griff thought for a moment, then remembered meeting Eply at Stein, Baylor and Stein. "He's one of Lance's guys. Does corporate. I met him once."

Article 15

"Makes sense. Lance kept asking about him every time he called his office."

Griff kept his mouth shut hard, hoping to avoid complications.

"That Hannah seems nice…" Helena said in a teasing manner. "I think she has a crush on you."

Griff prayed for their food to arrive and, thankfully, it did.

"So, you want to go to Alcatraz tomorrow?" Helena asked. "I love that place."

Griff just shrugged his shoulders.

"Come on, now. You know the rules. Whatever Helena wants…"

"Helena gets."

She smiled, slipped off her shoe, and massaged Griff's crotch with her foot. "And then, Helena gets grateful."

Griff grinned stupidly. He asked for the check, trying not to squirm noticeably, but got a curious look from the waitress.

Helena laughed and excused herself from the table.

Griff texted Lance, "Eply?"

Just as Helena came out of the Ladies Room, Lance answered, "MIA. 5 days. We need to talk."

Griff pocketed his phone as Helena and the waitress converged on the table. He paid cash. "Keep the change."

Griff's guilt over not calling Lance dissipated as he savored Helena smiling like a child on a Disneyland attraction as they rode the cable cars to Union Square. His angst was completely gone by the end of the elevator ride up to her suite with the view of the Golden Gate Bridge. He silenced his phone so Helena's expressions of gratitude would not be interrupted with business.

The next day Helena and Griff visited Alcatraz.

"He finally gave up, didn't he?" Helena asked as they leaned on the railing at the bow of the ferry coming back to Pier 33 after their tour.

"Who, Lance?"

"You twitched every time your phone vibrated. I'm glad he finally stopped."

"I really should call him."

"Tomorrow...*please?*" Helena stared straight ahead through her Jackie Ohhs.

Griff's fingers chased the wind through her hair as it blew her locks back in waves like a blonde flag. "Well, I am with a client."

"And he's probably never used that excuse before, huh?"

"Law School 101: Intro to Billable Hours." Griff's inside voice involuntarily reminded him of his conversation with Maura on the subject of clients, *They're only right as long as they pay their bills.*

Helena leaned into Griff.

"I suppose one more day won't hurt."

Helena kissed him on the cheek.

After they docked, Helena and Griff went back to the St. Francis, ordered room service, and exhausted themselves in bed.

Griff gazed out on the fog, which had rolled in over the bay and glowed in the darkness like a Chinese lantern from the ceaseless traffic crossing the Golden Gate.

Helena snored softly beside him.

~~~

Fargo

Griff left the St. Francis having extracted a solemn promise from Helena—she crossed her heart and hoped to die—that she would stay in San Francisco until Griff checked out her home in Taos and found it safe.

As he sat in the Cirrus on the tarmac in Hollister waiting for the engine oil temperature to come up, Griff sent a text to Lance: "Home tomorrow."

Lance replied: "Saturday. Meet you halfway. Code 2."

Halfway meant Fargo, North Dakota. Griff typed "10-4," hit send, then taxied out to depart Runway 13.

He made Taos in four hours with a fuel stop at Page, Arizona, south of Lake Powell.

Helena's bedroom window had been repaired, arranged by the property management firm contracted to look after her house in her absences. Their cleaning service had disposed of the abandoned derby pie and made the bed. All looked normal. Griff checked in with International Protective Services. The IPS residential security patrols reported no incidents and no alarms. He considered giving Helena the all clear, but his inside voice nagged him to wait until after he met with Lance.

With plenty of daylight left, Griff decided to head home. He topped his tanks in Ft. Collins, then by-passed Laramie to land at the ranch. Ben was still working in the barn and helped him push the Cirrus into his hangar as night fell.

"Please tell me it's been quiet around here," Griff said to Ben as they pulled the hangar doors closed.

"No more hunting accidents—if that's what you mean," Ben answered.

"Here or in the county?"

"Deputy Walt said ours is the only incident that's been reported."

"What are they making of it?"

"Nothing, like we talked. City folks on safari. Walt wrote a report, and that'll likely be the end of it."

"Good."

"How is Helena?" Ben gave Griff a big grin.

"You and Swannie sure have taken a shine to her."

"There's definitely entertainment value there and, you know us, we're easily amused."

"Glad to be of service. She'll be the death of me."

"Huh. You never noticed how women live longer?"

Griff whistled for Rodya, who came bounding out of the darkness. "Come on, boy. Let's enjoy what little time we evidently got left."

"Squaw fever, my friend. There's no cure."

Griff gave Ben the international sign language for being on your way, forthwith, in a carnal fashion.

Ben laughed.

"Give my best to Swan."

Rodya followed Griff into the house. It was good to be home.

~~

Article 15

Griff arrived first at Hector International Airport in Fargo. He paced the North Ramp tarmac as the fuel truck filled his tanks. Twenty minutes later the Stein, Baylor & Stein King Air 200 taxied up, spewing Jet-A fumes on the parking apron. The doors opened and Lance bounded down the stairs dressed like a golf pro. He inhaled deeply.

"You gotta love it." Lance beamed his white phosphorus smile.

"You solo?"

"We gotta talk. Your ears only." Lance eyeballed Griff's Cirrus. "Take me for a ride?"

Griff nodded. "Sure. I'm topped off. Where to?"

"Doesn't matter. I just want to be alone."

They piled into the Cirrus. Griff called Clearance Delivery for a westbound departure.

Fifteen minutes later, Departure Control advised Griff to Squawk VFR and ended their flight following with, "Frequency change approved. Good day."

"Kind of an expensive conversation we're going to have, huh?" Griff asked Lance as he throttled back to the best economy power setting. "You're not in a hurry to get anywhere right?"

"No. Just back for my round tomorrow morning. I've really been spanking the ball hard lately. Feels great," Lance said. "But, anyway, how are you doing?"

"Eh, I have my good days and my not so good days. Got no extra holes in me, so pretty good today. So far."

"And our favorite client?"

"Hopefully staying put like she's supposed to. Why didn't you take her to New York?"

"Have you met our client? She's very persuasive. And, you know, family is always important in times of crisis."

"Yeah, well, I was figuring she might not stick out like a sore thumb in New York City."

"Like I said, she made a compelling argument."

"With her checkbook?"

"Be that as it may." Lance scanned the horizon that seemed to go on forever. "We've got some catching up to do."

"Eply?"

"In part. I wasn't really worried until I learned about the sniper that seems to be stalking you two."

"And Junior."

"Him, too? Man, these guys are busy."

"Yeah. Real go-getters." Griff engaged the autopilot.

"Well, Eply and Wilkinson have been looking into...*things.*"

"Corporate things?"

"Mainly. Seems as though Mr. Nickolson had been steadily and increasingly divesting himself and Hornet out of the consumer tech sector."

"Meaning?"

"Mainly social media companies: Facebook, Twitter, Google."

"Meaning?"

"Wilkinson made the rounds with the vulture capitalists on the coasts. Evidently the guy—besides being wicked smart and almost always right—was an industry bellwether. You know, the old E.F. Hutton, thing. When Helena's dad talks, people listen, usually follow—and sometimes panic, especially if they're on the wrong end of the money flow."

Griff looked over at Lance. "You hungry? Seems like this is going to be a long conversation."

"Why not. No calories in an airport burger, right?"

"Wanna see some dead Presidents?"

Article 15

"Sure."

Griff checked the navigation display and angled the Cirrus southwest towards Rapid City. "Now, who was panicking over where daddy parked his money and why are they taking it out on my cows?"

"It's funny, really, how when it comes to high finance, perception is reality. Not hard to start a bear market stampede if you know how to spook the herd."

"So, was Nickolson trying to spook the herd?"

"Actually, no. He was being very discreet. Only a few of the bigger players had just started taking notice when his bird went down—oh, and you may be right about that. I talked to an old Army buddy of mine in Maintenance who's now running a fleet of choppers servicing Gulf oil rigs. He told me there were issues with a catastrophic failure mode in the FADECs on the Bell 407s causing the engines to run erratically and sometimes lose power when the throttle was advanced. Bad news if you're down low. It was a hard fault failure that didn't generate any cockpit warning signals."

"So, it wasn't nefarious?"

"Well…this goes back almost ten years ago. A guy in New Hampshire sued Bell and company. So, the NTSB should have gotten it resolved."

"Should have…"

Lance turned his palms up and shrugged.

"So, Facebook killed Cliff Nickolson and my cows?"

"I didn't say that."

"Who did it then?"

"Goddamn it. Now, *I'm* going to sound like Alex Jones."

"Conspiracy theory?"

"Well, let's just say there are other non-private sector interests involved."

"The Highlands Group."

"You know the night he was killed, Nickolson was going to Singapore, right?"

Griff nodded.

"Well, the Singapore Defense Ministry was the host for the international edition of the Highlands Group with China being target *numero uno*. You don't think Google bending over and grabbing the ankles to get into China is just about expanding into new markets for their search engine ads, do you? It's still the same wizard hiding behind the curtain."

"The one that put them into business in the first place."

Lance nodded. "Bingo. Good old Uncle Sam."

"Wait, so Nickolson was active in the Highlands Group at the same time he was divesting on the corporate side?"

"Sometimes a sound national security policy doesn't always make for a good private investment. Ever since Snowden blew the whistle on NSA surveillance of every John Q. Public on the planet, people—besides just the alt-right loonies—have been connecting dots between social media's obsessive personal tracking and the likes of Clapper and Brennen. Those guys make the *Stasi* look like Keystone Cops. Only nobody was ever supposed to know."

"So, the CIA is after me and Helena?"

"Come on, man. You know how this works. You don't really think your name is being taken in vain in the Executive Offices at Langely, do you? Behind some key-coded locked office somewhere in a big white building in, around, or somewhere near the Beltway, there's a patch of turf that some nameless, faceless drone believes is in need of protection."

Article 15

"From Helena?" Griff turned southwest of Rapid City towards the Black Elk Wilderness Area and began a descent.

"From the implosion of their digital house of cards. Social media is the fentanyl of the masses. And if the masses stop believing and trusting and using..." Lance shook his head. "Well, tell me, how much actionable intelligence do you think the NSA is harvesting from MySpace for targeting Hellfires off Predators in sand country?"

Griff nodded.

"You and I, we did our bit for the War on Terror and we know what's going on—especially, you."

"And Helena?"

"You read Nickolson's journals?"

"The most recent ones."

"Me, too. She left them with the firm for safekeeping. Put them in context and you can read between the lines that he was getting his money out of the spy business. And why. Others were sure to follow, so he had to be stopped and he was."

"The crash."

Lance nodded. "Then Helena hired me to hire you to find Nickolson's journals and..."

"And I got them before they did."

"And it's game on...*again.*"

Griff slowed as they drifted past the stone-carved visages of Washington, Jefferson, Lincoln and Roosevelt at seventy-seven hundred feet. From four miles away, outside the restricted airspace around the national monument, Mt. Rushmore was underwhelming.

Griff continued on to Custer County Airport and landed. They took a cab to the Sage Creek Grille for burgers.

"Sorry about the calories," Griff said when they ordered.

"Eh, life is short."

"So I hear."

~~

Mount Rushmore

Griff and Lance understood without saying that no business would be discussed at lunch. Instead, they talked airplanes, with Lance querying Griff on the Cirrus specs and performance. They compared notes on the Aeronca Champ versus the Cessna O-1 Birddog. Lance waxed nostalgic on the different aircraft he flew in the Army, then in civilian life.

"Never had a Cirrus. Maybe you can let me have some stick time on the way back," Lance said.

"Sure, but do you mind if we plan Fargo after dark? I'd rather not have any prying eyes putting a visual on my N-number."

"No problem. What do you want to do in the meantime? Dead Presidents?"

"We can do."

"So…I have to ask, how *is* our client, if you know what I mean," Lance sneered. His eyebrows bounced like a ventriloquist dummy.

Griff scowled across the table. "No business talk."

"Right, right, right. Soooo…how about Hannah?"

"I can't believe you."

"Come on. Throw this old dog a bone. *Please,*" Lance pleaded.

"All I'll say is that lemon bars and pecan pies are not her most impressive talent."

Lance grabbed his heart and panted.

"Here you go, fellas." The waitress stared at Lance as she dropped off their check. "Ah…thanks for coming in?"

"Jen, would you do us a huge favor?" Lance smiled up at the waitress.

"Maybe…"

"Would you mind calling a cab for us? We'd like to see the monument."

Griff peeled off a twenty and a ten to pay for lunch, handing them to Jen with the check. He gave her a second twenty, nodding towards Lance and rolling his eyes back in his head. "And that's for you."

"Sure thing. I'll call right away." Jen smiled at Griff, then turned and headed towards the register.

"She might be sweet on you," Lance said.

"Shut up."

"And thanks for lunch."

"Don't mention it."

As they waited for their cab in front of the Sage Creek Grille, an older gentleman, showing considerable gray hair at the bottom of a Vietnam Veteran baseball cap, came out of the restaurant and approached them.

"Name's Roy," the man said. "Didn't mean to eavesdrop but couldn't help but hear you fellas talking. I flew the Birddog a bit."

"I'm Lance. Good to meet you, Roy." Lance and Roy shook hands. "This here is Griff. I'm Army. He's Navy. Special Ops."

Griff shook Roy's hand. "Air Force, I take it."

Roy nodded. "Least ways we ain't got no jarheads to contend with here."

Article 15

Griff smiled, thinking of Cliff Nicholson, Donald Wallace, Johnny Leonard, Cap, and Maura. "Yeah, they can be a pain."

"Flew Forward Air Control."

"In Nam? Wow, high pucker factor," Lance said.

"My friend, here, chauffeured generals around," Griff said. "Got a Purple Heart for his luggage-inflicted hernia."

"It wasn't Afghanistan, but I did my share of heavy lifting in the War on Terror," Lance said.

"Eh, wasn't 'til Laos that it got real interesting." Roy gave a sly smile.

"Ravens?" Griff asked.

Roy nodded.

"That's funny. A raven and a Crowe," Lance pointed to Roy, then Griff.

"The Ravens were a CIA black op," Griff said.

"You make it sound more glamorous than it really was."

"And what do you do now, Roy?" Lance asked.

"Designated Examiner on occasion. Mainly retired, enjoying the peace and quiet here in the Black Hills. The O-1 was a good bird. Anyway, hearing you boys talk gave me pause. Brought back memories, you know?"

"Sure."

"Hey, Roy." A lean bald man with the hungry look of a salesman on the prowl walked up. "Friends of yours?"

"Hey, Ned. This here's Griff and Lance," Roy answered. "Fellas, Ned's my insurance guy."

"Pleased to meet you." Quicker than Wild Bill Hickok, Ned drew two business cards and handed them to Griff and Lance.

"We were just swapping war stories," Roy said.

"You boys are vets, then. Well, thanks for your service."

"You bet," Lance said. "And, hey, thank you for picking up the tab, citizen."

A confused expression gripped the insurance agent's face.

Their cab pulled up.

"Good to meet you, Roy," Lance said getting into the back seat. "You too, Ned."

Griff shook Roy's hand, saluted Ned, then followed Lance into the cab. He closed the door and waved at Roy and Ned. "Fucking spooks are everywhere."

"I'd say you're just being paranoid, but, lately, maybe not so much."

Lance pestered Griff for salacious details about his Assistant, Hannah—for the first fifteen minutes in earnest and for the second fifteen like an annoying little kid on a road trip, just for the pure joy of aggravating his friend.

"Keep the meter running." Lance handed the cab driver a twenty when they got to the National Park. "We won't be too long."

They toured the Lincoln Borglum Museum, hiked the Presidential Trail, then strolled out through the Avenue of Flags to the Grand Viewing Terrace.

"That is a special kind of crazy." Lance gazed up at the stone visages of Washington, Jefferson, Lincoln and Roosevelt. "Carving the mugs of politicians into a mountain in the middle of nowhere. Just crazy."

"And yet, here we are," Griff said, looking at the monument through the clunky pedestal-mounted binoculars. He stepped back. "Take a look."

Lance leaned in for a magnified view of the Presidents. "You know, Helena could pull it off."

"Pull what off?"

"The Eva Marie Saint thing."

"Hitchcock?"

"Yeah, but you're definitely no Cary Grant." Lance looked at Griff, then back through the binoculars. "But I could see you hanging from George Washington's schnoz like a big old booger."

"Yeah, well, this big old booger is getting more than just lemon bars."

Lance closed his eyes, leaned his forehead against the binoculars, and sighed. "You're killing me, Whitey. You're killing me."

"Who you calling 'Whitey,' Paleface?"

"Come on. Let's go. You've ruined the moment."

The cabbie dropped them off at the Custer County Airport, where Lance slipped him a couple of C-notes.

The first hour of the flight back was an impromptu flight lesson with Griff familiarizing Lance with his plane's systems and handling characteristics, then letting him fly the return route. The sun set behind them as the lights of Fargo came into view in the windscreen.

"So, what's going on with Eply?" Griff asked.

"He made a swing through blue grass country on his way back from DC."

"Blue Wing, LLC?"

"Yeah. He said he had a lead on it or something."

Griff thought of Johnny, Cap and Maura. "Did he find anything out?"

"Don't know. He fell off the radar. Wasn't worried at first. He's single and twenty-one and roaming the countryside on the firm's expense account. I started thinking maybe he got caught in some kind of *Justified* or *Deliverance* type scenario. But then, I hear somebody's throwing lead around in the vicinity of our client and…"

"You want me to go check it out?"

"Oh, yeah. You met with that Leonard guy, right?"

Griff nodded.

"Let's give it a day or two. Maybe he found himself a hillbilly honey pot."

Maura.

"Your airplane," Lance said.

Griff took the controls of the Cirrus and called Fargo Approach. He dropped Lance off at the King Air, then headed home to Wyoming.

~~~

Learjets and Lingerie

Griff landed on Runway 21 at Laramie Regional. As he turned back on Taxiway Bravo, a wave of exhaustion broke over him. First, he noticed the row of symmetrical cabin windows glowing like a short pearl necklace, then the silhouette of the now familiar Learjet 31 took shape in the darkness. He taxied over and parked wingtip-to-wingtip with the business jet. Griff tidied up the cockpit, grabbed his go-bag, and stepped out on the tarmac. It was nearly midnight and quiet enough to hear the wind whisper.

A man pushed open the door on the Cowboy Aviation offices and ran towards Griff, the slaps of leather soles reverberating on the asphalt.

Griff instinctively drew his pistol and held it behind his leg.

"Mr. Crowe."

As he came near, Griff recognized Helena's co-pilot but kept his SIG Sauer in hand.

"Mr. Crowe. Let me get the door for you."

The co-pilot motioned Griff towards the Learjet. He unlocked and opened the clamshell doors. Soft light spilled out on the tarmac from inside the fuselage.

Griff stepped up into the cabin. He turned and looked over his shoulder.

The co-pilot's eyes locked on Griff's pistol. He looked up at Griff, then slipped out of view from the doorway. The sound of his steps faded as he walked hurriedly back to the office.

Griff dropped his bag, checked that the cockpit was empty, then holstered his pistol. He looked back into the passenger cabin. Helena lay sleeping curled up across the bench seat against the back bulkhead.

He quietly pulled the cabin door closed, then went back to sit in the seat facing her. He picked up the well-worn, hardcover book which had fallen on the floor: *The Little Prince* by Antoine Saint-Exupéry. Griff flipped through the pages. A first edition. On the title page was handwritten, "To Helena, Love Dad."

Griff gently covered Helena's shoulders with the Navajo blanket she lay beneath and tucked her in. He sat back down, reclined the seat and watched her sleep peacefully.

Griff dozed off, holding Helena's book in his lap.

It was dark still when Griff felt hot breath and moist lips on his neck, then the press of Helena's body on top of his in the seat. The cabin lights were off, but he kept his eyes closed and searched the darkness with his hands, grabbing silk fabric into bunches until he felt the warm, soft skin of her hips…then her waist…then her breasts.

Helena's hands slid beneath Griff's shirt, up to caress his neck, then down to his belt. Effortlessly, they found their way into his pants.

Griff lifted his hips off the seat to free his BDUs, and suddenly they were together. He opened his eyes. Helena's eyes were closed. A soft smile lapped gently on her face as she slowly undulated against him.

Griff reached up to stroke her cheeks. He gently brought her lips down to his, and they kissed until their bodies clenched and she melted on top of him with her head on Griff's shoulder.

They lay until the rosy fingers of dawn reached down Runway 3.

Helena sat up and smiled. "Will you see me home like a gentleman?"

"Of course."

After they dressed, Helena called the crew waiting across the tarmac on her cell phone. They sat with their backs towards the entryway, slouched down out of view when the pilots came aboard.

"We'll be ready to go in just a few minutes, Miss Nickolson."

Helena and Griff traded naughty smiles across the aisle.

"Thank you, Roger."

Forty-five minutes later they landed in Taos.

~~~

Eply

Griff woke, naked in Helena's bed and alone. A faint aroma of frying bacon wafted in from the kitchen. He closed his eyes and listened. Helena hummed a random melody, accompanied by the percussion of cooking bacon.

Griff opened his eyes again and looked out the window at the soft light of dawn spilling out from around the Sangre de Cristo Mountains. From the moment he stepped into the cocoon of the Learjet 31's fuselage, life had become suddenly and remarkably easy and carefree—at least for the past thirty-six hours.

Funny what a difference five hundred million dollars can make, he thought. *Even if it is illusory.*

Reality stalked his thoughts from the shadows like a black panther. Griff tried to ignore his cell phone on the nightstand hovering in his peripheral vision. He closed his eyes again, breathed deeply and happily replayed the erotic escapades with Helena since she woke him on her Learjet to the present moment. She seemed insatiable.

Reluctantly, Griff opened one eye and looked over at his iPhone. He reached for it and checked his notifications:

A voicemail from a number in Virginia Beach—T-Rex, *no doubt.*

A text from Maura: "Call me."

Three texts and a voice mail from Lance.

"No honey pot. Need boots on the ground."

"Give me a call. RE: Eply. Make it snappy."

"How soon can you get there? Code 3."

Griff pulled on his pants and shirt, then dialed Lance. He stepped over to the window facing the mountains and stared as the phone rang, subconsciously wishing he was calling Maura instead.

"I heard from him. FUBAR," Lance answered. "A total fuster cluck."

"What?"

"An email dump from the week before last. Written off-line—probably on the flight in. What is it? Don't they have Internet in hillbilly land? I had IT check the logs. Eply hadn't signed on to the firm's servers for nine days. I called, but nada. I had Wilkinson check Eply's Facebook page. Nada."

Griff smelled coffee.

Helena reached around and handed him a mug. She nibbled on his bicep, then slid her hand inside his pants.

"I, ah—mmm…I don't get it."

"Looks like somebody down there finally turned on Eply's laptop. It must have been in sleep mode and replicated when it came alive. Of course, that was two days ago—when I got back from our visit at the rock."

Helena came around Griff. She mouthed, "What is it?"

"Lance," Griff silently answered. Then into the phone, he said, "What was in the emails?"

"Routine updates on his trip. A couple of emails about other cases he's working. But nothing from after last Thursday."

Article 15

"Okay. I'll get home and get there tomorrow."

"I can have the boys take you and you can be there tonight," Helena said softly.

There was a long pause on Lance's end of the line. "Where are you?"

"The Land of Enchantment," Griff answered.

"And is that who I think it is?"

Helena smiled up at Griff. She squeezed him and took her hands out of his pants. "Good morning, Lance Baylor, Esquire. I'll go call the boys and have them start flight planning." To Griff she whispered, "Then I think I'll go to New York, like you wanted me to."

Griff watched Helena head to the kitchen for her phone. "Apparently, I can be there later today."

"Good. IT traced the IP address to a public Wi-Fi in Cincinnati. I'll text you the address. Call me when you're there."

"Roger, Wilco."

"Griff…"

"Yeah?"

"Oh, never mind."

~~

The flight to Lunken Field in Cincinnati took just a bit longer than the drive to Taos at Flight Level 410 where a tail wind gave Helena's Lear 31 a one hundred twenty-three knot push.

Helena read *The Little Prince*, while Griff searched on the address Lance texted him to find where Eply's laptop was last turned on and connected to the Internet. The Flying Pig Cafe was just north of Fountain Square downtown on Vine Street. He decided to listen to T-Rex's voicemail and call Maura, once Helena departed for New York City.

"Will you miss me much?" Helena asked as they waited in the plane while it was being refueled.

"Of course," Griff answered.

"But will you miss *me?* Or, you know, just this?" Helena leaned over and gently grabbed Griff's crotch.

Griff smiled. "It's a package deal, isn't it?"

"Mmmm…one would think." Helena let go and sat back as the crew boarded the plane and went into the cockpit. She smiled seductively. "Off you go, then."

Griff stood and leaned over, coming nose to nose with Helena. He smiled and grabbed her crotch gently beneath her skirt. He kissed her lightly on the lips once, then started to stand up straight, but Helena took his head in her hands and pulled him in for a long, passionate kiss.

"Mmmm…" Helena let go and leaned back in her seat.

Griff stood up.

"I just might miss you, too," Helena cooed.

"Promise?"

"No."

Griff smiled.

Maura watched Griff deplane from inside Signature Flight Support. He stepped down and walked away from the Learjet as the doors were pulled closed behind him.

Griff stopped halfway to Signature. He turned to look back as the engines started.

The Learjet began rolling forward. The Captain gave Griff a big grin and snapped a crisp salute his way.

Article 15

Griff returned the salute and watched the plane taxi away, getting bathed in Jet-A fumes as it turned onto Taxiway Alpha, heading for the departure end of Runway 25. He watched Helena fly away in a roar directly overhead, then turned towards the door to Signature Flight Support. Through the chain-link fence, he noticed a familiar Jeep Rubicon in the parking lot.

Maura emerged from Signature and marched towards Griff. She met him halfway.

"I was going to call you," Griff said as she came up to him.

"You here for Wes Eply?"

Griff nodded slowly, not liking the curt edge to Maura's voice.

"He's dead."

"How do you know?"

"I have my connections." Maura searched Griff's face for a reaction. "Did you kill him?"

"No—what? *No*. What the hell's going on?"

"Then, you gots some 'splainin' to do, mister."

~~~

Murder One

Griff sat across the desk from Johnny in his downtown Newport office staring at the familiar mugs of Cincinnati celebrities shoulder-to-shoulder with the beaming lawyer. His eye was inexorably drawn to Lonnie Anderson. It almost seemed as if Bill Clinton, in the next frame over, couldn't help but look at her, too.

Johnny sat with his chin on his palm, his elbow on the desk, staring at his office door, tapping a #2 pencil on a stack of briefs over and over and over again: Tap…Tap…Tap…Tap-Tap.

Griff looked at Johnny and cleared his throat, but he just kept staring…and tapping. So, Griff resumed his scan of the eight-by-tens on the wall: with Hubert Humphrey …with Jack Nicklaus…with Roy Rogers and Dale Evans…with Jerry Springer—*in the Mayor's office…*

Maura came in, closed the door and locked it. She handed Johnny a manila file folder. "You need a new printer, Papa. Seriously. And maybe some Wi-Fi."

Johnny waved her off as he read the papers in the folder.

"It shouldn't be that hard to get something off this," Maura waved her cell phone, "and onto a piece of paper. It just shouldn't."

Griff nodded, but watched Johnny read.

Finally, Johnny closed the file folder and locked eyes with Griff.

When he couldn't take the silence any longer, Griff asked, "So…what are we doing here?"

Johnny sighed. He looked at Maura.

She shook her head.

Johnny looked back at Griff. "You might want to take a moment to recollect that you recently retained me as your attorney. Consideration was given and all—unless, of course, you no longer desire the services of the Leonard Group."

"I need a lawyer?"

"I believe you, your own self, opined how everybody needs a lawyer, but most folks remain blissfully unawares of that particular fact."

"I need a lawyer?"

"Generally, a charge of murder against the peace and dignity of the Commonwealth of Kentucky does present itself as an adequate occasion wherein legal representation is deemed most appropriate."

"Me?"

Johnny held up the file folder. "One Eply, Westcott Sinclair, age thirty-four of Skokie, Illinois, recently relieved of his mortal coil as evidenced by his battered corpse filled with a number of nine-millimeter holes, found in Bellevue Beach Park—just this past week."

"Up the street from Christopher's Bed and Breakfast where I stayed."

"That fact was, indeed, noted in the probable cause affidavit."

"I tried to warn you," Maura said. "You don't mess with the Man upstairs."

"Have you ever had occasion to find yourself in Bellevue Beach Park?"

Article 15

Griff nodded. "The day we went to Pine Hollow. I went for a walk after dinner."

Johnny made a note on a legal pad. "I'd expect to see that stroll memorialized on surveillance camera footage, then."

Griff sat back in his chair. He shook his head.

"Of course, I presume you are innocent of this heinous crime and wish to challenge these scurrilous charges in the most vigorous fashion possible."

"*Papa!* Of course, he is innocent."

"*Of course.*" Johnny smiled at Griff. "Though that particular fact is of little import to the task presently at hand."

"This does not make sense. How?" Griff asked.

"Oh, we shall get to the bottom of that deep mystery in due time. It does give me pause—knowing our local constabulary resources as I do—how they were able to connect this particular set of dots in such an expeditious fashion."

"Outside help?"

"I would certainly have no need of assuming a shocked expression on my face upon learning that was the case."

"Can you excuse me for just one moment?"

Johnny held his hands out, palms up.

Griff stood up and stepped away, fishing his iPhone out of his pocket. He listened to the voice mail left by T-Rex:

"Griff—you fucking twat—what in the hell have you gotten yourself into—and she damn well better be worth it. Don't have names, ranks or serial numbers yet, but there is vile swamp stink on your name. You definitely stepped on the wrong bureaucratic sperm squirt—whatever it is you're doing. Selection never ends, so watch your fucking six. More when I got it."

Griff sat back down across from Johnny. "Seems as though someone in DC isn't a big fan of my work."

Johnny's impassive expression did not change. He smiled. "And there you have it. Do I look surprised?"

"Can you handle this? And the *Federales?*"

"Son, in your present state of distress at recent unsettling news, you may not have noticed a distinct twinkle in my eye."

"There's no one better to have on your side," Maura said.

Griff looked at Maura, then Johnny. "I presume this is going to cost more than twenty dollars."

"You'll be good for it, I'm sure, so let's not fret about mere trivialities."

"Okay. So, what do we do now?"

"Well…what might your feelings be about the color orange?" Johnny winked at Maura. "Sartorially speaking, that is."

"Careful, though, stripes tend to make you look fat," Maura said. "But it's just for a week."

"Ten days to be precise. We shall forego seeking bail and force their hand at the preliminary hearing."

Griff sighed.

"Can you handle it, son?" Johnny asked softly.

Griff nodded, thinking how easy life had been for the past forty-eight hours—and how unpleasant it was soon to be. "You're sure you can beat this at trial?"

"Mr. Crowe, there will be no trial. Do not let this suit and my fine silk tie, the diplomas on my wall or the company I keep fool you. I know crap when I smell it." Johnny held up the copy of the arrest warrant. "And this here, my dear sir, is crap."

"How can you be sure?" Griff asked.

"A good manager gives serious study not only to his own roster, but to the fellas in the other dugout. Our County Attorney may have always been a—let's be kind and say—a mediocre practitioner of *juris prudence,* bless his heart, but he is a damn fine politician. And the particular minion he's assigned to this case…" Johnny pointed to a name on the Complaint. "Well, let's just say the boy's about three At Bats from a one-way ticket down to Triple A ball. No doubt the DA's olfactory senses are unimpaired, as well."

"So, I guess I turn myself in, then."

"What is your hurry, son?" Johnny laughed. "In spite of what you may have heard about our glorious southern hospitality, the food sucks, the beds are hard, and the amenities in jail are, well, lacking."

"The ink isn't even dry on the warrant," Maura said. "And I'd think you might want some time to get your affairs in order."

"Besides, you and I have some prep work to do. Maura, darlin', how about we park him at Dewey's for a day or two. He's a nice enough fella—under that roughhewn exterior."

Maura shook her head. "No, Papa. There's a revolving door on his place. We shouldn't take a chance."

Johnny scowled at his granddaughter.

Maura suppressed a smile.

"Dang it all." Johnny pointed at Griff. "You…you are a client. Remember that."

"Come on, Griff. I'll take you home."

"No hanky-panky," Johnny called after them as they left. "No hanky-panky—or I'll let your flea-bit carcass rot in that damn jail."

~~~

Birdtown

"I told you on the way that I don't cook," Maura said, dropping a stack of carry out menus in front of Griff at her kitchen table—mostly from the pizza, Mexican, and Chinese restaurants in downtown Amelia.

"No problem."

Maura studied the confused look on Griff's face. "What?"

"So…how well do you get along with all the soccer moms here in suburbia?"

"Just peachy. We all swap Jell-O salad recipes at the PTA meetings and whisper scandalously amongst ourselves about the how-to-keep-a-man hints in Cosmo."

"Sorry. I just didn't picture you as living in a cookie cutter kind of neighborhood like this."

"Hey, Birdtown is nice. It's clean. It's quiet. The people are…well, they're not the type of people I have to deal with at work."

"I'll bet not. But…" Griff looked out the sliding glass door. "But I can see into, what ten or fifteen of your neighbors' back yards."

"Yeah, well, nothing happens in here for them to drool over."

"What a crime."

Maura blushed.

Griff smiled.

"And it won't. And if you don't behave, I'll make you sleep on the futon in the rec room downstairs—in the basement."

"Rec room?"

"Stop it. Just stop it. I'd rather be back across the river with Johnny, but Ohio residency is a licensing requirement."

"Well, I guess this is as good a place as any to hide out from the law—ironic as it is—what you being a bounty hunter and all. I still can't picture you pushing a lawn mower around the yard on Saturday mornings."

"That's why God created snot-nosed neighbor kids. Now, what do you want for dinner?"

Griff shuffled through the menus. "Chinese sounds good. Something hot. Szechuan or Hunan chicken works. How's the Peking House?"

"I like their beef lo mein. Pork fried rice and egg rolls?"

Griff nodded. "How about some crab Rangoon, too?"

"Sure. I'll call."

When Maura left to get their food, Griff called Lance.

"What did you find out?" Lance answered.

"Eply's dead. And I'm Number One with a bullet on the suspect list."

Silence.

"You're going to need to get someone to the ranch, pronto, to clean things up," Griff said.

"You're serious."

"As a fucking myocardial infarction. There's an arrest warrant out already."

"How does that happen?" Lance asked.

"The same way Cliff Nickolson and Donald Wallace get themselves dead."

Article 15

"Call Ben." Lance exhaled loudly. "Wilkinson and I will take care of it—personally. What do you need there? Who should I call?"

"This E.J. Leonard guy says he can make this all go away."

"The old guy? You think he can handle it?"

"He does seem to know everybody in town and anybody who's somebody that's ever landed a Learjet in this berg. And he's got a plan."

"Yeah, well, Custer had a plan, too, until he ran into you people," Lance said. "It's your ass on the line, not mine. What about bail?"

"He intends to quash this thing at the preliminary hearing. If I sit it out in jail, they have to do it in ten days. Not so, if I'm out on bail. So, the quicker the sooner is better for me."

"Anyway, whatever you need."

"Thanks, Lance."

"Where's Helena?"

"New York City."

"Good. Does she know?"

Griff shook his head. "No. I haven't called."

"Maybe it'll blow over before she finds out."

"Not likely. She's got family here about, remember?"

"Anyway, give this Leonard guy my number—*my cell number*—and tell him to call me when the hearing's scheduled. And tell him if he needs anything—anything at all—to call."

"Thanks."

"Let Ben know we'll be out there tomorrow. Wait 'til you hear from me before you turn yourself in."

"Okay."

Griff was on the phone with Ben when Maura got back from the Peking House. She asked, "You need a minute?"

He shook his head. "Yeah. You know what to do. He'll be there tomorrow, but make sure you give him a call if something—*anything*—comes up. I gave you his number, right?"

Griff listened.

Maura set out plates and silverware, then pulled the square white buckets of Chinese food out of the bag.

"Take good care of Rodya, and I'll see you in a couple of weeks—or maybe a couple of decades." Griff hung up and set down his phone.

"Rodya?" Maura asked.

"My buddy. Of the four-legged variety."

"What kind of name is that for a dog?"

"Well, he's a Siberian Husky—and the name is from Dostoyevsky. *Crime and Punishment,* as a matter of fact. Ain't that ironical?"

"Don't worry. Papa will take care of this for you. Now, come on, let's eat."

Griff just nodded.

Maura retrieved a couple of Budweiser longnecks from the fridge. They filled their plates in silence and ate.

"You sure you want to get involved in this mess? And get your grandfather involved?"

"What mess?"

"You know what I do, right?"

"Actually, no. What's your MOS?"

Griff smiled. "I don't think there's a code for it."

"I kind of figured we're sort of in the same line of work, though on opposite sides of the aisle."

"Let's just say I get things done that need getting done."

"Yeah. Me, too. And what is it that Helena needs done?"

Article 15

Maura squinted at Griff over her fork full of lo mein. "Come on. I am part of your legal team. And, I've got a few semesters of law school under my belt."

"Going into the family business?"

"I might. Might not be as action-packed as my present-day job, but, you know, suburbia kind of grows on you."

Griff laughed under his breath. "Create some snot-nosed kids of your own someday to cut your neighbors' lawns?"

"Maybe. If I find the right fella." Maura smiled, then scowled at Griff. "So, what does Helena need to get done?"

"She said…" Griff skated a nugget of Szechuan chicken around on his plate. He took a deliberate breath. "She said she wanted to get back some personal items of her father's that went missing. He died in a helicopter crash, but…"

"But?"

"But…it was definitely no boating accident."

"And she knew?"

Griff speared the nugget and shoved it into his mouth, thinking as he chewed. He slowly nodded his head. "She knew. I mean, deep down she knew something wasn't right. That'd be my guess. But whether she knew what a cluster fuck it would all turn into…I don't know. Maybe. But how could anyone ever imagine such a mad conspiracy? The government. Google. Assassins and some uber-rich blonde…"

"And you."

"And me." Griff shook his head. "You sure you want in on this?"

"I don't scare easy." Maura smiled. "And neither does Papa."

~~~

Into the Belly of the Whale

Griff stood at the sliding glass door in Maura's kitchen looking out back. A half-hour before, Johnny left after a second full afternoon of going over every minute of every day since he first met Helena at Chicago Executive Airport. Lance had just called. He and Wilkinson finished at the ranch and were back in Chicago. Rodya was with Ben and Swan. Maura was at work chasing some bad guy for J-Bonds 24-Hour Bail Bond Service...*some bad guy like him.*

Griff was not sure which of the two deserved more of his empathy.

In the soft light of the summer evening, Griff watched the "snot-nosed" neighbor kids romp and play in their backyards, quarter-acres of suburbia cordoned off with cedar privacy fences. Griff had been at Maura's only two days and he was already feeling stir crazy.

He looked back at his phone on the kitchen table and wondered. *No calls...no texts from Helena?*

"Hey, Griff," Maura called out when she came in the front door. "I brought home a pizza. Is Papa still here?"

"He left." Griff looked back out the sliding glass door.

"Good. He's a pizza snob. Gotta be Angelo's or it's trash." Maura set the pizza on the kitchen table and put a twelve-pack into the refrigerator. "What's going on out there, Gladys Kravits?"

"Oh, nothing. Did you and Dewey get the skel?"

"Well, look at you, using grown up technical terms of the law enforcement profession and all. Ain't that just the cutest thing."

Griff shrugged.

"Well, a bird in the kitchen is worth two in the wind."

He turned around to face Maura. "Lance called."

"Oh."

"Then, I guess it's on. Huh."

Maura stepped over and took Griff's head in her hand, gently stroking his cheek with her thumb. She nodded slightly. "But not until tomorrow. Okay?"

They ate pizza and drank beer, sitting together on the couch, feeding the DVD player classic horror movies from Maura's collection—*Halloween, Nightmare on Elm Street, The Texas Chainsaw Massacre,* and *Night of the Living Dead*—until Maura fell asleep sprawled against Griff.

He did not know how long he watched the TV screen saver bounce the time around in random patterns before he dozed. The next thing he remembered was Johnny pounding on Maura's front door to take him to jail in his Cadillac El Dorado.

~~

"Hey, Maura," the desk sergeant at the Newport Police Department called out when they came in. "How's it going?"

"Hey, Andy."

"Whatcha doin' on this side of the river?"

"Officer, we understand there is an arrest warrant outstanding for our client," Johnny said. "One Griffith Crowe."

Article 15

"Oh, yeah? What did he do?"

"The Commonwealth claims—erroneously, of course—that he violated KRS Chapter 507."

"Huh?"

"Criminal Homicide, section zero-two-zero, to be precise, murder."

Andy looked at Maura.

She nodded her head.

"This guy?" Andy pointed at Griff standing between Maura and Johnny.

Griff nodded, too.

"He is here to surrender peaceably, officer." Johnny smiled broadly.

"And who are you?"

"He's my grandpa," said Maura.

"Andy, I am E.J. Leonard, attorney-at-law. I represent Mr. Crowe and I am merely here to keep tabs on those pesky rights he is duly afforded by our great and noble justice system."

Andy looked from Johnny to Maura. "Your grandpa?"

Maura nodded.

"Huh." Andy scratched his bald head. He picked up the handset on his desk phone. "I better check with someone about this. Would y'all mind having a seat?"

"Certainly," Johnny said. "Take your time, officer."

And so began Griff's arrest and detention with all the attendant personal indignities involved in the process.

~~

I'd Rather Be In Philadelphia

Maura and Johnny got to the courthouse early the next morning and sat against the back wall of Courtroom 2 watching the proceedings before Griff's arraignment.

"But, Papa, why are we here so early?" Maura asked like a little kid as she surfed the web on her smart phone.

"We are reconnoitering, which as a general rule involves much more watching than talking. In your line of work, I should expect you to be well acquainted with this immutable truth." Johnny casually scanned the courtroom, watching the comings and goings of his fellow bar members attending to the docket of criminal hearings.

As the judge shuffled paperwork in the lull before Griff's arraignment, the prosecutor handling his case came in and chatted with his colleague from the County Attorney's office at the table on the right near the jury box before unpacking his briefcase.

Johnny perked up and nudged Maura.

"What?"

They watched the doors into the courtroom. There had been few visitors in the gallery for the series of motion hearings and arraignments. A clean-cut man in a dark suit, white shirt, and red tie came in, looked around, then sat against the back wall on the prosecution side of the courtroom.

"There. Him." Johnny gave a slight nod in the man's direction and stood up. "Come on."

"What?" Maura followed Johnny up to the defense table but stood outside the bar.

"The Commonwealth versus Griffith Crowe," announced the bailiff.

Johnny looked to the back of the courtroom. He whispered to Maura, "Get that fellow's picture on your phone there. Be discreet, naturally."

"Naturally," Maura said. She looked over and saw Griff step up and fill the flat screen TV monitor positioned between the jury box and the witness stand. He stared intently into the camera, dressed in standard prisoner garb with horizontal orange and white stripes. "He looks healthy."

"He better. It ain't even been twenty-four hours, yet." Johnny looked over to study Griff's image. "I do believe you are correct about those stripes creating an illusion of enhanced girth."

"And don't forget, the camera adds ten pounds, too."

"Is the defense ready?" the judge asked.

"Just conferring with my associate, your honor."

"Johnny? It's good to see you," said the judge. "Been a little while."

"Judge Hemmings…" Johnny scowled toward Maura, then turned towards the bench with a huge grin. "I am downright tickled to be pleading before you in court again."

"Yes. Well, I pray we will have no recurrence of the unfortunate incident as in the McGreevy trial."

"Oh, no, your honor. I am only here in service of my client, Mr. Crowe."

"Very well. And how is Patty Ann?"

"I regret to inform your honor that she retains that virulently nasty vein of surliness not yet mined out."

"You know, somehow that pleases me to hear. We all have our crosses to bear." The judge, who was nearly Johnny's age, gave him a squinty-eyed smile, then put on a serious expression. "I do sorely miss Mrs. Leonard's apple pie."

"Everybody does."

"William Sewell for the Commonwealth, your honor," Griff's prosecutor interjected.

Judge Hemmings and Johnny both looked at the younger man as if he had emitted audible evidence of a bodily function.

Maura snapped a surreptitious photo of the man Johnny pointed out and quickly sat down in the gallery row directly behind the defense table.

"Mr. Crowe, can you hear us?" Judge Hemmings asked.

"Yes, your honor." Griff's voice was thin and trebly over the link to the Campbell County Detention Center.

"Very well, I'll call this proceeding in the matter of the Commonwealth versus Griffith Crowe, case number 17-CR-00074, to order." The judge looked at the prosecutor. "Now, Mr. Sewell."

"William Sewell for the Commonwealth, your honor."

"E.J. Leonard, appearing on behalf of defendant Crowe. And the court may dispense with the formal reading, your honor."

"As you wish. Let the record show the defendant waives reading of the charges." Judge Hemmings looked at Griff. "Mr. Crowe, you are charged with violations of Kentucky Revised Code 507020, Murder, a capital offense, and Kentucky Revised Code 507030, Manslaughter in the first degree, a Class B felony, in the death of Wescott Eply. How do you plead to these charges?"

"Not guilty, your honor."

"The Commonwealth is asking that the defendant be held without bail," Sewell said. "You should have the Pretrial Services Officer report there before you."

"Mr. Leonard, do you wish to be heard on the subject of bail?"

"No, not at this time, your honor."

"Does your client wish to waive his right to a preliminary hearing?"

"No, your honor. I must respectfully disallow my client being slathered up with mayonnaise and mustard like the proverbial ham sandwich." Johnny smiled and gave a sideways glance at the prosecutor. "Would tomorrow be too soon?"

"Tomorrow?" Sewell's voice betrayed a hint of panic. "I just—"

"Now, Johnny…"

"Your honor, the evidence here is thin—dang near anorexic—there just ain't no pork in the bun and…well, the quicker the sooner."

Judge Hemmings shuffled papers around. "Very well, next Tuesday, the twenty-third. Ten AM."

"Ten AM. Thank you, your Honor." Johnny smiled across the aisle at Sewell.

"Adjourned." Hemmings banged his gavel.

"Good to see you again, Judge Hemmings." He looked to the back of the courtroom and made eye contact with the stranger in the suit.

"You as well. So, until next Tuesday."

Johnny turned to Maura. "Did you get it?"

Article 15

Maura held up her phone and nodded.

The prosecutor approached the defense table and held out his hand. "Bill Sewell, Mr. Leonard."

Johnny's handshake was far firmer than Sewell expected and elicited a slight grimace.

"I noticed your boss elected not to be here this fine morning—what this being a capital case and all. He must have great confidence in you, young man."

"Yeah…I guess." Sewell looked over at Maura.

"How rude of me," Johnny said. "This is my associate, Maura Wiley."

Maura gave the prosecutor a snake-eyed look.

"Pleased to meet you," Sewell said with a leering smile but was dismayed that her grip was every bit as strong as Johnny's. "Would your client entertain a plea deal?"

"Like what? Disturbing the peace with a fifty-dollar fine? Perhaps, but unlikely."

"More like manslaughter with a sentencing recommendation."

Johnny looked at Maura, then back at the prosecutor. "Enjoy your weekend, Mr. Sewell. We shall let you to it, as you surely have much to see to before next Tuesday. Come, Maura."

Sewell watched them leave, then went back to the prosecutor's table to pack up his files.

The man in the suit followed Maura and Johnny out.

~~~

"So, does this outfit make me look fat?" Griff tugged at the sides of his orange and white striped prison shirt when he came into the conference room where Johnny and Maura sat waiting at the Campbell County Detention Center.

"You look like a damned highway construction barrel." Maura laughed.

"Thanks. It's good to see you, too." Griff winked at Maura as he sat down across the table from her and Johnny. "Boy, I have to say you guys sure seem to have a lot of friends behind bars here."

"Son, take a moment for yourself to practice a measure of quiet reflection and recollection." Johnny stared Griff in the eye. "Can you identify even a solitary soul hearkening from your new found community whose visage graces the wall of my office? I have certainly observed you perusing such with great intent on prior occasions."

Griff shook his head. "Well, you two have quite the renown in that *community.*"

"And well we should. You have seen fit to retain a highly regarded legal professional, to which any of the Leonard Group customers and business associates currently enjoying the hospitality of the Commonwealth will gladly attest."

"Business associates?"

Johnny sighed. "Surely you are aware that the best source of new clientele is word-of-mouth, and a highly proactive network of referral agents is an invaluable marketing tool."

"Referral agents?"

"Yeah, you know, like Amazon Associates," Maura said.

"Well, that might explain Johnny's renown amongst my new…*colleagues…*" Griff turned to Maura. "But what about yours?"

Maura shrugged her shoulders and rolled her eyes innocently.

"Show him." Johnny began a great show of pulling legal-sized file folders out of his brief case. He handed one to Maura.

"What's all this?" Griff asked.

"Just for effect my boy. We have to make this visit look all official and sufficiently legalistic-like for benefit of watchful eyes."

Maura pulled a printout of the picture off of her phone for Griff to see the man in the suit from court.

"You know this here fella?" Johnny asked.

Griff took the paper and studied the man's face. He shook his head. "No. Why?"

"You good with remembering faces, are you?" Johnny asked.

Griff nodded. "Yeah. Part of the trade. I don't recognize this guy, but he sure has 'Men-in-Black' written all over him."

"He's some kind of law enforcement. He was carrying inside the courthouse." Maura noticed the questioning look on Griff's face. "Part of *my* trade to recognize when someone's packing heat."

"And the only way to get one's self by the metal detectors with a firearm is with a badge," said Johnny.

"Well, he sure does have the stink of Fed on him. Let's find out. Give me a pen." Griff started writing on the back of the picture then handed it back to her. "Send this message to that number."

Maura read what Griff had written out loud, "T—ID guy in pic ASAP for Captain's Mast. ~Geronimo."

"Geronimo?" Johnny asked.

"Yeah, *not* Tonto." Griff gave Maura a sideways glance.

"Who's T?" asked Maura.

"T-Rex. A connected guy who might be able to help."

"But—"

"Trust me. I trust him."

"Fair enough," said Johnny. "Now, the next time you are afforded phone privileges, give your old pal, Lance, a ring. He will be expecting your call."

"You've talked to him?"

"Just bear in mind that all calls are recorded, so be especially particular in your choice of words."

Griff nodded.

"But be sure to inquire into the lovely and gracious Miss Nickolson's well-being." Johnny smiled.

Maura frowned.

"The pre-trial is scheduled for Tuesday morning at ten."

Griff searched Johnny's face for hope.

"Trust me." Johnny started packing up his file folders again. He paused to give Griff a fatherly look. "How are you holding up, son?"

"All in all, I'd rather be in Philadelphia."

Johnny smiled. "I cannot fathom why, but we shall see to it on Tuesday."

Maura started to say something but stopped, smiled, and reached over to pat the top of Griff's hand to reassure him.

Johnny got up and knocked on the door to get the guard's attention.

They were shown out and Griff was taken back to his cell.

~~

Summer Camp

"Hey, Griffie, how's summer camp?" Lance answered his phone in a sing-song voice.

"Camp North Star all the way."

"Have you met any...*special* friends?"

"Oh, trust me, they're all special."

"Good for you, little fella. Good for you."

"I was instructed to ask how Mrs. Lincoln is enjoying the play."

"Oh, you mean our most very special, favorite-ist *femme fatale* ever?"

"Does she send her love?"

Lance's voice became suddenly curt and business-like. "Haven't heard from her. I've reached out, but…"

"Nada?"

"Nada."

"Well, she got her dad's journals and medals back," Griff said.

"I don't think that's the reason."

"What is it?"

"Rumor has it that she will be putting in a grand appearance next week."

"And not at E.J.'s behest."

"Nope. So, deal with it," Lance said. "He thinks it would be best for you not to have an…adverse reaction in court."

"I'll leave my shocked face here at home, then."

"Be for the best."

"But it might be good, no? Maybe alibi-wise?"

"Oh, Griff, Griff, Griff—I tried to warn you. I tried. Different rules, man. Different rules. Just never underestimate the power of a political campaign contribution to turn steel-hard truth into Silly Putty."

"I'm fucked, aren't I."

"As your attorney, I advise you—"

"But you're not my attorney."

"Griff, you're going to have to trust E.J."

"Do you?"

"Honestly?"

"Yeah, honestly."

"If he was fifty years younger, I'd be hiring him for our litigation team. You're in good hands."

"How's Hannah taking this?"

"I had to talk her out of baking you a pecan pie with a file in it."

Griff sighed.

"You'll see her soon. Trust me."

"Yeah, but you're a lawyer."

"Trust me anyway."

~~

Maura came to the Detention Center Sunday afternoon to visit Griff. They sat in an awkward silence in the visitation center surrounded by the chattering of other inmates and their families under the watchful eyes of guards.

Article 15

"We only have an hour," Maura finally said.

Griff just nodded. "Been to any games lately? How are the Reds doing?"

"I've been a little busy with things and all, you know?"

"So, lots going on at work, then, with you and Dewey?"

"We've been helping Johnny."

Griff just nodded. "So, seen any good movies lately?"

Maura shook her head.

Another awkward silence.

"Anyway, I talked to Lance."

Maura sighed and looked around the visitation center, then back at Griff. "Do you really want to talk about the case or just chit-chat?"

"Chit-chat."

"Okay, so tell me about home."

"What do you mean?"

"When we went to see Cap, you said Pine Hollow was a lot like home. So, tell me about home. Tell me about the ranch. Tell me about Wyoming. I've never been west of the Mississippi."

And for the next forty-five minutes Griff told her about his land, his Arapaho mother and cowboy father, Ben and Swan, Shep and Johnny Eagle, Rodya, Winston, the special place with no name, and his dead brother.

~~

Office Hours

Tuesday morning, just before ten AM, two bailiffs led Griff to the defense table in Courtroom 2 dressed in his jailhouse stripes.

"Good morning, Defendant Crowe. How was your ride over to court?" Johnny asked.

"Hiya, fatso," Maura said. "Ready for Office Hours?"

Griff scowled at her. "Office Hours?"

"It is what we Marines call an Article 15 hearing," Johnny said. "I recollect you referring to it as the 'Captain's Mast' in your communication with Mr. Rex, which is the Navy equivalent of the same."

"Excuse me, but a murder trial is a bit more serious than that."

Johnny looked Griff in the eye, then shook his head. "Nah. Not this one. Trust me."

"Everybody keeps telling me that." Griff looked at Maura. She smiled and nodded.

Their attention was drawn to the entrance as the County Prosecutor entered the courtroom with the man in the suit Maura had photographed at Griff's arraignment. The two sat in the last row of the gallery.

"All rise," called out the bailiff.

Judge Hemmings walked in from his chambers and took his seat on the bench.

After dispensing with the proceeding's formalities, the

prosecution called Newport, Kentucky, Police Detective Paul Douglas to the stand with his murder book to lay out the Commonwealth's evidence in the case against Griff.

Douglas testified dispassionately that late on the night of June 7 or in the early morning hours of June 8, Griff shot Wes Eply five times with a nine-millimeter handgun in Bellevue Beach Park, killing him and leaving the body along the shore of the Ohio River where it was found the next day by municipal workers emptying the trash receptacles. The evidence presented included the Medical Examiner's autopsy report, video footage of the park, receipts from Christopher's Bed and Breakfast, the FAA registration records for Griff's Cirrus, the rental agreement signed by Eply for the National Rental car found abandoned at the uncontrolled Claremont County Airport outside the Class B airspace of the Cincinnati/Northern Kentucky International Airport, and Griff's military service record.

The Commonwealth's theory of the crime was that Griff, fearful of incriminating information Eply uncovered in his research into the holdings of Cliff Nickolson for his and Griff's employer, Baylor, Stein and Baylor, flew into and out of the area under cover of darkness in his private plane, thus avoiding any airline ticket records and TSA surveillance video; killed his colleague; and stole his laptop—which was still missing—to suppress the information and documents collected for reasons which, William Sewell promised, would be made clear shortly, then sat down at the prosecution table.

Johnny looked to Griff sitting next to him and mouthed, "Helena."

Griff nodded, his face impassive.

"Mr. Leonard, cross?" Judge Hemmings asked.

Article 15

"Thank you, your honor." Johnny stood up and buttoned his suit jacket. "Just a point or two of clarification for my edification."

"Proceed."

"Detective Douglas, I am duly impressed at the speed with which you have dispatched this case."

Douglas clasped his hands together and rested them on top of the murder book. He nodded, watching Johnny come around to pace casually in front of the witness stand.

"And you, your own self, developed all of this evidence, yes?"

"I, ah, er…" Douglas looked at Sewell, then to the back row of the gallery. He took a deep breath, then addressed Johnny. "I, um, of course, the department made use of all available law enforcement resources."

"Local, state…and *federal?*"

"Yes. Of course."

"Of course." Johnny stopped to glance towards the back of the courtroom, then continued strolling about, pausing occasionally to look at Detective Douglas. "Now, I seem to recall the autopsy report tallied up five entry wounds, but only found stippling on his forehead from the final fatal shot. Did the folks in forensics happen to test Mr. Eply's clothes for gun powder residue?"

"Yes. There was gunshot residue on the victim."

"So, the four other shots—while not contact wounds—were thrown Mr. Eply's way from a fairly close distance. How close?"

"Mr. Eply and Crowe were acquainted from their work together at Stein, Baylor and Stein, so it is reasonable to presume that the victim had no cause to fear being in close proximity to his assailant. I'd estimate the shots were taken five to fifteen feet or so away—except, of course, for the *coup de grâce.*"

"Refresh my memory, please. Where was the victim struck before he was put down?"

"The right shoulder. Abdomen. Left arm and left thigh."

"Huh, only two shots hit center mass. But you also presented evidence that the defendant was a United States Navy SEAL, a highly trained military commando and expert in the use of firearms. Let me ask you, detective, if, during your own firearm qualification on the police range, you shot a grouping such as was found in the victim's body, would you have passed the Department's minimum standards?"

Douglas exhaled loudly. "No."

"Yet, you are suggesting fifty percent of a Navy SEAL's shots would have failed to leave even holes anywhere in a paper target from five feet away? That ain't right."

"Perhaps, the victim was moving around."

"And perhaps you would like to share the photographic evidence of footprints and scuff marks from your binder which might indicate such activity at the scene of the crime."

"I don't have any such photos."

"If Mr. Eply was moving around to get away from his assailant, then it might be reasonable to expect that he might have been hit from the side or from behind, but all of the five entry wounds were from the front, correct?"

"Yes, that is correct. Maybe the defendant just doesn't spend time on the range anymore."

"And would you have evidence of any such oxidation of Mr. Crowe's shooting skills in your binder, Detective?"

"No. I don't know one way or another."

"Did Mr. Crowe use a Glock 17 or a Walther PPQ to allegedly fire the five bullets into his work colleague?"

Article 15

"I don't know."

"You don't know? Why is that?"

"We did not recover the murder weapon. It is suspected that Crowe threw it into the Ohio River after shooting Mr. Eply in the head."

"Detective Douglas, there are thirty-nine billion rounds of small arms ammunition manufactured each and every year—forty percent of them being nine-millimeter parabellum. What physical evidence do you have to present to us here today linking the five particular bullets fired into the victim—out of the billions and billions and billions, nay trillions of bullets out there rattling around in this old world of ours—to the trigger finger of my client?"

"This is a circumstantial case."

"A circumstantial case which includes no weapon and no ballistics report."

"The victim was killed with jacketed hollow point bullets."

"What is the caliber of your service weapon?"

"Excuse me?"

"Your department issued weapon. When you load its magazine, what caliber bullet do you use?"

"Nine-millimeter."

"Your honor," Sewell said impatiently. *"Please.* The detective is not on trial."

"Seems he could be."

"Move along, Johnny," said the Judge.

"Getting back to this circumstantial evidence. You showed a video of Mr. Crowe in Bellevue Park—and maybe my eyesight isn't as hawk-like as it once was in my misspent youth—but I don't recall seeing a date and time stamp on the screen. Was that particular footage from June seventh or June eighth?"

"The video shown was from May."

"But the Medical Examiner determined that Mr. Eply expired sometime between, say, ten PM the evening of June seventh and three AM June eighth, based on lividity, liver temperatures, and other such scientific medical facts and all, right?"

"That is correct."

"Well, was there a malfunction in the surveillance equipment that particular night or a careless mishandling of the video footage wherein it was misplaced or erased?"

"No."

"Thank goodness. Would you be so kind as to show us the actual video footage from the actual night Mr. Eply was killed?"

"I could, but the defendant does not appear in it."

"Well, that seems to be quite the circumstance, does it not? How could that be?"

"As you noted, Crowe was a Navy SEAL, so he would have likely approached this killing much like one of his SEAL team missions, which would involve reconnaissance and planning. The video footage from early May—the third or fourth, I believe—establishes that he knew the park and, likely, identified the locations of the cameras to avoid detection on the night of the murder."

"The night of the murder being definitively the seventh or the eighth of June."

"Correct."

"And this reconnoitering happening the first week of May, makes this murder premeditated?"

"Definitely."

"Well, then, in addition to being a Navy SEAL, how in the

world did you come to determine that my client is clairvoyant? Or was that in his military service record as well?"

"I don't know what you mean."

"If Mr. Eply only began his inquiry into the holdings of Cliff Nickolson after Memorial Day, then how in tarnation did Mr. Crowe know beforehand that he would need to kill him?"

"Uh, Mr. Eply's laptop has not been recovered."

Johnny stopped facing the witness stand and slowly shook his head. "Well, at least the one indisputable circumstance in this circumstantial case is that Mr. Eply expired in the darkness of June seventh or eighth, correct?"

"That is correct."

"Thank you Detective. No more questions." Johnny returned to the defense table and sat down next to Griff.

"What more do you have for us, Mr. Sewell?"

"Just two more witnesses, your honor."

Johnny looked across the aisle at Sewell. "Bring them on, Mr. Prosecutor."

"Now, Johnny, it's almost eleven-thirty," said the judge.

"I apologize, your honor, for my unseemly salivations at the prospect of fulfilling my duties as an advocate for Mr. Crowe and seeing fit to restore his liberty in the most expeditious fashion possible."

"Down, boy. Down. Let's recess for lunch. Reconvene at one-thirty." Judge Hemmings banged his gavel.

Maura watched the bailiffs take Griff back to the holding cell. She came around to stand by Johnny, placing her hand on his shoulder. "You did good, Papa. No?"

"Won't be enough. Let's see what the afternoon brings."

"Come on, let's get some lunch."

"Better to hunt when you're hungry, my dear."

"Well, let's at least get some fresh air."

Maura and Johnny were the last ones to leave the courtroom.

~~~

Family Affair

After lunch, the occupancy of the gallery in Courtroom 2 was near capacity with the section behind the defense table full. A number of years had passed—nearly a decade—since Johnny last litigated a criminal case, much less one for the capital crime of murder. Reports of his cross examination of Detective Douglas eviscerating the Commonwealth's evidence circulated through the courthouse, arousing the interest of legal professionals, most especially amongst public defenders who were so often outmatched in terms of money and manpower by the government prosecutors, that Griff's preliminary hearing suddenly and unexpectedly found an audience, though few of them knew who E.J. Leonard was.

As Griff was led to the defense table, he noticed Lance sitting in the back row on the prosecution's side of the courtroom, right next to the County Prosecutor and the anonymous Fed. Maura was nowhere to be seen.

I can't believe she would miss Helena testifying, he thought.

"The Commonwealth calls Clifford Nickolson, Junior."

"Hmmm…" Johnny looked at Griff. "Well, he did fairly announce he had two more witnesses. This should be interesting."

Griff nodded.

"Mr. Nickolson, do you know the defendant, Griffith Crowe," asked William Sewell.

"I have met the defendant on only two occasions. Once in the offices of my father's company, the Hornet Investment Group. The second time at a sushi bar at home in Silicon Valley while I was having lunch."

"What was the purpose of those meetings?"

"I believe he was working some kind of scheme to extort or blackmail money from our family."

Griff looked at Johnny and whispered, "Maybe an objection, here?"

Johnny smiled at Griff and patted his arm.

"What makes you think that?" asked Sewell.

"Well, the first meeting, at Hornet Invest, Crowe was actually there to see the Managing Director, Donald Wallace. I just happened to be in Los Angeles to review the quarterly results with Don. I was concerned for his safety, so I made sure I was there in the conference room when Crowe got there."

"Why were you concerned for Mr. Wallace's safety?"

"The night before I received an entry notification text from the security system of my parents' house in Bel Aire, which is on the market. Usually, the realtor gives me advance notice of showings, but hadn't, so I asked the security services company I use to check it out. Three of their men were overpowered, restrained with zip ties, and assaulted with a stun gun."

"After they were zip tied?"

"Yes."

"And their assailant was the defendant?"

"Yes, though we did not know that at the time. Nevertheless, a complete stranger showing up at the Century Tower offices out of the blue the very next day after that incident struck me as just too much of a coincidence."

Article 15

"So, the next day, did the defendant threaten or assault you and Mr. Wallace?"

"Not exactly. Don said the pretext given for the meeting was that Crowe was *helping*," JR paused to gesture air quotes, "Helena recover some missing items of my father's. When I challenged his intentions, he stared at me with a look in his eyes…honestly, I swear he looked like he was trying to figure out how to kill me. It was creepy."

Griff, recalling the meeting, covered his mouth to mask a quiet snort of a laugh.

"What?" Johnny whispered.

"General Mattis. That's exactly what I was thinking."

Johnny smiled. "I knew there had to be a good reason I took such a shine to you."

"That is all? A look?" Sewell asked.

"No. Despite my gut feeling about this guy, I let him and Don have a brief meeting. A couple of days later Don was shot dead in the parking garage. The LAPD said it was a nine-millimeter Glock."

"And you suspect it was the defendant?"

"I didn't connect the dots at the time, 'cause the police said it was a carjacking and Don's Beemer was gone and—you know, you don't really see things so clearly when you're dealing with an unforeseen tragedy like that."

"Are the Los Angeles Police looking into Crowe for this murder?"

Johnny stood up. "At this point, I feel compelled to object, your honor. Relevance, hearsay, or whatever. Perhaps we should focus our attention on crimes which have actually occurred here in the Commonwealth, rather than trying to assist California in solving theirs."

"Sustained."

"Crowe claimed to be working with your sister, correct?" Sewell asked.

"That's what Don said."

"Do you think your sister was involved in this extortion scheme?"

"Trust me, Helena does not need money. Our father's estate was valued at well over a billion dollars and she got half. She's got her Learjet and her home in New Mexico and her apartments in New York, Paris and San Francisco, and a bank balance some small governments only dream of having."

"If not for money, would Helena have other reasons for joining the defendant in his scheme?"

"If I can speak candidly, my sister is a ball buster."

Griff looked to Johnny for an objection.

Johnny just stared at JR like a hungry predator.

"How do you mean?"

"I mean, I am sorry that her mother caught brain cancer and died. That wasn't *my* mother's fault. Or mine. Or that poor sap she married, Edward. She took it out on everyone except our father. And when he died—I mean it was bad enough dealing with the loss of him and my mom in the crash, but she doubled down and fought me every step of the way as executor of his will. It was fair, though. She got half. Just like Dad wanted. And she got all her mom's diamonds, but not my mom's jewelry—not that she really wanted it. She just wanted to twist the knife in my heart, you know?"

"Was she a part of the defendant's scheme?"

"I really didn't think so until the second time I encountered Crowe."

"At the sushi bar?"

"Yeah, he kind of ambushed me at lunch. Must have been stalking me for a couple of days or how else would he know that was my regular place. I had a security detail with me that day because somebody had been taking pot shots at my car and my home. I had found bullet holes in the fender and through the living room window."

"By Crowe?"

"I hadn't gotten any death threats or anything and the cops had nothing to go on, really. But then one day, this guy," JR pointed at Griff.

"Let the record show that the witness identified the defendant," Sewell said.

"This guy gets by my security and sits himself down at the table and starts talking like he knows all about the sniper attacks. How can that be?"

"Did he threaten to kill you?"

"Not in so many words, but he knew. How could he know unless he did it? A short time later, Helena comes in and sits down beside him. And it's like they're Bonnie and Clyde or something."

"What did Helena say?"

"I don't recall exactly. Nothing specific, but the vibe coming off those two was…you know, menacing like. I warned them to leave me alone, because I had taken steps to protect myself. I pointed out my security detail at a nearby table. After that, they left together and all I can think at the time is 'good riddance.' The next thing I know I get a call from Kentucky police about the murder of some guy named Eply who was digging up dirt on my father. It doesn't take a rocket scientist to start figuring out who was behind it."

"Objection," Johnny said wearily. "I do not recall the witness being put forth as an expert in rocketry."

"Sustained. Mr. Sewell?"

"I have nothing more, your honor."

"Mr. Leonard?"

"Thank you, your honor." Johnny sat with his hands flat on the defense table, shaking his head. "Gosh, dang it all, if this don't sound like some kind of tall tale from a Harold Robbins novel—what with all the money and mansions and jets and diamonds and danger and intrigue and whatnot."

"Does the defense actually have any questions?" asked Sewell.

"Of course. Of course." Johnny stood up and stepped in front of the witness box. "You mentioned that your sister, excuse me, your half-sister engaged Mr. Crowe to find items belonging to your father, which had gone missing, correct?"

"That's what he said, anyway."

"What items?"

"I'm not sure. Some notebooks. I think his medals from the Gulf War and some personal trinkets and memorabilia."

"Did you or do you now have possession of these items?"

"No. I did not and do not now"

"Had Helena asked you about these items in the past—being the executor of your father's estate and all."

"She kept harping on it. But it was trivial stuff in the grand scheme of disposing of my father's considerable assets—"

"He was her father, too. No?"

"Yes, of course. Anyway, I figured the items would show up eventually at one of the residences—there were nearly a dozen properties all over the world. You have to understand finding that stuff was way down on the priority list at the time."

"And these notebooks were some kind of diary, correct?"

"Journals. My—*our* father kept a journal for himself. Not some kind of trivial 'Dear Diary' garbage, but an instrument of recollection and reflection, as he always used to tell me. A habit of great men down through history. He tried to get me to do it, too, but it never stuck with me. Besides, who needs it with social media nowadays? Same thing."

"Hardly."

JR casually shrugged off Johnny's opinion.

"It does appear as if there might be quite the trove of *invaluable* information and insights contained on those pages, given your father's experiences, what, from high over the deserts of Iraq in a jet fighter to clawing his way to the very pinnacle of this here planet's financial pyramid. It would be a fascinating ancestral family record and, perhaps, even a window into these contemporary times for future historians. Can you see why Helena might have concern to preserve them?"

"Yeah. Maybe."

"But you cared not about it."

"I got other things on my mind."

"What other things?"

"You mean, besides getting my own tech sector startup company off the ground and still dealing with probate issues and trying to keep on top of managing Hornet Investments—especially now with Don's death? Not to mention dealing with my crazy sister?"

"Oh, that's right. You now own half of your father's company and Helena owns the other half, correct?"

"We each own forty-two-and-a-half percent. Don owned the other fifteen."

"So, Mr. Wallace was the deciding vote, should you and your half-sister have a difference of opinion on corporate matters."

"You could look at it that way, though there haven't been any votes taken. No need, really."

"Do you think any of the recollections and reflections in your father's *journals* might touch on matters of import to Hornet Investment Group? Perhaps about all the companies and individuals and other entities he worked with during his career? Certainly, I'd expect incisive observations on the same from a man of your father's powerful intellect and keen financial acumen. Not to mention a clearly focused documentation of behind-the-scenes corporate activities, strategeries and power play machinations? Who knows, perhaps even government intrigue."

"Yeah. Probably. But what difference does it make? They're missing."

"What if I informed you that they are not, in fact, missing?"

"He found them?"

In his peripheral vision, Lance noticed the suspected Fed's spine stiffen abruptly, so much so, it caused the County Prosecutor to look that way.

"He did. And they make for quite interesting reading." Johnny stopped directly in front of JR and smiled a crooked smile.

"Do you, sir, in all honesty believe your sister was in cahoots with Mr. Crowe to cause you or Donald Wallace or Wes Eply any physical harm?"

Article 15

"I think those two were using one another. That's the kind of person my sister is. A user. And he seems no better. But Helena is not a killer, like him. She likes to squeeze, not crush. So, no. I do not believe she had anything to do with murder."

"I believe the defense is finished with Mr. Nickolson."

'You may step down, sir," said Judge Hemmings.

After JR left the courtroom, Sewell announced, "The Commonwealth calls Helena Nickolson."

Helena entered dressed in a conservative black skirt, matching jacket, and white silk blouse which neither detracted from her beauty nor constrained her sexuality. She took her oath and sat in the witness stand, staring blankly into the gallery, avoiding eye contact with Griff.

"Miss Nickolson, what is your relationship with the defendant, Griffith Crowe?" Sewell asked.

"I have no relationship with Mr. Crowe. He is an employee of one of the law firms I have retained."

"One of the law firms?"

"Isn't that what I just said?"

"And you have no relationship with the defendant?"

"Do you have a relationship with the fry cook at the McDonald's you so obviously frequent?"

"Have you had sexual relations with the defendant?"

"Having sex does not constitute a relationship."

In exasperation, the prosecutor turned to the judge and said, "Your honor, permission to treat this witness as hostile."

"Mr. Leonard?" asked Judge Hemmings.

"I most certainly was not absent from that particular class in law school where they instructed us if your opponent is suicidally destroying his own case, just stand back and enjoy the spectacle. Who am I to object to the Commonwealth presenting a witness so obviously hostile to their own cause, your honor?"

Judge Hemmings shook his head. "A simple 'yes' or 'no' would have sufficed. You best not be so verbose in the presence of a jury, Mr. Leonard. Proceed, Mr. Sewell"

"Have you had sexual intercourse with the defendant?" Sewell asked.

"Of course. Look at him. Who wouldn't? Surely *you* understand exactly what I mean," Helena answered, smiling at Sewell and licking her lips.

The prosecutor blushed visibly.

The judge gaveled down the snickers percolating in the gallery.

"How many times?" Sewell asked.

"Do you mean on how many occasions or how many specific acts of fornication we performed?"

"Your honor, instruct the witness to answer."

"I am so sorry, judge, but my attorney warned me to be very, very careful not to fall prey to—what is it called—oh, yeah, a perjury trap." Helena waved at Lance at the back of the courtroom.

Lance flashed an "Okay" sign to Helena, then leaned over towards the County Prosecutor and the Fed to whisper, "That's my client. Lucky me, huh?"

"Perhaps, you might want to rephrase your question, Mr. Sewell," said Judge Hemmings.

"Okay. Have you had sexual intercourse more than once with the defendant?"

"Yes."

Article 15

"Have you had sexual intercourse with defendant Crowe at your home in New Mexico?"

"Yes. Yes. Yes, and yes. Four times—no. Yes. Five times."

"Quiet." Judge Hemmings gaveled down a ripple of laughter in the gallery.

"Have you had sexual intercourse with defendant Crowe at the Beverly Hills Hotel?"

"Yes. In Bungalow Seven."

"Have you had sexual intercourse with defendant Crowe at his ranch in Wyoming?

"Yes."

"Have you had sexual intercourse with defendant Crowe at the St. Francis Hotel in San Francisco?"

"Yes."

"Do you have a relationship with defendant Crowe?"

"No." Helena looked at Griff for the very first time. "Not yet."

"Were you in Los Angeles at the time Griffith Crowe met with Donald Wallace and your brother, Cliff Nickolson, Jr.?"

"I know who my brother is. Yes."

"Did you kill Donald Wallace?"

"No."

"Did you conspire with the defendant to kill Donald Wallace?"

"No."

"Did you and the defendant meet your brother, Cliff Nickolson, at the Sushi Shack in Menlo Park, California?"

"Yes."

"Did you threaten your brother with harm?"

A clear look of disgust came over Helena's face. She shook her head. "No."

"Did defendant Crowe shoot at your brother's car and home?"

"No."

"How do you know?" Sewell smirked at Helena.

"How do you know he did? My brother? Yeah. Right. Take that to the bank for a laugh."

"Did you hire Defendant Crowe to find your father's journals and war medals?"

"Yes."

"Did he find the journals and medals?"

"Yes."

"Do you have any further need, then, of Mr. Crowe's services?"

Helena sighed. "No. I suppose not."

"I have nothing further, your honor."

"Mr. Leonard?"

Johnny stood up, cocked his head to the side and gave Helena a sympathetic look. He took a photograph out of a file folder and held it behind his back. He walked slowly up to the witness stand, his head bowed as if examining his own shoes. "Miss Nickolson…"

Helena looked at Griff, then back at Johnny. "Yes?"

Johnny looked over to scowl at the prosecutor's table, then turned back to gaze directly into Helena's gunmetal blue eyes. "Please forgive me for the necessary follow up to the Commonwealth's insatiably prurient interest into your romantic life."

Helena shrugged.

"We heard in prior testimony that you are the proud owner of a Learjet. Is that correct?"

"Yes. A Learjet 31."

"What is the N-number of your aircraft?"

Article 15

"November Six-Nine-Six-Papa-Romeo."

"Papa?" Johnny smiled. "I do so sincerely apologize, now, but have you had sexual intercourse with defendant Crowe on Lear Six-Nine-Six-Papa-Romeo?"

Helena smiled. "Yes."

"Your honor, I'd like to have Defense Exhibit A submitted into evidence." Johnny handed the photo to the bailiff to hand to Judge Hemmings. After taking it back, he showed it to William Sewell.

"Any objection, Mr. Sewell?"

"No, your honor."

Johnny handed the photo to Helena. "And is the Learjet 31 which appears in this photograph, the very same aircraft aboard which you hosted said tryst?"

"Yes. Yes, it is."

"Do you recognize the aircraft parked next to your Learjet in this photograph?"

"I do. It is Mr. Crowe's cute little airplane. A Cirrus, I believe he said it was."

"Would you please read the time stamp in the lower right-hand corner?"

"Cowboy Aviation Security Camera Three; June 8, zero four one eight."

"Four eighteen in the morning. And would that have been the night of your romantic encounter with Mr. Crowe?"

"Yes. I believe it is."

"Where is Cowboy Aviation located, Miss Nickolson?"

"Laramie, Wyoming."

"A mere one thousand, two hundred sixty miles from here as the crow flies." Johnny looked at the prosecutor, then back to

Helena. "Thank you, darling. And again, I apologize. Nothing further your honor."

"The Commonwealth rests, your honor," said Sewell.

"Mr. Leonard, will you present a defense?"

"I have only one witness, your honor. We shall require a mere ten or fifteen minutes...or so of the court's time."

"Very well, let's take a twenty-minute recess."

Johnny came over and leaned with his hands on the defense table in front of Griff. "Poor Judge Hemmings. He's got one angry prostate bedeviling his bladder relief schedule. Gives me pause to count my blessings I am haunted only by Patty Ann to aggravate my quickly fleeting days. You need to use the head, Griff?"

"No, but just one witness?"

"Why use more when one will do?" Johnny looked over the people milling about the gallery.

"Who is it?"

"You've drawn quite a crowd, son. I ain't seen this much public interest in a case since O.J."

"And you're going to get me off like O.J., right?"

"If it does not fit, you must acquit. I always did favor that Johnny Cochrane fella."

"And you're going to get me off, right?"

Johnny smiled. "Trust me."

"But you're a lawyer."

"But I am *your* lawyer. And a one damn fine practitioner of *jurisprudence.*"

~~~

Buffalo Burgers

Once the hearing reconvened, Johnny stood up and said, "Your honor, the defense calls Roy Estes to the stand."

Griff turned around to watch Maura lead a slight, bald-headed man into the courtroom, who looked vaguely familiar. Griff looked at Lance at the back of the gallery and caught his eye.

Lance smiled broadly. He cocked his head towards the County Prosecutor and the Fed sitting beside him and rolled his eyes up in their sockets.

Griff nodded and watched Maura sit down in the first row behind the defense table as Estes went through the swearing-in protocol.

Maura winked at Griff.

Johnny came around the defense table into the well to address the witness. "Mr. Estes, do you recall what entrée it was you enjoyed for your lunchtime sustenance on June seventh?"

"Objection. Relevance, your honor?" the prosecutor stood up. "What could this man's menu selection possibly have to do with the matter at hand?"

"If it please the court," Johnny said, "I may have to amend my prior estimate of the time required of this proceeding to indulge the defense its sole witness, if the answer to my every question is going to be interrupted all jack-in-the-box-like."

"*Johnny.*" The judge sighed impatiently. "Mr. Sewell, why

don't we just get a few of this witness's answers under our belt before we draw our conclusions. It's the only one he's got. Proceed, Mr. Leonard."

"I apologize, Mr. Estes, for the rude interruption."

"No matter. Don't have any place else I need to be at the moment."

"Now, you were about to share with us information about your noontime repast on June seventh."

"I had my usual."

"And what is your usual?"

"A buffalo burger."

Griff suddenly recognized the witness. He sat back and smiled.

"Would this buffalo burger have been served here locally at one of this area's fine dining establishments?"

"No. This was at Nancy's place, the Sage Creek Grille."

"Pray tell, Mr. Estes, where is Nancy's place situated?"

"Back home in Custer, South Dakota."

Sewell sighed loudly as he rested his chin on his palm at the prosecutor's table, affecting a bored expression on his face.

Johnny looked back at him and smiled, then continued. "Was there anything of note which occurred that noontime in the dining room of the Sage Creek Grille in Custer, South Dakota, while you were enjoying your bison sandwich?

"Well, there were two fellows at the next table discussing airplanes. I'm embarrassed to admit eavesdropping on their conversation, but, you know, it struck a chord with me."

"Why is that?"

"Well, I'm a pilot, myself."

"Oh, Mr. Estes, do not be so modest. What sort of work do you do?"

Article 15

"I'm an FAA Designated Examiner, so I give check rides for the issuance of pilot licenses. Before that, I took full retirement from the Air Force. Flew combat missions in Vietnam—these two other guys were veterans, too."

"Do you see either of these two men here in court today?"

"Yeah. I saw Lance in the back row. And Griff, there, sitting at the table."

"Could we let the record show that the witness pointed to the defendant, Griffith Crowe, please?" Johnny said. "So, you know these two men by name? How did this come to pass?"

"After lunch, I approached them outside Nancy's place while they were waiting for a cab to introduce myself and engage in a little hangar talk—you know, compare notes on our rides. I mean, the different airplanes we've flown."

"What time of day did this session of hangar talk occur?"

"It was one-thirty. I had a check ride scheduled for three and was heading out to the airport."

"One-thirty in Custer, South Dakota, which would be three-thirty back here in Newport. Am I close?"

"That's right."

"You say they were waiting for a cab?"

"Lance and Griff were going up to the Monument for a little sightseeing, then they were flying to Fargo for Lance to pick up his King Air to head back home to Chicago."

"And would this particular monument happen to be of the national variety?"

"Mount Rushmore."

"And how far—by cab, that is, not airplane—would Mount Rushmore be from Nancy's place?"

"Takes about a half-hour or so to get to the park from Custer."

"Do you know how long the defendant and Mr. Baylor spent gazing upon our most revered Commanders-in-Chief?"

"No, not directly. But Griff's Cirrus was still parked at the airport when I finished with the check ride at seven."

"Let me attempt to wrap my mind around the events of this particular afternoon, the seventh of June. After lunch, around one-thirty, the defendant, Mr. Crowe, and his pal, Lance Baylor, took a cab from the Sage Creek Grille to Mount Rushmore; toured one of our nation's most iconic National Park monument sites and all it has to offer; returned by cab to the Custer County airport sometime after seven PM—local time—then departed for a flight to Fargo, North Dakota. What would the estimated time en route be for such a flight from Custer County Airport to Fargo, North Dakota?"

"A couple of hours or so in Griff's Cirrus. Depends on the tailwind."

"Depart Custer after seven PM. Arrive Fargo after ten PM—'cause they are on Central Time, so I add an hour if I am not mistaken. Drop off Mr. Baylor and see to refueling the defendant's plane. So, a half-hour or so on the ground before Mr. Crowe departs Fargo. At the moment of his takeoff, the clock on the wall there in Fargo would likely read, say, ten-thirty, maybe close to eleven local time, or approaching midnight here in Newport. Further, that we have seen photographic evidence of Mr. Crowe's Cirrus aeroplane being parked on the tarmac at the Laramie, Wyoming, airport at four-eighteen the morning of June eighth for a romantic encounter of the type the prosecution finds so disturbingly interesting. Mr. Estes, as an aviation expert and a man of good character—what you being acknowledged as such by this here country's Federal Aviation

Article 15

Administration bestowing upon you the sacred role of keeping our nation's airspace safe by appointing you as one of their Designated Examiners—what would your opinion be if I told you that the Commonwealth of Kentucky has arrested Mr. Crowe for the murder of one Wescott Eply between the hours of ten PM June seventh and three AM June eighth here in Newport, Kentucky?"

"I'd have to say they've arrested the wrong man."

"Why is that—speaking as an aviation expert and man of good character and all?"

"There is just no way to travel those distances in the time allotted without somehow warping the time-space continuum—not even in an SR-71 Blackbird."

"And what is the unladen cruising speed of this Blackbird of which you speak?"

"Three times the speed of sound. About two thousand two hundred miles per hour."

"So, faster than the muzzle velocity of a nine-millimeter pistol?"

"Sounds about right."

"And faster than Mr. Crowe's cute little airplane?"

"Yes, sir. An order of magnitude faster—I mean, ten times faster."

"Thank you, Mr. Estes. No further questions." Johnny sat down next to Griff and folded his hands on the table in front of him.

"Mr. Sewell?" Judge Hemmings asked.

"Thank you, judge. I'll be brief." The prosecutor stood up behind his table to ask his questions. "I thank you for your service and certainly mean no disrespect to you, but we only have your word here with regards to the defendant's presence in Custer, South Dakota, on the date in question. Would there be any corroborating evidence to support your testimony?"

"Well, I believe Jen waited on Lance and Griff. She might recall them being there. My insurance guy, Ned, might remember meeting them outside Nancy's place, but then again, they didn't buy any policies, so maybe not. And, of course, the cab driver—"

"But none of these individuals are here today."

"I suppose not."

"So, do you have any evidence to corroborate your testimony?"

"Well, I know Hank Thacker. He's a local controller at Fargo, and I gave him his instrument check ride. I called Hank and he—"

"Is Hank Thacker here in court today?"

"Not that I am aware of, but he gave—"

"Then, no. Hank Thacker is not here either."

"Your honor, I must object. Mr. Sewell has twice asked for corroboration and has twice interrupted the witness as he has struggled mightily to have his answer heard by this court. I suggest, perhaps, we give a listen to what Mr. Estes has to say. I must admit my own curiosity has been sufficiently aroused."

"Sustained. The witness may answer."

"I was talking to Hank about Lance and Griff and their airplanes and that they had recently passed through Fargo. He said he was working that night and took a picture of the tower logs with his phone and sent it to me." Roy held up his phone with the picture of a document on the screen." It shows the times they arrived and departed Hector International."

"All you have is a picture of these logs, correct?"

"Yes, sir."

Article 15

"Have you seen the actual physical paper logs themselves?"

"No, sir."

"So, you still have no tangible proof to support your testimony. After all, we cannot very well admit your cell phone into evidence, can we?"

"Don't know. I'm not a lawyer. I don't know how all this works."

"No further questions, your honor."

"Redirect, your honor?" Johnny stood up and dug into his briefcase. He pulled out a couple of documents and a pair of DVDs. "Mr. Estes, you testified that Mr. Hank Thacker is a local controller at the Hector International Airport in Fargo, North Dakota. What does a local controller do?"

"He works in the tower cab and, depending on which position he's working, Hank might be clearing aircraft for takeoff or landing, positioning aircraft on the ground, or issuing IFR clearances."

"IFR? What does that mean?"

"Instrument Flight Rules."

"Part of Hank's responsibilities would be to scribble down the N-numbers of the various planes being handled, along with their times of arrival and departure. Correct?"

"Yes. That's what this log is." Roy held up his phone again.

Johnny stepped over and handed Roy one of the documents. "Is this the tower log that appears on your phone?"

"Objection." Sewell stood up. "Just because Mr. Leonard printed out the photo from the witness's phone, doesn't make it official."

"Oh, no, your honor, this here certified copy of said logs was obtained officially from the Federal Aviation Administration, themselves. Not Mr. Estes' phone."

"And you are going to submit this into evidence?" asked Judge Hemmings.

"Indeed, that was what I was endeavoring to do when, once again, Mr. Sewell interrupted." Johnny handed the bailiff the log to pass to Judge Hemmings.

"Mr. Sewell, do you care to examine this document?" The judge motioned the prosecutor to approach the bench.

"We also made a point of asking the FAA for a copy of the recorded tower radio transmissions for the night of June seventh at Hector International Airport in Fargo." Johnny handed the Bailiff one of the DVDs, then the second document. "This here is a transcript of those tower communications with arriving and departing aircraft that night. I have taken the liberty of highlighting the radio communications between Mr. Crowe and Air Traffic Control for your convenience. The Laramie Regional Airport has no control tower, so no tapes are available of his arrival there. But, of course, we do have the Cowboy Aviation security camera photos previously entered into evidence of Mr. Crowe's Cirrus parked on the tarmac. Further, the FAA was kind enough to provide radar track videos of Mr. Crowe's aircraft departing Fargo westbound at ten thirty-seven PM local time on the seventh and arriving in Laramie area at one twelve AM the morning of June eighth. The defense proposes to play these recordings and videos for Mr. Estes, in order for us laymen to get his expert aviation opinion on the information contained therein to alleviate the Commonwealth's trepidations overshadowing this witness's veracity."

Judge Hemmings handed the logs, transcripts, and DVDs to Sewell for his examination. "This witness's testimony that

Article 15

you might have the wrong man, is, evidently, not without *corroboration*, Mr. Sewell."

"It does give one pause," Johnny concurred.

The prosecutor looked at the stack of evidence about to be admitted and sighed heavily. "Your honor, may I have a moment to confer with the County Prosecutor?"

"Gosh, who would have seen that coming?" Lance leaned over and asked the County Prosecutor.

"You would have, you asshole."

"I kinda did."

The County Prosecutor stood and went to meet his employee at his table when Sewell waved him forward.

"I'm Lance Baylor, Senior Partner at Stein, Baylor and Stein." Lance offered to handshake the Fed.

The Fed scowled at Lance's paw as if it were maggot infested roadkill. He folded his arms across his chest and looked back to Sewell conferring with his boss. "He was right. You are an asshole."

"Well…that *is* my job."

The County Prosecutor stormed out of the courtroom.

William Sewell skulked back up to the bench.

Concluding the sidebar, Judge Hemmings motioned the attorneys back to their respective tables. "The court hereby accepts the FAA Tower logs into evidence as Defense Exhibit 2; the FAA recordings of Tower radio communications into evidence as Defense Exhibit 3; the transcript of FAA Tower radio communications into evidence as Defense Exhibit 4; and the FAA video of Air Traffic Control radar tracks into evidence as Defense Exhibit 5. The parties further stipulate that this evidence shows the Cirrus S-22, owned by and piloted by Defendant Crowe, departed Hector International Airport in Fargo, North Dakota, June seventh at zero-one-three-seven Universal Coordinated Time and arrived in Laramie, Wyoming, June eighth at approximately zero-five-one-two Universal Coordinated Time."

"Your pal, Lance, really came through for you in procuring these evidential items," Johnny whispered to Griff as they listened to the judge. "I sincerely hope he exercises some modicum of restraint from lording it over you in the future."

"Mr. Estes, you are excused. Thank you for coming all that way." Judge Hemmings watched the witness leave the courtroom. "Mr. Sewell?"

The prosecutor rose. "Your honor, in light of this new evidence, the Commonwealth moves to drop all charges against Griffith Crowe."

"Mr. Leonard?"

"No objection, your honor."

"So moved. The defendant is ordered released from custody. I apologize, Mr. Crowe, for any inconvenience or hardship caused by the Commonwealth, but justice has been served here today. You are free to go."

The Fed got up and left the courtroom.

"Court is adjourned," declared Judge Hemmings, rapping his gavel.

"Thank you," Griff said to Johnny as he and the lawyer stood up from the defense table.

"Oh, no. Thank you for choosing the Leonard Group." Johnny packed up his briefcase. "I do trust you might see fit to refer your friends and...*colleagues* to us for all of their legal and judicial needs. After all, word-of-mouth is the best marketing."

"Of course." Griff looked Johnny in the eye and smiled.

Article 15

"Congratulations, Griff," Maura reached over the bar to grab his hand.

"Glad it worked out for you, son. Maura and I will meet up with you after you have shed those stripes." Johnny gave Griff's bicep a squeeze. "Then, you can take care of the scoundrels who dared to perpetrate this foul deed."

Griff looked over his shoulder at them as the bailiff led him away to process his release.

"Just don't get caught," Maura called out.

"But if you do…" Johnny grinned at Griff.

~~~

Freedom

When the Kentucky legal system spit Griff back out dressed in civvies with his personal belongings returned, Lance was there waiting for him.

"Where's Johnny and…"

"Maura? Yeah, you know, she's kind of cute—in a wayward daughter sort of way." Lance correctly read disappointment in Griff's eyes. "They're soaking up the lime light of the local news media over his victory. Man, the guy looks so happy. But I figured you really wouldn't want to be part of that whole circus."

"No. Not at all."

"So, let's make this pop stand a memory." Lance put his arm around Griff and pulled him towards a back exit. "Besides, I could have sworn I caught the aroma of fresh baked pecan pie when I left the office."

Forty minutes later they were on the ramp at Lunken Field in the cockpit of the Stein, Baylor & Stein King Air, Lance in the left seat going through the checklist to bring the Pratt and Whitney PT6 engines to life and Griff in the right slowly coming to the full realization that his legal ordeal was over.

Ground control told Lance to stand by as his IFR clearance to Chicago Executive Airport was on request.

"Chicago Exec?" Griff asked.

"What? Did you think I was kidding? Hannah's got a special home-cooked meal all planned for you. Or did you develop a liking for institutional cuisine and all male companionship?"

"I just want to get home."

"Sure, I understand. Tomorrow. It's been a long day, and I've got the Citation on call in the afternoon to take you."

"Thanks." Griff watched a Gulfstream G-5 taxi across their nose heading out of Signature Aviation. He recognized the N-number from the NTSB accident report. "That's Hornet Investment's bird."

"Cliff Junior, riding in style," Lance said.

"Rat bastard."

"Eh…"

"Johnny says I owe you for the FAA data dump."

"Big time. I got rope burn pulling strings for you."

"Well, thanks."

"Oh, I'll get my payback. Don't you worry your pretty little head about that."

"Just not today."

Lance gave Griff a sideways glance and smiled. "Not today."

Ground control called with their clearance. After Lance repeated it back, she said, "Eight-Six-Bravo, read back correct. Taxi to Runway two-five via Alpha. Give way to the Lear turning off Charlie."

The props bit the air loudly as Lance increased the blade pitch to get them rolling. He pulled a U-turn to exit the Signature Aviation ramp just in time for them to see a very familiar Learjet 31 make a right turn onto taxiway Alpha.

"Looks like everybody hung around to catch the compelling

conclusion to your little legal drama," Lance said as he pulled out to follow Helena's jet to Runway 25. "I do hate rush hour traffic."

Griff stared out the windscreen, his face set hard in an unsmiling expression.

"I wouldn't think too harshly of her. She might not exactly have been a willing nor particularly cooperative witness for the prosecution."

Griff thought for a moment, then asked, "Was that by design?"

"I don't know," Lance said in a sing-song voice. "Maybe."

They stopped behind Helena's Learjet at the departure end of Runway 25.

"Eight-Six-Bravo, contact tower at the line. Number three. Waiting on release."

"Anyway, she asked me to give you this." Lance reached into his flight bag and pulled out a bottle of fifty-year-old Balvenie single malt scotch. He handed it to Griff. "We'll crack that bad boy when we get to Chi-town. Never had fifty thousand dollar a bottle hooch before."

JR's Gulfstream departed in a roar. Lance crept forward as the Lear pulled up to the runway hold line.

"My bonus." Griff looked at the bottle, then set it back into the flight case.

"She instructed me to put Johnny's fee on her tab and doubled yours."

"Soothing a guilty conscience?"

"No. I don't think so."

"A pat on the head for a job well done. *Good boy. Good dog.*"

"Lear Six-Papa-Romeo, right turn to three-zero-zero.

Cleared for takeoff," came over the radio from the tower controller.

The Lear rolled onto the runway and spooled up its engines.

Lance turned ninety degrees and pulled up to the hold line.

Griff watched out his side window as Helena's jet jumped off the runway and flew away to the west.

Déjà Vu

The next morning, Griff sat in a shadow in the dimly lit and extremely well-appointed war room, sipping coffee from a massive, dark mug with Stein, Baylor & Stein gilded on the side. His psyche struggled mightily—as Johnny put it in court—to allow the memory of a delicious home-cooked meal and the warm, naked embrace of a beautiful and sensual woman the night before to triumph over and mask the deep and foreboding sense of *déjà vu* haunting him.

"Miss me?" teased Lance, baring his canines in a huge smile as he burst into the small, oak-paneled conference room tucked away back among the partner offices.

"That did not help," Griff said.

"What?"

"Oh, no. *Oh, no.*" Griff suddenly realized he was reliving the very day he first met Helena Nickolson.

"I have a little surprise for you," Lance said.

"I *hate* surprises," Griff growled lowly. In spite of his inside voice's warning, he felt himself instinctively grasp at a slender thread of hope.

"I know, but…" Lance winked. "You owe me. remember?"

"How could I ever forget?"

Lance stepped back out of the room and waved to someone down the hall to join him.

"Goddamn it, Lance."

Lance just looked back into the war room and smiled.

"You have got to be fucking kidding me," Griff said as he rose to his feet when the tall, buff man who looked like the illegitimate spawn of Richard Nixon and a blonde surfer dude came through the door.

"I believe you know Cliff Nickolson, Junior," Lance said, following JR into the room.

Griff and JR stared one another down.

JR finally looked away. "I, ah, apologize."

Lance put his hand on JR's shoulder and led him to sit in the chair catty-corner across from Griff, next to his seat at the head of the conference table. "Griff. *Griff.* Down, boy. Sit. Sit."

Griff slowly sat back down at the same time as Lance.

A pretty Asian woman pushed a serving cart into the room. She placed a platter of pastries and a small tray with cream and sugar on the table. She poured a cup of coffee for Lance and JR. She came around to top off Griff's mug.

"Thank you, Mae Lynn," Lance said.

She placed the pot on the table and left, closing the door behind her.

Lance took a sip of coffee. He looked at JR sitting beside him, then down the table at Griff, as the two glared at one another like rival pack animals. He took another sip. "So, this is nice. Making amends and all."

"Steve and Allen. They here, too?" Griff asked

"Downstairs in the Starbucks," Lance said. "Cooling their heels."

"Wonderful."

"You know, Griff, it seems to me you fellas have

something very important in common. Think about it." Lance took a sip of coffee, then noticed both Griff and JR had turned their alpha male stares his way. "No, no, no. Not her."

"Maybe this isn't a good idea," JR said.

"Just because Johnny so ably disposed of your legal problem doesn't mean your troubles are over." Lance set his cup down and looked Griff in the eye. "Maura heard back from your buddy in Norfolk, T-Rex."

"The Fed in court?"

"Yeah. He's an all-star evil doer seemingly headed for the bad guy hall of fame."

"Great," said Griff.

"Yeah. And now I'm on his shit list, too," said JR. "Along with you and my sister."

"Too bad for you," Griff said. "But welcome to my world."

"And you know how misery loves company and brings folks closer together in common cause," Lance said, smiling broadly. "God, I love my job—helping people, that is."

"And now I'm supposed to save his ass, too," Griff said. "After what he tried to do to me in court."

"Now, I thought we were going to let bygones be bygones—and you better, Griff," Lance said. "Besides, he and Helena really didn't have much choice."

Griff winced at the mention of her name. His inside voice told him to keep his fucking mouth shut. "There is always a choice to be made."

"And you best make the right one," Lance said. "We can't put down Goliath if all the Davids keep squabbling amongst themselves."

"So, what was the point—the *real* point—of finding those journals?" Griff asked JR. "Not sentimental, was it?"

"No." JR sighed. "I honestly don't know if she was trying to drown me…or save me."

"This is all about Hornet's tech sector divestiture, right?" Lance asked.

JR nodded. "But they had their hooks in me, too."

"So, what was it? Did Daddy Warbucks come down with a bad case of the morals all of the sudden about taking dirty government money?" Griff asked.

"Fuck no." JR shook his head. "You know what my very first lesson in business was at Dad's knee? He asked me why Willie Sutton robbed banks."

"Because that's where the money is," said Lance.

"Yeah. Then he asked me, who printed all the money in all those banks?"

"The government," said Griff.

"Lesson One: Willie Sutton was a chump change chump."

"I wouldn't think Silicon Valley types would want the government all up their skirts," Lance said. "Tax dollars usually come with strings attached."

"You gotta understand these guys. They're the Masters of the Universe. The smartest guys in any and every room they walk into. And greedy bastards to boot—they don't play whose dick is the longest." JR took a sip of his coffee. "And if you think these guys aren't picking the pockets of the Treasury all the while laughing out loud behind the backs of the lame-oid bureaucrats sent to babysit them…well…"

"Lame-oid bureaucrats with Predator drones, Hellfire missiles, and Navy SEALs on speed dial," Lance said, looking at Griff.

Article 15

"Not to mention Spook Central in Langely." Griff shook his head.

"Yeah, well, remember the Arab Spring? Social media toppling the Tunisian and Egyptian governments?" JR asked. "You don't think that didn't go to their heads? I mean the President of the United States was coming to Silicon Valley to have lunch with all these guys."

Lance and Griff looked at one another and shook their heads.

"Who's pulling whose strings?" Lance asked Griff.

"Yeah. Right." Griff looked at JR. "You don't think the aforementioned spooks didn't have anything at all to do with Murbarak getting the boot? Off camera from all CNN's pretty boy stand ups from Tahrir Square?"

"Perception is reality." JR shrugged his shoulders. "Especially in cyberspace."

"And who had their hooks in you?" Lance asked.

"Likely the *aforementioned* spooks. I took Dad's lesson to heart. While I was making the rounds for VC funding, I moonlighted by muling code back from India."

"What kind of code?"

"Data mining social media mainly. They'd give me the parameters. And I'd bring back algorithms from Mumbai. The NSA has a boat load of RAID arrays to fill in Utah. What did I care as long as their money was green?"

"Do you care, now?" Lance asked.

JR hung his head low and nodded. "Yeah."

"So, why did your father decide to divest?" Lance asked.

"Strictly a business decision. Dad was a master tea-leaf reader. I guess when you fly MACH two, you learn to think and react way ahead of where you are right now. Business Lesson

Number Two: buy low; sell high. He tried to warn me. He saw rough waters ahead for the tech sector. Facebook, Twitter and YouTube reaching critical mass, getting to the point where they really had to decide what they wanted to be when they grew up. That's going to be a painful process, as you can see, what with these guys picking censorship fights with their own users and pissing off half the political population. Then you've got the smoldering tire fire of tracking people's every whim and folly online to abuse their privacy for fun and profit and...*whatever*. Thank you, Edward Snowden for bringing *that* to everyone's attention. Not to mention internal rebellions. It ain't pretty having Google employees demand the company stop doing business with the Department of Defense. Yeah. Right. As if money *isn't* the only thing more addictive than crack cocaine. And like Alphabet is going to just let Bezos walk away with all that cash being pocketed by Amazon Web Services. It's all kind of a mess. And cleaning up messes tends not to be very profitable. So, Dad decided it was time to move on and find the next shiny new thing—which, of course, got some people's panties all up their cracks—perception being reality on Wall Street, too."

"I can't believe they'd actually start putting metal on meat because of it," Griff said.

"You'd be surprised how protective people get of their cash flow," said Lance.

"And it's not like we're curing cancer or actually putting food into people's mouths," said JR. "It's all just a house of cards nobody really needs that can come tumbling down faster than a cocaine addict's heartbeat. Believe me, when you catch lightning in a jar, you'll do anything to hold on to it."

Article 15

"I find it hard to believe your father could really bring down Google." Lance shook his head.

"The big guys—they'd be okay. Maybe their quarterly reports might not be so rosy and their share price might take a hit for a little while, but they'll lumber on," JR said. "It's the little guys who die hard. Not so much a bubble bursting as a financial tide going out sucking up all the cash. The lucky ones survive—if their little tide pool is deep enough or a big kahuna swims in and takes advantage of a fire sale. Either way, the early investors take it in the shorts. The unlucky ones lose it all."

"I reckon it does take only one shot to start a stampede." Griff looked at Lance and asked, "So, who's the ambitious black hat you befriended in court?"

"According to T-Rex, his name is Seth Valance. Former 75th Ranger Regiment, former Company Cowboy, former Blackwater Associate. Evidently, he is currently pursuing a career as a ten ninety-nine independent consultant in the anti-hospitality industry. He's kind of like you, only for the Dr. Evils of the world."

"And which Dr. Evil is picking up his tab at present?"

"Talon Technology Group is the eight-to-five favorite on the Vegas betting line," said Lance.

"I've heard of it," JR said. "A small consortium of Highlands Group guys. Mostly government types trying to cash in for themselves."

"You'll have to forgive Wilkinson," Lance said to Griff. "He's still pretty spooked about what happened to Eply and didn't really want to take this meeting, so I let him off the hook."

"Does he blame me?" Griff asked.

"No, not at all. And he's pretty pissed off about it, so he's still digging hard into Blue Wing, Talon and the other names in Nicholson's journals. Can't hold it against him, though, for wanting to keep a low profile."

"Yeah. Me, too," muttered Griff.

"So, what do we do now?" JR asked.

"Me? I'm going home. You best stick close to Allan and Steve—better yet, get yourself some real protection. Your sister, too." Griff looked at Lance. "Tell Wilkinson I'm sorry about Eply. Tell him I'll make sure it gets taken care of—and get me everything he's got so far."

"I love it when a plan comes together." Lance rubbed his hands together.

"Plan? What plan?" JR asked.

"Trust us. We know what we're doing."

~~~

Homeward Bound

Hannah drove Griff to Chicago Executive Airport, while Lance tended to the collection of a retainer from JR and issuance of the engagement letter. They sat on the sofa in the Atlantic Aviation passenger lounge waiting for the NetJets Cessna Citation to arrive under Tiffani's watchful eye. Not unaware of their audience, Hannah took Griff's hand and gently massaged it.

Griff stared at the sign pointing down the hall to the pilot lounge. He could not help but feel a sense of *déjà vu* all over again, so much so, he could almost smell Ralph Lauren Perfume Notorious in the air.

The high-pitched whine of turbine engines grew as the Citation taxied up. With a last look over her shoulder at the reception desk, Hannah walked Griff out on the tarmac. They watched the jet stop and the line boys roll out the red carpet on the asphalt. The cabin door opened. The co-pilot motioned Griff aboard while the engines idled.

Griff took a step forward, but Hannah pulled him back. Too loud to speak, he pulled her to him and gave her a long, smoldering kiss.

Hannah gave Griff a last peck on the cheek, then let him go. She watched him walk over and step up into the jet. The doors closed. A moment later the engines spooled up.

When he stepped into the fuselage, Griff was brought up

short by the two passengers already on board. "Wilkinson? And *you*...Does your grandfather know where you are?"

"*What is it* with you and blondes?" Maura pointed out the window at Hannah on the tarmac watching them taxi away. "Papa warned me about boys like you."

"What are you doing here?"

"Unfinished business...and I figured it was about time I explored the land on the other side of the Mississippi River...and you promised me the day I visited you in jail that I could come see the ranch. Remember? Or were you just being your typical lying skel?"

"A promise is a promise." Griff sat down across the aisle from Maura and strapped himself in. "And I keep my promises. How's Johnny?"

"Anxiously awaiting your next call from jail. He ain't had that much fun in a long, long time."

Griff laughed. "I've had my share of that kind of fun."

It wasn't long before they were cruising nearly eight miles high over the corn fields of western Illinois. Maura watched out the window as they crossed the Mississippi River.

When the "Fasten Seat Belt" light went out, Roger Wilkinson came up from the back row and sat down at the table across from Griff. He set a stack of file folders down on the table.

"I'm really sorry about Eply," Griff said. "I thought you didn't want to be seen with me."

"I don't, particularly—and hopefully haven't been."

"Can you blame him?" Maura asked. "Besides, I don't trust Helena's brother any farther than I can throw him. How could you stand to be in the same room with him?"

"The mental exercise of planning the death of the person sitting across the table from you sometimes has an oddly calming effect."

"I don't know if I want to be hearing that," Wilkinson said.

"I am represented by Stein, Baylor and Stein, which means you're my lawyer, too. So, it's covered by privilege."

"Yeah…but I happen to be sitting across the table from you."

"Come on, Griff. We need Roger," Maura said.

"For what?"

Over the next two hours, Wilkinson briefed Griff on the information gathered on the Talon Technology Group and its two principal partners. He also handed over maintenance files on Cliff Nickolson's Bell 406 and information on an upcoming Highlands Group meeting the following week.

Maura went through a very disturbing file full of information from T-Rex on Seth Valance.

"I'm not getting off," Wilkinson said when they landed and parked at Harvey Field in Rawlins, Wyoming. "I'm meeting JR in Los Angeles to go over the Hornet Investment Group books."

"I'll get this guy, Valance," Griff said.

'We'll get this guy," Maura corrected.

"We will get him—and the rest of them, too." Griff held out his hand.

"Just have Lance let me know what I can do to help," Wilkinson shook Griff's hand.

"You be careful, Roger," Maura said. "I still don't trust him."

When Maura and Griff stepped off the plane, Rodya bounded towards them across the ramp. Griff went down on one knee and let the Husky lick his face as he scratched his head.

"Who's that?" Maura pointed to the gate.

Griff stood up. "That's our ride home."

Rodya sniffed at Maura's feet, then sat down next to Griff. Ben walked over.

"Maura, this is Ben, the best friend and ranch hand a guy could have. Ben, meet Maura. She's a bounty hunter—"

"Recovery agent."

"I stand corrected."

"Pleased to meet you, ma'am." Ben tipped his Bullhide leather cowboy hat, then gave Griff a wayward glance. "Though I can't say as I speak for Swan."

"It's not like that," Griff said.

"It never is, is it? We'll see." Ben grabbed Maura's duffel bag. "I hope you brought your appetite, ma'am. You made it in time for dinner."

They piled into Ben's Silverado for the drive home to the ranch.

~~~

Milky Way

The kitchen fell dark again as Griff pulled out two bottles of Bass Ale, then shut the refrigerator door. He stepped back out on the deck behind the ranch house and paused to consider Rodya's head laying in Maura's lap, eyes blissfully closed as she gently scratched behind his ear.

"Man's best friend, huh?" Griff handed her one of the bottles. "Mangy mutt."

Rodya opened his eyes to watch Griff sit down beside Maura, then closed them again with a dismissive soft snort.

"How quickly they forget—and I wasn't even in jail for a whole week."

"Maybe he can still smell it on you. It is a stink that lingers."

"And what would be your professional recommendation? Tomato juice?"

"Couldn't hurt."

Griff took a swig of his beer and stared into the clear night sky.

"That steak was amazing." Maura looked over at Griff and smiled. "Even better than the one you bought me at Ruth Crist."

"Fresh off the hoof."

"Does Ben do that every Thursday?"

"Just once a month."

"So, why are you getting to be as bad as Johnny Eagle?" Maura asked.

"Who says that?"

"Swan. And what makes Johnny Eagle so bad, anyway?"

"Nothing. He's just well-known to reservation raconteurs for his...*conquests*. A source of tall tales, not half of which I believe."

"People tell tall tales about you, too?"

"Not if I can help it."

"So, you don't kiss and tell."

Griff smiled cryptically.

They pondered on the Milky Way's arc over the Medicine Bow Mountains and chased their thoughts with a pull off their beers.

"And I thought Pine Hollow was way the hell out in the middle of nowhere. Doesn't it get lonely out here?"

"Quiet, yes. Lonely, not so much."

"So, what are we going to do about this Valance guy and the rest of them?"

"Don't know yet." Griff leaned forward and put elbows to knees. "Are you sure you want in on this? Might get ugly."

"I'm sure."

"Why?"

"If you knew skels, like I knew skels, there'd be no doubt. These Talon guys went to all that trouble to kill Eply and frame you for it, then Papa gets you off scot free? No self-respecting bad guy is going to allow that to stand."

"Johnny..."

"Maybe Cap, too, if they find out about him and the journals and all. Just can't let that stand."

Griff nodded.

"I'll bet you can't wait to kick that Ranger puke's ass after what they did to you."

"Yeah, but…he who flanks first, wins."

"What do you mean?"

"We've got to out maneuver these guys."

"How?"

"If I had all the answers, I'd go on *Jeopardy.*"

"You mean questions?"

"Huh?"

"Don't forget to frame your answer in the form of a question."

Griff hung his head low and shook it wearily.

Maura punched him in the shoulder. "I'm beat. You want to show me to my room?"

Griff sighed. He led Maura upstairs to one of the guest rooms, then came back down to sit out on the deck for a Task-Condition-Standard meditation on Seth Valance and the Talon Group.

When Griff finally went to bed, he slept alone as Rodya curled up at the foot of Maura's bed in the next room.

~~~

War Plans

By five the next morning, Griff was at the table in his hideaway going through all the files from Lance, Wilkinson and T-Rex again. He called Lance at six-thirty, knowing he was on his way to the office. Griff asked to have Wilkinson look into the health and well-being of Talon Technologies' most recent investments and for JR to put into play Spook Central's social media data mining algorithms from Mumbai and point them at Talon's partners.

"Add Andy Rousch to the list, too," Griff said.

"Who's he?" Lance asked.

"A-and-P at Reid-Hillview Airport in San Jose. South Bay Avionics. He was the last guy to sign off maintenance on Nickolson's Bell 406. Logs say he pulled a radio and did a transponder check."

"Worth a look for sure."

"Oh, what a tangled web we weave..."

"When first we practice to believe."

"How would you feel about playing Spyglass next week?" Griff asked.

"Can I bill it back to JR?"

"Absolutely."

"I'm in. Why?"

"There's a Highlands Group outing, and it looks like one of the Talon guys is a golf nut. No doubt he's playing."

"I'm there. Got me a new Calloway Rogue driver I'm dying to put through its paces."

"And I'll need to borrow JR's credentials and accommodations—at least for the first day of the conference. Make sure he's signed up for the golf outing. And get two extra tickets to the banquet Tuesday. And one for yourself."

"This is exciting, no? Business and pleasure all wrapped up in a big flour tortilla. Covered in cheesy mystery sauce."

"Yeah. Exciting."

"Come on, Griff. You and me. On the case—*on the client's dime.*"

"I'm all tingly inside."

"It doesn't get any better."

"I'll be in touch."

Griff hung up and dialed Norfolk.

"You lucky twat," T-Rex answered his call. "I hear you skated from Johnny Law."

"Thank you, Dewey, Cheatum and Howe."

Rodya wandered in and put his muzzle on Griff's thigh.

"Now what? It never fucking ends with you, does it?"

"Got your info on Valance. Thanks." Griff scratched the Husky's neck.

"I hate guys like that. No soul. They're the fucking worst."

"I gotta deal with this situation. Pronto. His body count is six blue—so far. Gotta stop."

"How's that?"

"Cover and move."

"And…"

"I need some cover. Next week. Three teams."

"Where?"

"Kentucky. Newport, Maysville, and Pine Hollow."

"I'm on it. Put this dog down already."

"Gotta flush him out first."

"Then what the fuck are you waiting for, you twat?"

"I love you, too, Chief. I'll send the details." Griff hung up and set down his phone. He patted Rodya's flank and, without looking back, said, "Well, well, well...look what the dog dragged in."

"Damn it, I thought for sure I got the drop on you." Maura's voice came from the doorway behind Griff.

He shook his head and pointed to a convex mirror in the corner by the ceiling.

"Rodya made me do it."

"Just don't know who I can trust anymore."

"Trust me." Maura stepped in and surveyed the hideaway, barefoot and dressed only in a large Denver Broncos #7 jersey. "Hope you don't mind. I found this in a drawer. The orange reminded me of...you and home."

"Very funny."

"So, what is this? Your Crowe's nest? Ha, ha. I make myself laugh."

"You are hilarious."

"I know."

"Welcome to my lair."

"That sounds nefarious." She stepped over beside the table.

Rodya turned his attention from Griff to Maura. She knelt down to let him lick her face.

Griff sighed.

"So, what was that all about?" Maura pointed to Griff's iPhone.

"Did you happen to pack any girlie things?" Griff asked.

"What for?"

"Didn't think so. Then, we'll have to go shopping when we get there."

"Where?"

"Ca-li-for-nee-ya," Griff said in an Austrian accent like Arnold Schwarzenegger.

~~~

My Fair Lady

It was her first time in a single-engine General Aviation plane. Maura barely spoke the entire flight, except to point towards the horizon at the Grand Tetons, the Great Salt Lake, Lake Tahoe, San Francisco Bay, and the Pacific Ocean, then ask, "What's that?"

She was uncharacteristically quiet through dinner, half the time staring at Griff like a teeny-bopper mooning over her idol of the moment, then avoiding direct eye contact.

Griff was at first amused, then annoyed, and finally bored.

Back at JR's Fairway One cottage at Pebble Beach, she went straight to her room and did not come out.

Griff went out on the patio and listened to the Pacific Ocean pound the California shore in the darkness.

The next day he took her to the Stanford Shopping Center where they made the rounds of the Women's departments at Macy's, Bloomingdales, Neiman-Marcus and Nordstrom.

"Too long. Too baggy. Too...*Amish,*" Griff said when Maura came out. He slouched down wearily in the chair outside the fitting rooms. "You don't get a second chance to make a first impression."

"I'm not some dress-up Barbie doll, you perv."

"You do understand what we're trying to do here, right?"

"I know. I know." Maura pouted. "But you're not getting me in CFMs."

"CFMs?"

"Come Fuck Me shoes. You know, stiletto heels."

"Whatever. Try that blue one on."

"Perv." Maura turned and went back into the fitting room

Griff closed his eyes, cleared his mind, and made a conscious effort to listen to himself breath in and out.

"You'll probably like this one," Maura said when she came back out in a tight-fitting, low-cut, navy blue cocktail dress.

Griff opened his eyes and smiled. He sat up straight in the chair. "Is that the right size?"

"Any tighter and I won't be able to breath."

"Yeah...*yeah*..." Griff nodded as he looked Maura up and down.

"Stop drooling like a horny old hound dog, for Christ sake. It's embarrassing."

"Let's go look at those CFMs."

After a reluctant purchase in the shoe department, a makeover in Cosmetics, and the acquisition of three hundred fifty dollars' worth of chemical compounds for female enhancement, they drove to the Palo Alto Airport where the Cirrus was parked.

Griff paid his fuel bill and tie down fee while Maura changed into her new blue cocktail dress. He whistled when she came out of the woman's lounge, squirming and pulling at her dress.

"Put a sock on it, Pablo."

"Is he still there?"

She pulled her phone out of her tiny new purse and tapped on the screen. "Yeah. You know, Facebook sure makes the life of a bounty hunter easy."

"Recovery agent."

Article 15

"Whatever." She gave Griff a quick spin. "You really think this is going to work?"

"You'd make a bulldog bite his chain."

"That's cool. Can we get this thing over already?"

Griff handed her the keys to the rental car. "Text me when you get there. I'll give you a half-hour, then land. Remember, South Bay Avionics."

"I know. I know. This isn't my first rodeo, cowboy."

Maura drove to the Reid-Hillman Airport.

Griff departed to the south and loitered over Gilroy, awaiting her text. By the time he landed and taxied to parking, Maura and Andy Rousch were standing side-by-side, waiting on the ramp. Rousch pointed to the Cirrus. Maura waved enthusiastically, like the little sister she was pretending to be. As the prop wound down to a stop, Griff watched Andy gently shake Maura's daintily extended hand with a huge smile on his face, then go back to work in the South Bay Avionics hangar.

"So, you got dinner plans for Tuesday?" Griff asked when he walked over from the Cirrus.

"Easy, peasy." Maura looped her arm in Griff's. "Melted his will to even live like butter on a hot skillet. I get to keep the dress, right?"

"Oh, you scamp, you."

When they got back to the cottage at Pebble Beach, Lance was sitting out back on the patio. Seeing Maura, he grabbed his heart and hyperventilated, gasping, "You can take me now, Lord—I can die a happy man."

She blushed and hurried into her room to change.

"She dresses up nice, huh?" Griff said. "And you can put your eyeballs back in your head."

"You dog, you. You know, I'm going to need pics if you intend on charging those threads back to the client—let me see your phone. I know you got some."

"You perv."

"Your point being?"

~~~

The Links

Griff walked along the tees at the Spyglass driving range in the soft morning light, carrying the putter lifted earlier from Lance's bag. He spied Lance down the line working the duffer in the next tee box over as they traded shots. He stopped to admire his friend's easy, fluid stroke as he effortlessly pounded drive after drive straight down range three hundred yards, much to the chagrin of his tee box neighbor.

Griff walked up behind the pair and said loudly, "Well, look at you showing off like you're the veritable Jack *Nicholson* of the Highlands Group."

The golfer on the tee to Lance's right arrested his stroke in mid-backswing. He looked over his shoulder at Griff.

Griff smiled broadly at the man, recognizing him as one of the founding partners of Talon Technology.

"I believe you mean Jack *Nicklaus.*" Lance said. "Not *Nicholson*—he's the actor. You know, *The Joker.*"

"Oh, yeah. Right. Anyway, you are really spanking the ball," Griff said. He had heard Lance use the term.

"Yeah, I love my new Calloway." Lance leaned on his driver. "Oh, this here is Larry Schmidt from Talon Technologies. He's playing the tournament this morning, too."

"Beautiful day for it. Glad to meet you, Larry. Griff's the name." He gripped Larry's hand hard and long until his wince was replaced by dawning recognition. "Griffith Crowe."

"Yeah…likewise." Larry pulled back, opening and closing his fist to restore circulation.

"Thought you might need this." Griff handed Lance the putter.

"Thanks. So, what are you and Maura doing today?"

Schmidt wiped the head of his driver clean with a towel, then bagged it, following the conversation between Lance and Griff closely.

"Touristy stuff. The Wharf. Cable cars. The Golden Gate Bridge." Griff looked at Schmidt. *"Alcatraz."*

"Gee, I'm sorry we're going to miss out on all that fun." Lance winked at Schmidt. "But, you know, duty calls. And…it's a write-off. How great is that?"

"A write-off?"

"God, I love my job. Don't you, Larry?"

"I, ah, I've got an early tee time." Schmidt shouldered his bag. "I should check in."

"Wanna make a little wager? Fifty a hole?" Lance asked.

Schmidt just shook his head and headed for the first tee.

"Well, good luck, Lar," Lance called out, then under his breath said, "Dickhead."

"Always making new friends, huh?" Griff asked.

"So, what are you and Maura really doing?"

"I told you: The Wharf. Cable cars. The Golden Gate Bridge."

"No Alcatraz?"

Griff shook his head remembering his visit there with Helena.

"Too soon after your stint in stir?"

"Yeah. That, too."

~~

The Highlands Forum

When Griff came back to the cottage from the fitness center and swimming laps the next morning, Maura was still asleep in her room. He shaved, showered, and dressed, then silently opened the door to look in on her. All he could see was a tangled mass of black hair spilling out from under the blanket which she had pulled over her face. The long, easy draws of breath gave evidence to the depth of her sleep cycle. He smiled at the memory of their day of innocent fun exploring Fisherman's Wharf, riding the cable cars, and crossing the Golden Gate Bridge for dinner in Sausalito with a view of San Francisco glittering across the bay, which ended innocently, despite his not so innocent thoughts and instinctual urgings when they got back to Pebble Beach as he watched Maura shuffle sleepily off to her room with visions of her in a blue cocktail dress dancing in his head.

Griff quietly closed the door and went to The Lodge for the Highlands Forum meeting. He lingered outside the Stanton Room, sipping coffee and watching for his prey. He was glad to see he was alone.

"Mark Dorsey, right?" Griff asked, approaching the other founding partner of Talon Technology at the coffee buffet. Conveniently, the man was wearing a Department of Defense picture ID on a lanyard around his neck. A second, engraved plastic badge pinned over his heart echoed his name and "OASD(C3I)," indicating he was an employee of the Office of the Assistant Secretary of Defense for Command, Control, Communications and Intelligence.

"That's right." The short, rotund man stirred the cream and sugar into his coffee, then turned to face Griff. He had to look up. "Have we met before?"

"Only by proxy. Not face-to-face. I'm Griffith Crowe."

Dorsey checked the roster on his clipboard. "I don't show you on the invite list. Who are you with?"

"So, you are here in your official government capacity, then."

"Yes, to help with the Forum. Is there something I can do for you, Mr. Crowe?"

"No. Not yet," Griff smiled. "I just thought it might be important to put faces to names."

"Mark, how are you?" JR called out as he walked up to Griff and Dorsey. "Long time no see."

"Mr. Nickolson. Good to see you again." Dorsey looked up at JR and extended his hand.

"It's been a little while." JR shook hands with Dorsey.

"I never got a chance to tell you how sorry I was about your father's accident."

"Yeah…" JR looked at Griff and smirked.

"My, ah, condolences." Dorsey looked from JR to Griff, then back to JR.

"I see you've met one of my guys. Here to help me out for the week." JR cocked his head towards Griff.

"Oh, right. We were just getting acquainted."

Griff smiled down on Dorsey and winked. "We'll talk more later."

Article 15

"Okay…" Dorsey frowned.

"So, the Stanton Room, nice." JR pulled Dorsey along with him as they went into the conference room. "How did Larry do yesterday in the tournament?"

"He had an off day," Dorsey answered looking back over his shoulder.

Griff gave a little wave.

~~~

Maura met Andy Rousch outside The Lodge at six-thirty that evening. From the big smile on the mechanic's young face and the uncomfortable tug at the collar of his dress shirt and necktie, her sleek and clinging off-the-shoulder little black dress met with at least as much approval as her blue cocktail dress.

She led Andy inside to the Pebble Beach room which was set up with round tables and a dais at the front of the room for the Forum banquet attended by guests and select support staff. She sent Andy off to the bar for drinks while she moved through the room scanning for Mark Dorsey and Larry Schmidt as the cocktail hour wound down. She found them huddled together at an otherwise empty table next to the terrace looking out on the eighteenth green.

"Is anyone sitting here?" Maura asked Dorsey and Schmidt.

Both men looked up at her, smiled, and quickly shook their heads.

"Please, join us," said Dorsey, breathing a bit too heavily.

Suckers, she thought, amazed yet again how such a small amount of artfully arranged fabric could reduce men to panting Pavlov's dogs. She waved Andy over and sat down. "Thank you."

"Hi. I'm Andy," He exchanged nods with Dorsey and Schmidt, setting down Maura's wine and sitting beside her with a beer.

"Larry."

"Mark."

"Save that seat next to you, too," Maura told Andy, putting the napkin from the place setting on the chair next to her. She looked across the table and raised her wine glass in a toast. "This is so nice. Cheers, fellas."

The three men returned tight-lipped smiles as if to hold back their salivating as they raised their glasses to Maura's toast.

"Hey. Hey, Larry," Lance called out. He circled the table, repeating his name as he shook hands with Dorsey, then Schmidt, then sat down between Larry and Andy. "Andy, right?"

"Yeah. How did you know?" Andy asked.

"We'll get to that." Lance winked at the young mechanic. He looked at Schmidt on the other side of him and shook his head sympathetically. "Larry...Larry...heard you had a tough day on the links. What, a ninety-five?"

"Ninety-two." Larry grimaced.

"Nothing at all to be ashamed of, Lar. Only ten percent of all us duffers shoot bogey golf—*legitimately*. And, what, with Spyglass being the toughest course in the world according to the PGA."

"How did you do?" Mark asked.

"I was up three going into eighteen. Birdied it to finish two over par." Lance smiled broadly at Mark.

Larry hung his head low.

"Wow," Mark said.

"Eh, I got lucky," Lance shrugged his shoulders and

looked around the room.

"Who are you here with?" Larry asked in an impatient, accusatory tone.

"Oh, here he is now." Lance pointed with his thumb as Griff sat down next to Maura. "You both know this guy. Griffith Crowe."

Larry's back stiffened.

"You're with JR. We met this morning," Mark said.

"JR is with us, actually," Griff said. "Nice act with him, by the way."

"What do you mean?" Mark asked.

Andy scanned around the table at the men in confusion. He looked over at Maura.

Maura patted his arm. "Wait for it."

"Andy, do you know these two?" Lance asked, pointing at Dorsey and Schmidt.

Maura's date shook his head.

"Then you probably never thanked them properly for the fifty thousand dollars they paid you for some special modifications…" Lance turned to Andy and made air quotes. "…that never made it onto the FAA Three-Thirty-Seven form for Major Repairs and Alterations done to that unfortunate Bell 406."

Andy swallowed hard.

"Cut the kid a break, Lance," Griff said. "He probably never met these guys. Did you at least thank Seth Valance?"

Dorsey wheezed at the mention of the ex-Army Ranger's name.

"I—I never saw him again," Andy said. "I didn't know."

"Hold that thought, son," Lance said, patting Andy on the shoulder.

M.T. Bass

"We don't have to sit here and listen to this crap." Larry raised his voice enough to draw looks from neighboring tables.

"Larry, please," Lance said in a soothing, lawyerly voice. "We're having a friendly little discussion here, and I think it might be in your best interest to hear my colleague out."

"You two are going down. Hard," Griff said in such a low voice, Dorsey and Schmidt reflexively leaned in to hear. "You can tell Valance that I'm going to take care of him personally for what he did to Eply."

"That was my guy, you assholes." Lance stuck his index finger in Larry's face. *"My guy."*

Schmidt and Dorsey exchanged worried glances.

"My firm is cooperating fully with the Newport police. So, I've seen all the data on Eply's laptop he collected on Talon Technologies. And, of course, JR has seen the light and been extremely helpful in sorting out some pretty interesting connections with the social media sniffers his company created for the NSA spy masters. "

"You can't prove anything," Larry said.

"You mean like the Gmail Drafts folder we found where you guys hatched your schemes?" Maura asked. She rolled her eyes back in her head. "Jesus, how did a moron like you ever get a job at the CIA?"

"You are going down, you bureaucratic cockroaches. We clear?" Griff stood up. "Now, Maura and I have to get back to Wyoming tonight. We have a long day of travel ahead of us tomorrow. I already know from boots on the ground that Valance is in Kentucky. You feel free to tell him I'm coming after him."

"And tell him if he puts hands on my grandfather..." Maura said, adjusting the tight black dress around her breasts.

~ 294 ~

Article 15

She looked up and pointed at Dorsey. "Me and Dewey will personally make that fat mug of yours all FUBAR—and that goes for you, too, ferret-face." She pointed at Schmidt.

The men looked at her all shocked-faced.

"You're kind of cute," Maura whispered to Andy as she stood up, too. "But kind of dumb. You better get some smarts, quick."

Griff and Maura left to fly back to the ranch.

"Do you think they bought it?" she asked him on the way out.

Griff nodded. "Absolutely. I already filed IFR. No doubt Valance will track us on FlightAware the whole way."

"Now, I am not your attorney," Lance said to Dorsey and Schmidt, back at the table, "but as a legal professional, I'd advise you guys to begin drinking heavily."

The Talon Technology partners got up and left quickly.

"What's going on?" Andy asked.

"Did I miss the big show?" JR asked as he sat down next to Andy.

"Here's what is going to happen." Lance turned in his chair towards Andy and put his hand on his shoulder in a fatherly way. "Tomorrow, you and I are going to pay a little visit to the local FSDO office and explain to the FAA what exactly you did to the FADEC and nav systems software on Cliff Nickolson's helicopter. At that point, I am sure that sworn law enforcement officers will be invited to participate in our discussions. I would suggest that you cooperate fully, if you ever hope to see sunshine again on the freedom side of barbed wire fencing. Believe me, son, those two slime-ball civil servants would sell out their moms to cover their own asses and save their pensions. Of course, you will still have plenty of time to contemplate new career opportunities."

Andy buried his face in his hands.

"Agreed?" Lance asked softly.

Andy nodded, still covering his face.

"But, first, you need to apologize."

Andy looked up.

"This is Cliff Nickolson, Junior," Lance said. "You killed his father."

Andy looked at JR. "I—I—"

JR stood up. Neck muscles taut, he leaned down over Andy, one hand on the table, the other closing into a fist and opening again, closing and opening over and over.

Andy slowly shriveled towards a fetal position.

"Say it," Lance said.

"I'm sorry," said Andy looking into his lap.

JR stood up and shook his head in disgust. He looked at Lance. "Thank you."

Lance nodded.

JR left.

"Come on, son." Lance stood and lifted Andy to his feet by the arm. As they walked out of the Pebble Beach room, he said, "I'll introduce you to Allen and Steve. They'll be babysitting you until our little tea party with the feds."

~~~

The Thin Gray Line

When Griff went in to wake Maura at four-thirty, Rodya was sleeping on the bed curled at her feet.

They were packed and in the air by quarter after five. With a fifty-knot tail wind at fifteen thousand feet and a fuel stop at Pekin Muni airport south of Peoria, Illinois, Griff touched down at Lunken Field just before two in the afternoon.

While Griff tended to the needs of the Cirrus with Signature Aviation, Maura called Johnny. "Papa, are you okay?"

"Of course I am—what with the two bruisers Griff has camping out next to Patty Ann's desk."

"Good. I was worried."

"I found them somewhat bothersome at first, taking up so much space and all in the office, but, you know, they've come to grow on me, especially since they give the appearance of having put the fear of the Almighty back into Patty Ann. She's been damn near personable. I'm getting fond of it."

Maura chuckled.

"Where are you now, darling?"

"We just landed in Cincinnati."

"We?"

"Me and Griff. There's unfinished business to be taken care of."

Johnny was silent for full twenty seconds.

"Papa?"

"I know it. Where are you headed?"

"Not sure, yet. Either Maysville or Pine Hollow."

"I reckon I'd put my chips on Pine Hollow."

"Why's that?"

"Oh, just an inclination that came my way."

"You're okay where you are, right?"

Johnny paused again. "We'll be fine. We'll see you soon, I suspect."

"Good."

"Maura, darling, you and Griff be careful."

"We will, Papa."

"And no hanky-panky. Be professional."

"Yes, Papa."

~~~

"Come on. Let's go." Griff said as he walked by Maura, pulling her along by the arm. He dialed T-Rex's number as they headed out to her Jeep in the parking lot.

"T, sit rep."

"Where you at, you twat?"

"Cinci-tucky."

"Well, you're getting warmer. At least you're in an adjacent state. Valance and his crew got there yesterday and crossed the river. Looks like he's got three guys with him. Loaded up a step van with gear and Triumph Tiger adventure motor bikes and took off into the hills."

"No idea where they're headed?"

"No joy on the other Xs."

"Tell the boys I'm feet dry and headed their way. If the bad guys show themselves, let me know."

"Roger that."

"Thanks, T."

"You know that old bastard is slippery as an eel."

"What do you mean?"

"Lost the boys a time or two."

"He's a crafty old coot."

"Yeah…but didn't get far. Anyways, what the fuck are you waiting for? Go out there and *be someone special already,* you twat."

Griff laughed and pocketed his phone,

"What?" Maura asked as they got to the Rubicon.

"Be someone special…" Griff shook his head. "A cheesy old SEAL recruiting video."

"I don't get it."

"Guess you had to be there."

"So, where are we going?" Maura asked with her hands on her hips.

Griff scratched the stubble on his chin, listening to his inside voice. "I'm thinking Pine Hollow."

"That's what Johnny said. Why?"

"Don't know. A family run greasy spoon doesn't strike me as a particularly target rich environment. Whereas Cap does present an air of mystery and intrigue. After all, that's where Nickolson's journals ended up. What else might be stashed in and amongst that hoarder's delight he calls inventory?"

"Now you're thinking like a skel." Maura got behind the wheel and started the engine.

Griff got in the passenger side.

"Pine Hollow it is."

"So how is Johnny doing, anyway?"

"Good. He likes your friends. Patty Ann…not so much—and that makes him like them even more."

"He best be careful. They'll be going home once we're done. And payback is a bitch."

Maura laughed and pulled out of the airport. She headed southeast on interstate that gave way to four-lane highway that narrowed to a thin gray ribbon curly-cuing through the Kentucky wilderness.

~~

Maura backed the Jeep into a parking spot at the Uptown Beauty Salon facing Cap's store.

"There. Our guys." Griff pointed to a late model sedan nestled among the cars awaiting repair at Mac's Garage. He sent a text. A moment later his iPhone dinged. "Nada. So, we wait. I'll take first watch. Catch some winks."

It started as a mental itch sometime after five. Griff ignored it at first, then scratched, which only made it itch more. He started to wake Maura but stopped himself. He kept puzzling things out in his head until he couldn't take it anymore and shook her awake. "Hey, wait here. I want to do a perimeter check."

Griff got out and walked behind Mac's Garage. He noticed the heads in the sedan turn to look back at him. He waved them off and sprinted across the country road and behind the Hot to Trot Tavern directly across the street from Cap's. He watched the storefront intently.

Just as he was about to move further on down to cross the road and circle back around in the woods behind the Pine

Article 15

Hollow General Store, a muffled shotgun blast came from across the street. A second shot shattered the front display window, followed by a third, louder blast which pushed a man through the front screen door and tumbling down the steps, leaving a trail of blood.

Two men scrambled out of the store and down the steps, jumping over the lifeless body.

Two more shot gun blasts came from the store.

Griff drew his SIG and ran into the road. He recognized one of the fleeing men as Seth Valance as they ran around the building.

The distinctive growl of metric motorcycle engines was followed by the spitting of gravel as three bikes sped out from around back and onto the road.

Griff instinctively started running down the road after them shooting on the run.

The two riders in trail of Valance turned on their seats and returned fire.

Behind Griff, Johnny stepped out on the front porch and began firing his Colt 1911 pistol, dropping one of the motorcyclists who tumbled under his bike in the middle of the road.

Maura skidded to a stop in front of the store. "Papa, are you all right?"

"Get them sons-of-bitches. Go on now," Johnny said, releasing the empty magazine and reloading his pistol with a full one.

Cap stepped out behind Johnny, pushing shotgun shells into his gun.

Maura pulled up to Griff and let him in, then laid rubber to catch up with the fleeing motorcycles, swerving around the dead man Johnny put down.

More familiar with the road, Maura was able to close the gaps in the corners but lost ground to the quicker acceleration of the bikes on straightaways. As she entered the next curve, she saw the sedan from Mac's Garage coming out of the last corner in her rear-view mirror.

The chase yo-yoed for miles until the lead bike turned off on an old mining road while the other kept going.

"That's Valance," Griff said. "Take him."

Maura turned off and climbed the rutted gravel road up the hillside, losing ground to the bike.

Griff held on as the Rubicon bucked hard like an untamed mustang.

Maura skidded to a sudden sideways stop near the crest of the hill.

Griff jumped out and ran the rest of the way to the top.

The motorcycle engine revved to the red line and faded away, followed by a distant splash.

Griff slid to a stop at the very edge of a bluff that looked out over a water filled quarry. Fifty feet below, waves rippled out from where the bike went into the water.

Maura came running up behind Griff. "Damn…that had to hurt."

Griff just nodded. "Guess I won't be needing Johnny's services again after all."

They sat down with their legs dangling over the edge to wait for Sheriff's deputies and the Kentucky State Highway Patrol to find them.

~~~

All in the Family

When the Highway Patrol cruiser dropped off Maura and Griff, Johnny and Cap sat side-by-side on the front porch of the Pine Hollow General Store, leisurely rocking and conversing between sips of sarsaparilla as they watched the crime scene techs work around the two dead bodies, marking shell casings, taking pictures, and collecting blood samples.

Mac's tow truck followed with the Rubicon hooked up, still dripping oil and coolant.

"Hey, Griff," Cap called out, "you need any more antiques? I got me some repairs that need funding."

Griff just shook his head wearily.

"Papa Johnny, you told me you were fine." Maura pointed at her grandfather as she skirted the dead man and his blood on the steps to get up on the porch.

"Well, I am fine," Johnny said. He turned to Cap and asked, "Do I not look fine?"

"The picture of health," answered Cap.

"What are you doing here?" Maura stood in front of Johnny with her fists firmly planted on her hips.

Griff leaned against the cruiser's rear quarter panel to watch.

"Did I not mention my inclinations? I distinctly recall doing so." Johnny took a pull of root beer, then muttered to himself, "Expect a man to leave his fellow Marine high and dry? *Semper fi,* darlin'. *Semper fi.*"

"It's a damn tragedy how soon the young uns forget nowadays," Cap said.

"You could have got hurt," Maura said. "You could have got killed."

"Oh, yeah? Maybe you should get that there fella's opinion." Johnny pointed to the man he shot dead laying in the middle of the road. "He just might beg to differ."

Griff stepped up on the porch and put his hand on Maura's shoulder. "There's no winning with him. You know that."

"Besides, I needed some legal advice," Cap said.

"And I am a lawyer, you might recall," Johnny said. "A damn fine one, if I do say so myself. Wouldn't you agree, Mr. Crowe?"

"That and that…" Maura pointed at the dead bodies, "…do not look like legal *advice.*"

"She's got a point there, Johnny," Griff said.

"It's true," said Cap. "I needed to dispose of some property."

"What property?" Maura turned her anger on Cap.

"My nephew left me some shares of stock I don't particularly want," Cap said.

"Nephew?" Griff asked.

"One Mr. Donald Wallace," Johnny said. "Recently demised."

"*Son…of…a…bitch…*" Griff slapped his forehead and turned away to lean on the porch railing.

"Just look at the trouble it brung me," Cap said, pointing to his broken display window, smashed screen door, then the dead man at the bottom of the steps. "I don't need this. I live here 'cause it's quiet. Got my fill of excitement in 'Nam."

Article 15

Griff looked back over his shoulder. "Hornet Investment Group?"

"Fifteen percent of said same," Johnny said. "A chunk of which is surely gonna make the day of a certain restauranteur and her family up in Maysville. About twenty, twenty-five million dollars' worth."

"A chunk?" Griff asked.

"A certain Mr. Lance Baylor, Esquire, of Chicago, Illinois, expressed an interest acquiring a portion. Evidently, he is of the opinion that Mr. Nickolson's heir will make a go of it."

"Son-of-a-bitch..." Griff moaned.

"And then..." Johnny said.

"Then?" Maura asked.

"This fella, here," Cap said, pointing at Johnny beside him. "Bought the rest."

"Bought?" Griff asked.

"I ain't a damn fool," Cap replied. "Ain't giving it all away."

"Papa?"

"Not for me, darling. For you." Johnny winked at Maura. "Perhaps the time has arrived to give consideration to a career change."

Maura looked at him in shock.

"Well, think on it some, why don't you." Johnny pointed across the street to Mac's where the tow truck was lowering Maura's Jeep. "Least ways it will come in handy for some unexpected expenses."

"Mr. Leonard?" A Highway Patrolman sauntered up to the bottom of the steps. "I think we've got everything we need from you for now."

"And my 1911?" Johnny asked. "There's a certain sentimental value to it."

"You'll get it back when the lab is done with the ballistics testing."

"Thank you, officer."

"You are free to go." The officer walked away.

"Now, how are we going to get home?" Maura asked.

"The El Dorado is parked out back," Johnny said. "I'll get it."

"No. Give me the keys." Maura held out her hand. "I'm driving."

"Now, darling, as much as I love you, your tendency towards reckless abandon on public roadways, gives me pause." Johnny looked across the street at the broken-down Rubicon.

"I have to side with Johnny on this one," Griff said.

"Fine, then."

~~~

Griff only had to endure five minutes of the tense silence inside the El Dorado as Johnny pulled out of Pine Hollow before he fell asleep in the back seat, too tired to pay attention to the warning of the little voice inside his head.

The next thing he knew it was dark, and they had pulled to a stop in front of Christopher's Bed and Breakfast in Newport.

"I took the liberty of booking you a room," Johnny said with a sly grin. "No need to hide out at Maura's abode any more."

"Thanks."

"You want some company?" Maura scowled at Johnny,

then turned and looked into the back seat with a defiant look on her face. "I ain't tired yet."

Griff looked at Maura, then at the deep frown on Johnny's face. "I don't know…It just doesn't seem right—you know, being a house of God and all."

"Former house of God," Maura said.

"Still, baptisms, weddings, funerals…"

"Ain't you two had your fill of tempting fate and the devil his own self for one day?" Johnny asked.

"Fine, then."

"Thanks, Johnny," Griff said getting out.

"Oh, no. Thank you."

~~~

The War Room

In the dim, indirect lighting of the small conference room, Griff found a shadow where he sat and sipped coffee from a massive, dark mug with Stein, Baylor & Stein gilded on the side, patiently waiting for Lance Baylor to come back with his check.

A soft knock came at the door.

"Yeah?"

The door opened and Roger Wilkinson stuck his head in. "Mr. Crowe?"

"Hi, Roger."

"I just wanted to thank you personally for…you know, Wes."

Griff looked Wilkinson in the eye. "I'm sorry for what happened to him. Please know, what you did for us was a big help."

Wilkinson nodded his head, then closed the door, again.

Griff sipped his coffee. He closed his eyes.

The door opened and shut quietly.

Griff opened his eyes and smiled. "Hi, Hannah."

She sat down next to Griff, setting a pie box down on the table. She took Griff's hand, then slowly slid the box in front of him.

"For me?"

Hannah nodded and squeezed Griff's hand.

"This isn't store-bought, is it?"

"No, silly. But it is a new recipe." Hannah smiled coyly. "Derby pie."

Griff hung his head low in defeat and pinched his eyes shut.

The door opened. Lance came in and stood at the head of the conference table.

"Don't be a stranger now, Griff. Ya hear?" Hannah petted the top of his hand, then got up and left.

"Ooooo, pie," Lance oozed.

"Don't. Do not go there," Griff said.

Lance sat down. He slid a check over in front of Griff.

"So, case closed?" Griff asked.

"Yeah, and, you know, everybody seems happy. Which is odd."

"Except the bad guys, of course."

"Of course. But nobody else is complaining. It's like Halley's Comet. Once a century it happens."

"I heard you made out pretty well with Hornet Investment Group," Griff said.

"We...*we* made out."

"What are you talking about?" Griff asked.

"Well, me and Johnny and Cap all pitched in a point for you off our shares. So, you're going home with a nice little seven figure bonus."

Griff's face assumed a shocked look.

"And, who knows, maybe you'll run into the Nickolson kids again at a shareholder's meeting—*God, I love my job.*"

~~~

Home on the Range

Clear of the Chicago Terminal Area, Griff found I80, throttled the Cirrus back, and descended below five hundred feet above the ground, flying IFR: "I Follow Roads." He skirted around the Quad Cities, Des Moines, Omaha and Lincoln municipalities with their Approach and Departure Control radars. He generally ignored the navigation data on the multi-function displays in the cockpit panel as he made his way west, measuring his progress instead by the town names painted on their water towers and posted on highway exit signs.

Crossing the Wyoming border by Pine Bluffs, a thought percolated up into his consciousness, *Lance is right. I love my job, too.*

Griff arced north to stay out of the Cheyenne control tower's airspace. Fifteen minutes later, he was on final approach to Laramie Regional Airport Runway 21. And fifteen minutes after that, he sat in the Cowboy Aviation offices slurping down a cup of coffee and shooting the breeze with Bones.

Swapping the Cirrus for his little rag-wing Aeronca to commute to the ranch, Griff felt himself relaxing back into a familiar, comfortable routine. By the time he landed, Ben, Shep, and Johnny Eagle were gone, the day's ranching duties done.

He missed Rodya's supervisory help pulling the Chief into the hangar. He sent a text message to Ben to bring him back home to the ranch with him in the morning.

M.T. Bass

Griff went upstairs to shower and change. He froze in the doorway to his bedroom, suddenly staring down the muzzle of a Beretta M9 pistol.

"Hey, squid. Welcome home," said Seth Valance, sitting in the chair by the window. "I thought you'd never get here."

Griff shook his head. "You know, you'd think I'd have learned by now."

"What? The little voice?"

Griff nodded.

"You always got to listen to the little voice inside your head, man." Valance stood up. "You've been a real pain in my ass."

"Sorry to have messed up your plans."

Valance shrugged. "Improvise, Adapt and Overcome."

"Please, enough with the jarheads, already. Had my fill of 'em."

"Shouldn't be a problem moving forward." Seth raised his pistol.

Griff's eye caught motion in the convex mirror in the corner of his hideaway.

Valance noticed and half-turned to look over his shoulder.

"Hey, moron," Helena said, stepping out from behind the vault-like door.

Valance noticed her gun and began to spin around to meet the threat.

"What's your favorite color?" she asked.

"Huh?"

In the Ranger's split second of hesitation, Helena emptied her Smith and Wesson M&P Bodyguard 38 into Seth Valance until he dropped.

Griff bolted forward to grab the Beretta away from

Article 15

Valance, but he was dead. Griff looked up at Helena. "I never expected to see you here."

"Yeah. Well, you're welcome."

"Thanks. Are we even?"

"I dunno. I never keep score."

~~~

Twenty minutes after he called, sitting out back on the deck with Helena, Griff heard Deputy Walt's SUV pull up.

"Upstairs. In my bedroom," Griff said, when the officer stepped up on the deck.

"Wait here." Deputy Walt drew his service weapon and went inside.

Griff looked at Helena, shrugged, and sat back down next to her.

They gazed on the Medicine Bow Mountains in silence.

"Dead as a doornail," Deputy Walt said when he came back out the sliding glass door, his gun holstered.

"Not a flesh wound?" Griff asked.

"Ah...no."

A second Albany County Sheriff's Deputy arrived. "Walt. How's it going?"

"Vic. Hey, ah, go on up to the second-floor master bedroom and secure the scene. I called the Coroner and DCI." He stepped over to Helena and Griff. "Talked to the Sheriff, and he would really prefer for you to come to the office and make your statement there, ma'am. Please?"

Helena sighed. She looked at Griff. "This really wasn't what I had in mind for the evening's...*entertainment.*"

"I'll call Lance," Griff said.

"Thanks." Helena stroked Griff's cheek and scratched behind his ear. She stood up. "Shall we, officer?"

As they walked toward his SUV, Griff heard Deputy Walt ask Helena, "Why did you shoot him five times?"

"Because when I squeezed the trigger a sixth time, it just went *click.*"

~~~

Crowe's Nest

July rolled into August. The days, though still hot, were noticeably shorter. Griff sat at a familiar spot with his back against a granite boulder looking out over his ranch and the high plains beyond. He closed his eyes and soaked up sunshine like a thirsty new sponge.

He heard a horse walk up the trail behind him and snort. He called out, "Hey, Ben, what's going on?"

When he got no answer, Griff put a grip on his P226 in its holster and leaned to peer around the boulder.

"Hey, Griff," Maura said from atop Hannibal. "Want some company?"

Griff nodded slowly. "Yeah...yeah, come on down."

She dismounted with ease and tied off the quarter horse next to Winston. "Ben said you were probably here and brung me to the trailhead. I found my own way up."

"Huh. I'd have figured you for a rice-burning dirt bike ride, not an oat eater."

"Papa Johnny has a horse farm south of town. Raised thoroughbreds for racing until Nana died and he sold them all off." Maura walked over to Griff. "I love that place."

"Have a seat." He slid over.

"Thanks." She sat against the boulder and took in Griff's special view of Wyoming. "This is awesome. What's this place called?"

"Crowe's Nest."

She nudged Griff with her shoulder. "I get it. That's cute."

"I wasn't going for cute, actually."

"Oh. Well, it's still awesome."

"So, what brings you out west?"

"Lance's jet. He dropped me off on his way to some meetings in Los Angeles."

Griff shook his head. "I mean—don't get me wrong, I'm glad to see you—but why are you here? Is Johnny okay?"

"Ornery as ever." Maura smiled, then looked down into her lap.

"So…"

"Papa actually sold me the farm for a dollar on the condition he could live there rent free. He had made it mine in his will anyways. I hope to get back to raising horses again." Maura took a deep breath and exhaled. "So, I put my house in Birdland on the market. It sold quicker than I thought, which is good. But now I don't have a place to live until classes start."

"Classes?"

"Yeah. I signed J-Bonds over to Dewey for a dollar."

"So, that's how you could afford to buy Johnny's farm." Griff nudged Maura back.

She smiled. "Anyway, I talked to Johnny and Lance and decided to go back full time and finish up law school. U of K, just like Papa."

"Going into the family business, then."

"Lance even promised he'd hire me, but I'd rather stay close to home in Kentucky."

"And work for Johnny?"

"He said he'd make me a full partner when I graduate."

"Sounds like you've got it all going your way."

"Yeah...I guess."

"Except..."

She turned to look Griff in the eye. "I was thinking that I'd like to spend the last of my summer vacation 'til fall semester starts here."

"Here?"

"With you."

Griff held her stare.

"Well...what do you think?" Maura took a deep breath and held it.

Griff smiled. "I think I'd like that."

Maura exhaled loudly, leaned back against the boulder and smiled. "Good, then."

Griff dug in his rucksack. "You want half a sandwich?"

"What kind?"

"Bologna."

"Yes, *please.*"

~~~

Thank you for reading my story.

About M.T. Bass

M.T. Bass lives, writes, flies, and plays music in Mudcat Falls, USA.

www.MTBass.net

Available in Paperback, eBook & Audiobook

Artificial Intelligence? *Fuhgeddaboudit!*

Artificial Evil has a name…*Munchausen.*

When androids are reprogrammed into hit men, detectives of the Artificial Crimes Unit repo the AnSub and track down the hackers. Partners Jake and EC's case of an "extra-judicial" divorce settlement takes a nasty turn with DNA from a hundred-year-old murder in Boston and a signature that harkens back to the very first serial killer ever in London.

www.MTBass.net

.

Available in Paperback & eBook

It was the case of a lifetime…but then it went sideways on her. The serial killer Maddie put behind bars might have been crazy but it turns out he was innocent, and now she finds herself hunting robot killers in the Artificial Crimes Unit. Worse yet, she's partnered up with Jake, her former lover.

When androids are hacked and reprogrammed into hit men, Maddie and Jake investigate and track down the hackers. But now, an evil genius is using droids to recreate the infamous Jack the Ripper murders.

www.MTBass.net

The
Invisible Mind
Murder by Munchausen #3

A NOVEL BY M.T. BASS

Available in Paperback & eBook

Now unleashed, the "Baron" is resurrecting history's notorious serial killers, giving them a second life in the bodies of hacked and reprogrammed Personal Assistant Androids, then turning them loose to terrorize the city. While detectives Jake and Maddie of the police department's Artificial Crimes Unit scramble to stop the carnage with the Baron's arrest, the cyberpunk head of the Counter IT Section, Q, struggles to de-encrypt his mad scheme to infect world data centers with a virus that represents a collective cyber unconsciousness of evil.

Artificial Intelligence? *Fuhgeddaboudit!*

Artificial Evil has a name…*Munchausen*

www.MTBass.net

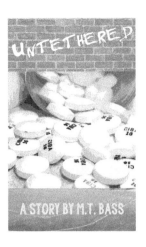

Available in eBook

At District High School #6241, Connor wants only to get close to Liz, the cheerleader whose locker is just across the hall, and forget the suicide of his father in jail, but his family's dark past and a rebellious nature force him to the fringes of student social circles and into an unlikely alliance to fight back against a tyranny of conformity.

www.MTBass.net

Available in Paperback & eBook

People ask me where I get the ideas for my books. In this case, I recall reading about Alaska bush pilots for fun. I must have watched *Animal House* and *Treasure of the Sierra Madre* around that time and…a few months later—Eureka! The words for the prologue and first chapter just started spilling out of my head. ("Clean up on aisle five.")

Seriously, what could go wrong? *Love & Betrayal…Murder & Mayhem…Friendship & Double-Crossing Partners in Pursuit of Buried Treasure…*

www.MTBass.net

Available in eBook

*Lodging — bending of the stalk of a plant (stalk lodging)
or the entire plant (root lodging)*

While World War II engulfs every nation on the globe, Rebecca
and her high school friend Sarah can only dream of escaping a
dreary, wind-blown existence in western Kansas, until their
boring, stodgy old hometown fills with handsome young men
learning to fly Army Air Corps bombers known as Liberators,
and their lives are suddenly filled with temptation and, perhaps,
true love.

www.MTBass.net

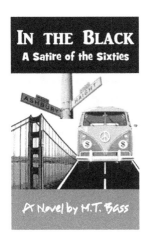

Available in Paperback & eBook

Kansas City, 1965 — Y.T. Erp, Jr. can't wait to leave for college at the University of California, Berkeley to escape not only the work, but especially all the phlegm-brained idiots at his father's aerospace company. Leaving behind a pregnant auburn-haired cheerleader, a sensuous red-headed siren plotting to usurp his familial ties, and his two best friends—one who ends up in Vietnam and the other in the Weather Underground—his "trip" on the wild side of the Generation Gap takes him from the psychedelic scene of Haight-Ashbury to the F.B.I.'s Ten Most Wanted list. Meanwhile, his father is consumed by the task of managing his unmanageable corporate team in the quest to help fulfill a President's challenge to "land a man on the moon."

www.MTBass.net

Available in eBook

Cleveland, 1977 — Grappling with a foreign policy crisis, the U.S. Government targets a hapless rock-'n'-roller as a Russian spy in a classic case of mistaken identity for an innocent, 'Wrong Man' hero…or *is he?*

Think of an unholy fictional union between the Rolling Stones and Alfred Hitchcock's *North by Northwest*.

Unlike any novel you have ever read, this one has a soundtrack. After all, a story whose characters are musicians should have…well…*music*. Right?

www.MTBass.net

Available in Paperback & eBook

Hollywood, 1950 — Former P-51 fighter pilot A. Gavin Byrd is on location for a movie shoot, when he gets a call from the police that his older brother, a prominent Beverly Hills plastic surgeon, has been found dead on his boat. The Lieutenant in charge of the investigation is ready to close the case as a suicide from the start, but "Hawk" doesn't buy it and decides to find out what really happened for himself.

With help from a former starlet ex-girlfriend, a friendly police sergeant whose life was saved in the war by his brother and a nosy Los Angeles Times reporter, Hawk's search for the truth takes him through cross-fire, dog fights and mine fields in Hollywood, Beverly Hills, Burbank and Las Vegas, and leads him into some of the darker corners of his brother's patient files and private life that he never knew existed.

www.MTBass.net

CPSIA information can be obtained
at www.ICGtesting.com
Printed in the USA
BVHW030155290422
635713BV00004B/13

9 781946 266118